CLOSE RANGE

SHANNON BAKER

Severn River Publishing
www.SevernRiverBooks.com

This is a work of fiction. Names, characters, businesses, places, events and incidents are either the products of the author's imagination or used in a fictitious manner. Any resemblance to actual persons, living or dead, or actual events is purely coincidental.

ISBN: 978-1-64875-580-4 (Paperback)

ALSO BY SHANNON BAKER

The Kate Fox Mysteries

Stripped Bare

Dark Signal

Bitter Rain

Easy Mark

Broken Ties

Exit Wounds

Double Back

Bull's Eye

Close Range

Taking Stock

Michaela Sanchez Southwest Crime Thrillers

Echoes in the Sand

The Desert's Share

The Nora Abbott Mystery Series

Height of Deception

Skies of Fire

Canyon of Lies

Standalone Thrillers

The Desert Behind Me

**To find out more about Shannon Baker and her books, visit
severnriverbooks.com**

1

Blood smeared the pavement, crimson streaks glaring in the afternoon sun. I jetted from my cruiser and raced toward the mayhem, squinting into the glare. My heart thudded and I shouted, though it couldn't be heard above the moans and shrieks rising from the center of the chaos. Amid the scene of destruction, I tried to make sense of what had happened, but my main concern was finding my people. "Sarah!"

I didn't see my best friend, who was also my favorite sister-in-law, amid the carnage. Steel and aluminum, black skid marks across the center line, all mingled with enough body parts I assumed there would be more than one casualty. Cattle skittered from the road, hooves slipping on the pavement, and their panicked howls raised the hairs on my neck. The musky scent of manure and blood hit me, ratcheting my heart rate further. "Sarah!" I skittered between two parked pickups and around the overturned stock trailer.

Sun heated the metal on the vehicles so a casual brush of my knuckles on the side panel burned. The trailer's back door had crashed open on impact, spilling the load of cattle onto the road and no telling how many were dead, mutilated, or injured. My heart climbed my throat because I knew cattle might not be the only casualties.

I spun in a frantic search to see Sarah bracing herself against the hood of an older blue Ford F250, head down, one hand rubbing her belly. My brother, Robert, leaned over her. Their two-year-old daughter, Brie, hugged Robert's leg, her mouth open, but if she cried, the cattle's bellows drowned it out.

Sarah's due date for their second baby was approaching and I worried that even if they hadn't been involved in the wreck, the stress of the accident might kick her into labor or somehow complicate the pregnancy.

"Are you okay?" I shouted as I ran toward them.

The smell of hot engines, baking pavement and cow manure mingled in a nasty fug.

Sarah glanced up. "Kate. Thank God."

Robert plucked Brie from his leg and thrust her to me. "Ellie can watch the kids. I'll get the cattle off the road."

The cattle needed to be rounded up and the injured attended to so there wouldn't be another accident with someone approaching on the highway. Of course. But what about the people? Two pickups, along with the one pulling the trailer. "Who else is here?"

Sarah straightened and brushed wisps of her chestnut hair from where it stuck to the sweat on her cheeks. "Mom, Dad. Garrett and Tony." True to her nature, she brushed aside emotion and got to work. "I'll help Robert."

I held a hand up. "Oh, no. You sit in the pickup and run the a/c. I'll find the others." *Alive, please let them all be alive and as unharmed as Sarah.*

"Screw that." She wiped her palms on her widening hips and stomped off.

Brie wound her arm under mine and hunkered against me, a burning coal on the steaming day. Her bright eyes shone with tears, but she was her mother's daughter, fearless and tough.

With Sarah, Robert, and Brie accounted for, I spun around to find the rest. The Haney clan had been hauling a bunch of culled heifers to the sale barn. I guessed Sarah's older brother, Garrett, had been driving the white F350 dually pickup pulling a long gooseneck stock trailer. Alden and Ellie, Sarah's parents, must have been in the newer silver Ford pickup, making Robert and Sarah's blue pickup the only other vehicle. That left Tony, Garrett's ten-year-old son, with either Sarah's parents or Garrett.

A black heifer skittered by me, head high, tail whipping, eyes crazed. A gash in her side gushed blood and she let out a shriek of pain that sounded like an elephant's blare.

I'd been on my way to meet Sarah and Robert to take Brie with me, and I had topped the hill to find this devastation. The trailer in a mangled heap, with cattle strewn in the ditch and at least one dead on the road, blood pooling under her head. I stepped over a severed leg and scanned between the pickups for the rest of the cow but didn't see it.

It appeared only Garrett's vehicle had been involved in the wreck.

I breathed a sigh to see Ellie, a petite woman in her mid-sixties , standing in Alden's embrace. He patted her back while she buried her head in his chest. I didn't blame Ellie for falling apart. The blood, the noise and the heat made it feel like a war zone.

Amid a chorus of moos and snorts, one heifer let loose with a banshee wail. It curdled my blood.

With Brie riding my hip, I rushed to Alden and Ellie. "Are you hurt? Where's Tony and Garrett?"

Ellie pulled her head away from Alden, alarm hitting her teary eyes. "Tony. Oh, no. Where's my grandson? Where's my boy?"

Alden reached for her. "I'm sure he's fine. He was just here."

Crap. I hadn't seen the ten-year-old. Sounded like he was fine, but a kid didn't need to see the gore scattered on the highway. And what about his father, Garrett? I had to find them.

Ellie brushed Alden away. "I need to be with my boy."

"Now, honey. Let's get you into the air conditioning. We'll take care of everything."

Brie whimpered, a helpless mewling, not like her earlier efforts to be brave.

With one arm snugging Brie to me, I latched onto Ellie with my other hand. "The best thing is for you to keep Brie safe inside the pickup. We'll find Tony and Garrett."

Ellie let out a series of squeaks as I dragged her to the shiny silver pickup. We had to skirt a confused white-faced heifer who stood with her head down, knees scraped and raw from falling on the road. I opened the door, plopped Brie on the seat, and helped Ellie into the passenger side, fighting the urge to toss her in. She huddled in the seat. If the a/c was going to get turned on, I'd have to do it. That ate up precious seconds while I ran around to the driver's side and cranked the key.

The wrenching wail of an animal in agony sounded like an air raid siren. I prayed she wasn't the animal whose hind leg I'd hurdled in my search for Sarah. I felt for my gun, expecting I'd need to put her out of her suffering. I'd made sure to wear my sheriff uniform today of all days, and now I was glad. The polyester might be suffocating, but the gun might be necessary. First, I needed to find Garrett and Tony.

I whirled around and assessed the scene. Robert and Sarah were making their way away from the wreckage to round up the cattle that had wandered off . Ellie's head barely cleared the dash on the passenger side where she sat with Brie.

Along with the injured cow screaming in pain, other heifers let out long cries that made me clench my teeth against their torment. Several black cows skidded and lurched in panic on the pavement made slick with blood. Others had made their way to the barrow ditch on either side and were scattering up and down the highway.

I wiped sweat from my eyes and brushed the strands of curly hair that had escaped from my ponytail off my forehead to get a clearer view. Brie plastered two palms and a nose to the window, her eyes bright and worried.

That left the white pickup on its side attached to the upended gooseneck trailer, and Sarah's brother, Garrett, nowhere in sight.

A police siren sounded from the east. It would be Ted Conner, sheriff from Chester County and my ex-husband. Can't say I wasn't glad to hear him on the way, even if I didn't like him any better than a chicken likes a bull snake. I'd called the dispatcher and she'd alerted the ambulance crew and Ted had probably heard it on the radio.

I lunged toward the white pickup and bent to check the cab, my stomach in my throat for fear I'd see Garrett in a tangle of blood and guts. Blessedly, the cab was empty and though there was a fair amount of blood, it was free of guts.

I straightened and heard a string of curses rising above the continued screams from the cow I'd just located halfway under the trailer.

Alden, in his sixties, on the shorter side with a belly that rivaled pregnant Sarah's, shouted at Garrett, spittle flying. "What the hell is wrong with you? Get your shit together!" Blood dripped from his fingers. I hadn't noticed it before when he'd been with Ellie. Maybe he tried to free a heifer from the wreckage and sliced himself. I couldn't tell where or how bad his injury was.

A crimson gusher flowed from a gash on Garrett's forehead, and he looked pale. He towered over Alden and swayed slightly, a rifle dangling loosely from his hand. "Maybe we can save her." Normally handsome and assured, tall and square shouldered, he gave his father an imploring look, as if he needed someone to take charge.

The cow's bawling sliced through the air, shredding the world with her all-consuming pain.

Alden reached up and placed his palm on Garrett's shoulder, shoving him backward. "Put that damned animal down. It's your fault and you need to fix it."

Garrett wobbled, his head bouncing on his neck, but he only stared at his father. "It was an accident."

Bile rose in my throat, and I yanked my gun from my holster. Forcing myself forward, I strode to the cow. On her side, one spear of aluminum piercing her belly, she beat her head on the ground. A swath of rough white hair started between her glassy eyes and splashed down her face, now smeared with blood. Pain kept her from focusing on me as I lowered my barrel to the rough hair on her forehead and pulled the trigger, creating a single hole on the white blaze. The bawling stopped and her black head flopped to the ground in a puff of dust.

The shot vibrated up my arm and felt like it exploded in my belly, filling me with sour anguish. I sucked in a lungful of air and swallowed hard as sound started to filter into my head. Cows mooing, vehicle doors slamming, Alden still yelling at Garrett. I still needed to find Tony, but with a pickup and trailer blocking both lanes, a dozen or so cows scattered here and beyond, and debris cluttering the area, we needed to act now. Traffic in this lonely spot in the Nebraska Sandhills might mean a dozen pickups on a busy day, but if one of those vehicles topped the hill—never driving the speed limit—and found this mess, it could be fatal, and not only to the bovine.

We were along a curve in the bottom of a meadow. The road swept up on either side. I met Ted running toward me in the middle of the mess. "Park your cruiser on the top of the hill with your lightbar going and I'll get mine on the west."

Sarah was already lumbering east on the shoulder of the highway. I assumed she planned to herd cattle. Robert leaped down the borrow pit and up the other side and sprinted along the fence line, looking, I guessed, for a gate into the pasture. It would make sense to herd the loose cattle into the nearest pasture and get them off the road. In this case, it was Jade McPherson's range and Robert would arrange to round them up and take them away as soon as possible.

I turned to see Tony behind me, staring at the dead heifer. Like Sarah and Garrett, he had remarkably shiny and thick chestnut hair and their perfect symmetry of features. He raised his eyes to me. "Awesome."

Not for the first time I wondered if there was something wrong with this kid. I grabbed his wrist. "Wait in the pickup with your grandma."

He pulled back. "No way. I'm not a little kid." Brown eyes, bright with intelligence, he could be an actor with his flawless looks.

I may only be 5'3" but I'd wrangled bulls three times his size and a lot tougher, so his wrestling didn't slow me. I tuned out his complaints and shoved him into the pickup.

Ellie pounced on Tony and threw her arms around him. I shut the door to her cries.

For one second, I let my eyes rove over the hills surrounding the highway. Endless, serene, a sea of grass curing from the summer rains into the golds and reds of fall. Cows belonged munching grass amid the buzz of insects and the whisper of the breeze, not bellowing in terror, torn to bits in an accident.

I raced off to check on the men.

Alden advanced on Garrett. "It was a flat road. Can't you pay attention for two seconds?"

Garrett blinked and shook his head as if he'd missed a beat or two. He focused on Alden. "I have things on my mind."

"Like what?" I doubted Alden cared about the answer.

Garrett started to get steamed. "You think this ranch is the center of the world. But there's more to life than this."

"I suppose you know what that is."

Garrett stepped closer to his father. "You have no idea what a miserable little man you are."

Wow. Even if we needed to take care of the cattle and clear the highway, I wanted to cheer Garrett on. I suspected Alden had domineered and harassed him all his life, and I liked seeing Garrett fight back.

Alden didn't seem the least bit intimidated by Garrett's aggression. "Is that so? At least I'm not running off the damned road for no damned good reason and murdering three good heifers and setting the rest running around and taking pounds off them. You sorry excuse for skin."

Before there was any more bloodshed, I landed a hand on Alden's shoulder. "Help me get these heifers rounded up."

Alden opened his mouth to say something to Garrett, closed it and flipped his hand in disgust as if giving up on his son. To me, he said, "You drive on up there and I'll meet you coming down."

Garrett and I locked eyes. His held sorrow, apology, and a well of compassion I hadn't known he could feel. There might be more to this man than the arrogant lawyer and dismissive big brother I knew.

By the time I parked my cruiser and walked toward the three cows huddled next to the fence to head them toward Sarah and Robert's bunch, the Grand County ambulance topped the hill and idled alongside me.

Eunice Fleenor, the steely EMT who would make a drill sergeant look like the Easter Bunny, leaned her head out of the passenger window. "What are we lookin' at down there?"

"No fatalities, except a couple of cows. I think Garrett Haney might have knocked his head pretty hard. Alden is bleeding from his hand. Everyone standing when I left."

Eunice flicked her finger at Harold Graham, the old duffer who usually drove, and pointed forward. She didn't bother to respond to me. That's okay. Eunice would take care of business and that's what I needed her to do.

Alden caught up to me. His powerful body odor mixed with Old Spice in a nauseating way. "Damned idiot."

I gave him the benefit of the doubt and assumed he wasn't talking about me. "What happened?"

His arm flew up as if tossing all his frustration into the air. "How the hell do I know. Gave him one thing to do. Drive the damned trailer to the sale barn. And he can't even do that without costing me a damned fortune."

"Did a coyote or deer dart in front of him?" It seemed logical that something had caused him to jerk the wheel. There was a curve, but it wasn't sharp and there wouldn't have been traffic to get in his way.

Alden glared at me. His face, weather hardened and not handsome to begin with, looked like a tumble of dirt, sweat, and a case of number ten rage. "For all I know he had his damned head in his damned phone. That's all him and that danged grandson of mine want to do when they get away from home."

Sarah had said about the same thing to me last week. A couple of months ago, Garrett and Tony had moved from their upscale life in Scottsdale where Garrett was a highfalutin attorney, to one of Alden's isolated ranches. They had no cell service at their house, so couldn't seem to saturate themselves enough with all things tech when they emerged from home. Which, again according to Sarah, they did as often as possible.

I decided not to engage Alden on the topic and kept easing the heifers east.

In the fifteen minutes it took us to get the three agitated heifers beyond the wreck and on their way to the gate Robert had opened, Eunice and Harold had Garrett loaded in the ambulance.

Eunice motioned to me. "Says he wants to talk to you."

I hopped into the back of the ambulance where Garrett sat on the gurney, leaning against the wall. "Gonna have a headache."

He touched the bandage on his forehead already showing a shadow of red. "Keep an eye on Tony, okay?"

I glanced out the back of the ambulance. "I'm sure Alden and Ellie will look after him."

He shook his head. "Yeah. But check on him. Okay? Just do that for me."

He seemed worried and I could understand that. I even had twinges of concern when I left my silly dog in someone else's care. "Sure. No problem."

I jumped out and let Harold and Eunice ease their way from the scene and flip their lights on.

We managed to herd the heifers to join those Sarah and Ted brought from the other direction. After we pushed them into the pasture, my brother Robert pulled the wire gate closed, cinching it with the cheater bar.

He tipped a chin to his father-in-law. "Douglas is headed down with a truck and trailer and can load the mess. He's bringing a couple of kids with him."

Douglas, another of my brothers, managed the University of Nebraska (Go Big Red) research ranch at the northern edge of Grand County. The kids he'd be bringing were no doubt ag researchers working on PhDs.

Alden whipped a watch from his pocket and flipped it open. "How long do you 'spose that'll take?"

Not that my little problems came close to the suffering of the cattle or the financial loss of a wrecked pickup and trailer and the livestock, but I couldn't help calculating. With Douglas riding to the rescue, not to mention Robert and Sarah now wrapped up in this, and though I hadn't actually counted on Alden and Ellie, for sure they wouldn't help me out. This accident might make a difference on my future. I tried to put it out of my mind.

Robert's eye twitched the tiniest bit. You probably wouldn't be able to tell unless you'd known him all your life and knew every expression on his face. It meant he'd like to take a swing at Alden but tamped down the urge. His voice was terse. "Douglas will get here as soon as he can." He spun toward the east, where Sarah was plodding toward us.

Alden said, "You need to get hold of Jade and get these cows moved back home. And—"

The speed at which Robert doubled back was impressive. He leaned into Alden with attitude I was sure the older man wasn't accustomed to. "What I need to do is take care of my pregnant wife, *your daughter*, who has no business tromping up and down the highway in this heat." He didn't wait for a reply but took off again.

Alden's nose flared over his clamped lips for a second, then he shouted at Robert's back. "Don't think you can leave Brie with Ellie. She's been upset by this, too. She can't handle a little kid getting all fussy."

I'd witnessed Brie fussy exactly once in her short life. And that was on account of toddling into a red ant pile.

Robert swerved and stomped past us on his way to the silver pickup.

Brie started slapping the window and jumping up and down. Ellie rested her head on the seat back and looked washed out. Tony sat in the driver's seat, head down as if he was playing on a phone.

Sarah made it to us. She looked done in. Which was saying something because even at her worst, she was a beauty, in the same way Garrett was handsome. Lucky for them, they'd inherited their looks from Ellie. Who knows where they'd picked up their long legs, since Ellie was petite and Alden was stumpy.

Sweat dripped down the sides of Sarah's face and she circled one arm under her belly as if trying to take the pressure off her back. "What's going on?" She dipped her head toward Robert.

Alden sniffed and yanked up his jeans. "Don't know what good it was to have kids. One of you is an idiot that gets his butt hauled off to the hospital. And the other is useless."

Didn't matter to me if Alden was her father, I wouldn't let that stand. "Rounding up cattle when you're thirty-nine weeks pregnant is about as far from worthless as you can get."

Sarah shook her head at me as if to tell me to save my breath.

"Robert's getting Brie and then he's taking you home," I said to Sarah.

Underneath the bright slashes of heat marking her cheeks, Sarah looked pale and drawn. "We'll go home as soon as we get the road cleared."

Robert strode to us, Brie resting her head on his shoulder.

I'd planned to be cleaned up and hanging with Brie in town, giving folks a good impression of me before they walked into the courthouse to decide my fate. "I'll wait for Douglas." I pointed at Sarah. "Get home, put your feet up. Drink some ice water."

"Bullshit," Sarah fired back at me. She glared at Robert. "We're going to take care of this, then I'll let you rub my feet and bring me ice cream."

Alden snorted. "You let her talk to you like that? Women getting all bossy like that. No wonder this country's in so much trouble."

Robert shifted slightly to give Alden his back. "Doc told you to take it easy. You've already done too much. We're going home."

Ted wound his way around the white pickup, surveying the scene. "Well," he gave a breezy understatement, which wasn't funny. "This is messy."

"Got a trailer on the way and it'll be cleaned up quickly." I gave it a firm, official tone.

Ted, carrying off his suave, Ben Affleck cool and handsome, made a sympathetic cluck with his mouth. "This is a big day for you, Kate. Probably didn't need all of this, especially just before the voting closes."

Sarah leaned her head back and exhaled. "Balls. I forgot. We were going to vote on the way to Ogallala."

Alden scoffed. "I wasn't. It's a colossal waste of taxpayers' money to finance a family squabble between sisters."

Ted lifted his eyebrows and tilted his head as if to confirm Alden had a point.

Sarah, with sweat pooling in the divot at the base of her neck, motioned to Robert. "We have to go to town to vote for Kate."

Ted chuckled. "Oh, I doubt your two votes are going to make much difference. Dahlia's got a buffet at the Legion and she's been hauling folks in and out all day. I think she's got you beat this time, Kate." Dahlia being Ted's Medusa of a mother.

If Robert hadn't had his daughter in his arms, he might have taken a swing at Ted on my behalf. Instead, he snarled at him. "Don't you need to get back to Bryant? They'll be missing their village idiot."

Ted brushed his hands together with a gloating grin. "Yeah, I've got some packing to do."

If I had an ounce of confidence, I'd shoot back that he should save himself the trouble because I had no intention of losing.

Too bad I had too many doubts to swagger. Truth was, I feared Ted was right.

And the even bigger nightmare: the commissioners would appoint Ted to his old job, Grand County Sheriff.

2

Sometimes, your best isn't good enough. You throw your heart into it, punch, weave, duck, and slide and something can still shoot you out of your saddle.

If ever there was a sorrier looking garden, I hadn't seen it. All the tender care I'd lavished on those tomatoes, the backbreaking effort to haul fertilizer and till the soil, planting, watering, encouraging. I'd even made it through a nasty infection of potato bugs. I'd waited patiently for the harvest. I'd given my best and grown thriving green beans, carrots, onions, and, most of all, the red, juicy, sweet, perfect tomatoes. Last week's hail had decimated the whole lot and what had struggled for survival was being eaten by a grasshopper horde.

Perfect metaphor for this day. Grand County was having a special election.

Maybe one of the few times in my life I could officially be called special and not for a good reason.

The vote would decide if I'd be recalled as sheriff. Humiliation stung because Grand County had never held a sheriff recall before. It hurt that the community seemed to be split and the outcome uncertain. But what really gutted me is that my sister Louise, someone I'd thought would unfailingly be on my side against the outside world, had been the one to file the petition.

I picked a mushy tomato from a withered vine, looking like so much blood and guts, and I winged it past the yard into the prairie beyond the remnants of my garden. "Tomorrow we'll be back in business. Election over, all the foolishness behind us, and we won't need to worry about putting up any salsa or canning green beans."

Poupon, my shaggy standard poodle, shook his apricot curls and yawned at my optimistic proclamation. He sat beside me, eyes drooping in the evening gloom. We still had that glaring burn in the middle of the day, but fall was creeping into the mornings and afternoons, planning its siege on summer.

Freshly showered and dressed in a clean uniform, a chill spiked my skin. Maybe it was the night air seeping in, maybe it was nerves. I'd sent Robert, Sarah, and Brie home. Alden insisted on taking Ellie and Tony away from the scene of the massacre, and I'd waited for Douglas and his crew and helped them load the trailer and wrecked pickup. We'd lugged the two intact carcasses and the severed heifer's remains far off the road for Robert to deal with later.

I'd come home to Poupon asleep on my couch. But I'd need to leave again. I'd be expected to witness the vote counting, which would take place in the courthouse meeting room as soon as the poll closed and the county clerk/assessor, Ethel Bender, had her dinner at the Long Branch.

I considered Poupon sitting in the grass. "How about it? Do I look like I've got the world by the tail? Would I convince you I'm not worried about the good citizens of Grand County falling for Dahlia's lies and Louise's manipulation?"

He turned his head to watch the lake, his chin high in that regal posture.

"Yeah, me neither." Despite that, I climbed into the cruiser and took off for town.

In a matter of fifteen minutes, I pushed open the Long Branch's glass door and stepped into the entryway. About the size of two old-time phone booths, it separated the restaurant from the bar area, though that didn't make much difference. Anyone, including minors, could eat and drink on either side. I glanced into the restaurant side.

A dozen red molded-plastic booths flanked the long, narrow dining room along the windows that looked out onto the highway. The opening into the kitchen, the silverware station, the drinks dispenser, and the rest of the serving equipment took up the opposite wall, allowing for a walkway, about six feet wide, from the door to the end of the room. Ethel, the gray-haired battleship of a county clerk/assessor, sat at the first booth with a bloody steak nearly half eaten, a baked potato slathered in sour cream, and the remains of a dinner roll on a separate plate.

To the weak smile I offered through the glass door, she returned her usual scowl. I barreled through the door into the bar.

Aunt Twyla and Uncle Bud owned the Long Branch, the most popular restaurant and watering hole in Hodgekiss—and also the only one. Twyla knew most of the region's goings-on—if not from firsthand witnessing, then through gossip.

The place smelled like deep fryer grease and stale beer and as familiar as my childhood bedroom. I'd spent nearly as much time here as at home while I was growing up and beyond. In my teens, I'd worked here waiting tables and as a housekeeper for the four upstairs hotel rooms.

Most of the tables in the bar were full, with a lot of them shoved together to accommodate bigger parties. Only two bar stools sat empty, but one was my regular seat at the end, so I strode toward it. I fielded several greetings and a few well wishes along the way.

Twyla scurried from the kitchen a few seconds after I'd plopped on the bar stool. About my diminutive height, thin enough to make you wonder how her Wranglers stayed on her narrow hips, with a gray ponytail hanging down her back, she scowled at me. Balancing ceramic dinner plates of burgers and fries, she made her way around the bar. "This mess is your fault. You could at least pour those cowboys a beer."

I glanced down the bar to see Tuff Hendricks and my youngest brother, Jeremy, with empty beer mugs in front of them. If today's vote didn't go my way, maybe working for Twyla would be my next gig. No reason not to get a jump on it. I slipped around the bar and grabbed their glasses. "What're you drinking?"

Jeremy slid off his stool and walked away, leaving a nick in my heart. I'd hoped that today, no matter how the vote counted up, would put an end to our family rift.

So much for hope.

Tuff, a burly cowboy who'd been friends with Jeremy since before they'd pulled little girls pigtails in kindergarten, gave me a sympathetic nod. "Sorry he's such a dick."

I grabbed Tuff's glass. "Coors Lite?"

He nodded and watched me pour from the tap, leaving a half inch of foam. "It doesn't make sense. Him blaming you for your mom leaving. But he's let Louise get him all worked up about it and you know your brother, once he gets hold of a notion no matter how harebrained, it's hard for him to let go."

I didn't want to discuss family business, even with someone who had spent enough time at our house to almost be considered a Fox. "Thanks. He'll have to work it out on his own."

I'd like nothing more than to sit down with all seven of my brothers and sisters and get this whole Mom business cleared up. It'd been almost two years since she'd shot a man in the basement of the home she'd shared for over forty years with my father. And from that, her whole life, and ours as well, unraveled, causing her to flee, leaving us with fragments of our childhood in shards like a shattered wine glass.

But none of that was my fault. My oldest sister, Louise—oldest only because Glenda, the first born, had died going on ten years ago now—had followed some convoluted logic that said if I hadn't investigated the shooting, Mom would still be living with Dad and our lives wouldn't have been upturned in a wreck as bloody as the trailer accident earlier today.

Not content to rally Jeremy and another brother, Michael, to her side, Louise had filed a recall vote against me—as one does. Because the best way to bring a family together is to forcibly remove a sister from her job in a public and humiliating way.

The recall was the break my ex-mother-in-law, Dahlia, needed. She loved me the way a sow loves a coyote, which is to say, given the least opportunity, that old pig is gonna eat the 'yote. Louise didn't have to do much leg work collecting signatures on the petition. Dahlia and her sisters,

Rose and Violet, dispatched that chore in record time. Not that there was a record to break since there had never been a sheriff recall in Grant County. Ever.

Twyla stomped behind the bar, grabbed a round plastic tray from a shelf underneath and slapped it down. She muttered clearly enough for me to hear. "You get a herd of folks on a random Tuesday night, like we got the help to handle this ship of fools."

Tuff fought a smile.

I offered, "I heard Dahlia is having a free barbeque at the Legion. I would have thought everyone would be up there."

Her lip curled, not a great look for a woman who'd lived on Jack Daniels and a few stray French fries for the last thirty years. She was kind of like a sock monkey without stuffing. "You may have collected a few enemies since you been sheriff, but that Dahlia's been racking 'em up her whole danged life. It'd take more than free food to entice folks to her table."

The part about me collecting enemies stuck in my craw.

She grabbed a bottle of Jack and a small rocks glass. "Make yourself useful and pour two Coors Lites and a Bud."

While I pulled the spigot for the cold beer, I dished it back at her. "Think of the income you're getting off of this election. Not to mention the tips."

She reached for the soda sprayer to top off a gin and tonic. "Tell Bud we need a chicken strip basket with extra fries and a burger with onion rings."

I set the beers on the cork-topped tray. "Glad to help you out."

She lowered her voice, probably to keep anyone from knowing she was capable of a supportive thought. "Get that worried look off your face. If the folks in here are any indication, you got this election in the bag." She dipped her chin toward Tuff.

He startled at the sudden attention and jumped on it. "Right, right. It's not even close."

Lumbering movement outside the window made me home in on Ethel on her way back to the courthouse. Apparently, others noticed, too, because chairs scraped, people stood, and some filtered out, while a few others sidled to the bar to settle up.

I poured myself a mug of Coors Light, not my favorite beer, but the one that required the least effort right now. I tipped glasses with Tuff, and we drank in silence, my stomach feeling like a goldfish flitted inside. I'd take my time with this beer before making my way up the hill to the courthouse.

And what might be the end of another hopeful phase of my life.

3

A few more beers seemed needed to build up my nerves, but if I was getting ousted, it'd be better to bow out with dignity instead of a sloppy slur of tears. I washed out my beer mug. Tuff didn't feel the need to watch ballots counted, so I said good night, left Twyla cash for my beer, and stepped into the twilight.

Without the sun, a jacket would have felt nice. My boots made a lonesome thud on the sidewalk as I rounded the corner where the Long Branch sat on the highway and headed up Main Street. Only a smattering of businesses—the bank, a tack shop, Dutch's market, and the post office—made up the town center. The Legion hall surveyed it all from its throne atop the hill. Down the rise, across the highway, dipping into the right of way and BNSF tracks, up the other side and across a single lane stretch of blacktop, was my childhood home.

Lights spilled from Dahlia's party at the Legion and a group of about six or seven people clumped down the middle of the street on their way to the courthouse. That brick building, built more than fifty years ago, took up half the block around the corner from Main Street.

It sounded as if they'd drank those few extra beers I'd passed on as they laughed and teased. Lights snapped off and Dahlia stepped out of the Legion and turned to lock the door.

With no sidewalks in Hodgekiss, we all used the middle of the road, me climbing toward the intersection, them tromping noisily toward me. My flight instinct kicked in, but I fought it off, smelling the first scent of cheap men's cologne—probably used to mask BO instead of taking a shower—before they noticed me.

The laughter fizzled as the group recognized me in the dwindling light. Dahlia's sisters and their husbands, Deb Holt, Dahlia's best friend, and a couple who ranched down south walked past me. Rose, the sister I liked the best of the bunch, managed to say hello, guilt evident even in the faded light. It was echoed with diluted greetings by the others, who I assumed felt a bit uncomfortable.

With only five thousand people in the whole county, everyone has some relationship to everyone else. Even if it's not blood ties, and it often is, your best friend is someone's first cousin and married to the rancher who buys your heifers every spring. It gets way more complicated than that, but when I spoke to someone not from a county with a cow to people ratio of sixty to one, I'd learned to keep it simple.

Trailing behind the bunch with Dahlia's sisters, my ex-father-in-law Sid pulled his hat off as if paying respects at a funeral. "How do, Kate."

"Did you have a big turnout at your bash?" I tried to keep my tone friendly because Sid had never been anything but kind to me.

"Oh, well, you know how Dahlia is. She's got a bee in her bonnet about you, always has. But that's not nothing you don't already know."

We fell in together making our way behind the others. "How was your summer? Get a good hay crop this year?"

He let out a sigh as if it carried the weight of a thousand elephants. "Not as much as we should have. I didn't have the hands to get it put up before it got rained on. And that last hail- storm knocked down 'pert near a whole cutting of alfalfa."

After eight years of managing the ranch and doing a fine job of it by all accounts except Dahlia's, I knew all about the challenges of keeping up with the chores. "That's a bad break."

He sounded as if someone had shifted him to a lower gear. "I admit it's not as easy as it used to be when I didn't have all these years on me. I was hoping Ted could help me out some, but he's busy with that little sprout he's got, and Roxy keeps him hopping."

I was sure. When I didn't answer, Sid rushed on. "Oh. I didn't mean that I want you to be recalled so Ted can get back down here to help out. I guess you know that even when he lived at Frog Creek he wasn't much on the work."

I let out a *huh*. I managed the ranch and, when necessary, I could get Ted to help me round up or work cattle or even spend an afternoon in the hay field. Mostly, I traded help with my brothers and sisters. Sid didn't have that kind of back up. "It's a good place. You know how much I loved it."

He sounded as if speaking took more energy than he could summon. "I don't know how long I can keep this up."

At that, the clack of Dahlia's stacked-heeled cowboy boots gained on us. She started off with a strong stroke, probably because she swam in confidence I'd be voted out. "Don't you look official." She didn't add, "while you still can" but I was sure she wanted to.

Bless Sid's heart, he didn't hesitate to come to my defense. "Kate always did clean up nice."

Of course, Dahlia was way more than simply cleaned up. She wore tight jeans on her long, slender legs, with patches of colorful fabric tacked all over the denim. Some kind of peasant blouse puffed around her arms and tucked into a waist way thinner than a woman in her late sixties ought to be sporting. She and Roxy, Ted's second wife, always looked as if they shared a closet or else competed for most trendy and garish in Grand County. I didn't envy their wardrobe or taste, but I'd love to have their long legs and impressive cleavage. In fact, Roxy looked more like Dahlia's daughter than daughter-in-law. Or maybe even younger sister, though I'd never tell either one of them that in case they liked the image.

"Dahlia," I said, neither a hello nor go to hell, just acknowledgement she existed.

She took hold of Sid's elbow. "We should hurry so we'll get a seat. I'm sure it'll be standing room only for this show."

Even in the twilight I made out Sid's apologetic wince in my direction. "Good luck, Kate."

Dahlia yanked his arm, clearly as an admonition to not give succor to the enemy.

And the horse you rode in on. I didn't flip her the bird, but not because I didn't want to.

I wished Sarah and Robert were here. Always my wing woman in any situation from playground bullies in kindergarten to disastrous double dates in college, Sarah would have given me courage and made me laugh. Normally, there would be a brother or sister to gossip or joke with. But half of my clan couldn't make it in because of an accident or, in the case of my youngest sister and my oldest niece, were in Lincoln at school (Go Big Red). The other half supported the recall.

I hated the thought of Louise—named after Louise Fletcher, the actress who won the Academy Award for Nurse Ratched in *One Flew Over the Cuckoo's Nest* the year she was born—being all smug as votes against me were read. Even a bigger dread might be how she'd react if I won. All of that launched the war that had been raging inside me for the last three months about the crappy position she'd put me in.

On the one hand, filing a recall against me fired me up at the unfairness of the charges. Louise's petition stated I gave preferential treatment to my family. First, by not charging Jeremy with some kind of crime when he'd been duped by a pretty face attached to a drug cartel. And the ultimate insult, by allowing my mother, facing felony murder charges, to escape into Canada.

The petition didn't begin to tell the story. Louise blamed me for Mom's crimes coming to light—not my fault. And for chasing Mom away—again, not my fault. And as for Mom fleeing the country and causing our family to blow to pieces—that absolutely was also not my fault.

I'm the middle kid of nine, named after Katharine Hepburn, who won the Academy Award for *On Golden Pond* the year I was born. I don't know who handed out family roles, but I never asked to have the job of holding the family together. Apparently, Louise decided I'd shirked my familial responsibility and, for that, I needed to be punished.

I made my way to the front of the courthouse. Usually, I took the back door through the basement because the sheriff's parking spot was down there. I'd left the cruiser there earlier before I'd gone to the Long Branch.

Two glass doors opened to a wide corridor with caramel-colored linoleum so shiny it looked like glass. May Keller stood in the middle of the corridor patting the breast pocket of her threadbare cowboy shirt where she kept her smokes. May ran a good-sized ranch on her own and had managed to do quite well for herself for the last two-hundred years, or so it would seem by her appearance of a well-preserved mummy. With more nooks and crannies in her face than the leading brand of English muffins, and given her chain-smoking habits, it was a miracle of science she survived. I suspected that when the rest of us were dust, May Keller and the cockroaches would still be kicking.

A gurgling cough preceded her greeting. "There's the star of the night. I just saw that igit Dahlia and her henpecked other half. She's as full of herself as usual."

Newt and Earl Johnson, bachelor brothers Dad's age, stood with May. They swam in their too-large matching camo pants and jackets that made them look like preteens dressing up as soldiers for Halloween. Both wore buzz cuts I was pretty sure they gave themselves because they looked like gray sheep sheered by a blind shepherd. They smelled only slightly stale, which meant they'd probably been down to North Platte to see their sweet-heart recently.

Newt, the younger of the two, gave me a grave look. "We come by to be support."

May sounded like a shovel full of gravel. "Support would have been voting for her."

Earl, identifiable because his right ear was intact—he'd bitten Newt's off when they were toddlers—jumped in, "I told you we're sorry about that. We ain't registered."

"On account of the war," Newt said, helpfully.

Sure wished they'd added their two no votes to the tally, no matter what the obscure reason.

May scowled at them. "That's so much bull hockey."

Earl straightened his slight shoulders and spoke with more calm than normal. Probably out of respect for May, who'd had a hand in raising them. "The Man sent us to Vietnam and we're protesting that."

May patted her cigarettes. "By not voting for the best sheriff we've had in decades? We're likely to end up with that mud-brained Conner for all your protest. Also, you boneheads, you volunteered, no one sent you. I need a smoke."

She stomped off.

Newt watched her go with sad eyes. "We're sorry, Katie. We liked bein' your CIs."

I resisted the urge to pat his arm to comfort him. Their job was cleaning out private dumps and sheds, which created unique opportunities to be good confidential informers and explained my reluctance to touch them. "We haven't lost yet, boys."

Earl looked even gloomier than Newt. "Not yet."

I wandered down the stairs. The first floor, or the basement, depending on if you entered in the front or back, held the boiler room and a big meeting room. With no windows, a stack of folding chairs, and a couple of long tables, the space was used for everything from Girl Scout meetings to extension clubs, 4H, and the Grand County polling place. Tonight, all the chairs had been set up in neat rows in front of the tables.

Ethel Bender and the treasurer, Betty Paxton, sat up front with the metal ballot box in front of them. One of Betty's granddaughters bounced her toddler on her knee and sat at the same table with a spiral notebook and pen in hand. Garth Bender, Ethel's long-suffering husband, sat next to Ethel, with his own notebook and pen. The battle lines were obvious.

Ethel had always supported Ted and made it plain over the last three years that she considered me an interloper. Betty, the county treasurer, had lined up behind me, possibly because Ethel opposed me. The recorders on either side would take the tally and verify with each other.

Dahlia and her crew, who would have been the cool kids in the high school cafeteria, sat in front taking up two rows with their husbands, any children who still lived in Grand County, and the long-time friends too intimidated by Dahlia to move to a different social ring. She'd been right about one thing, there was standing room only.

I sidled up next to Zoe Cantrel, one of Susan's and Carly's best friends. Out of the three of them, Zoe was the only one to stick around. She'd gotten married two years ago and now had a three-month-old baby, Ivy, who she wore in a sling on her chest. She shifted rhythmically from one leg to another close to the back wall.

She offered a sober smile. "Sorry about Susan and Carly."

That spiked my concern. I hadn't heard anything about them. Susan, my youngest sister and a spittin' image of me, was a year older than Carly, my niece, who'd been my ward until she'd turned eighteen three years ago. They lived in Lincoln. "What do you mean?"

She winced. "Dang. I probably wasn't supposed to say anything. They're on their way home but they had a flat and didn't make it in time to vote."

I could have used those two votes. But I hadn't expected them, anyway. And knowing someone wanted to be here for me bolstered my spirits. "Don't worry about telling me. I'll be happy to see them when they get here."

She patted her baby's bottom. "I don't know if they decided to turn around since they couldn't vote."

"Oh." I leaned on the back wall. There were so many times when I was growing up in a house bursting with siblings that I'd prayed to be an only child. Then, being alone sounded like paradise. Though I still loved solitude, and my bungalow on Stryker Lake suited me perfectly, right now I felt as alone as a stink weed in a rose garden.

I scanned the room for Louise's not quite brown-not quite gray head.

Absent. The chicken.

May Keller shoved into the room and surveyed the crowd with her hands on her hips. She raised her voice so I could hear her, and that meant the whole room also listened in. "I'd like to be here just to see the gob smacked look on these yahoo's faces when they don't get you recalled. But I'll be damned if I'm gonna stand around to do it. I got work needs to be done tomorrow that won't happen if I'm stoved up."

Newt and Earl tried to squeeze past her into the room.

She shoved them backward. "If you didn't vote, you don't got the right to torture those that did with the stink you got on you."

They protested but there was no way they'd overcome May Keller and soon the buzz of conversations drowned them out.

On the far side about midway from the front, Deenie Hayward twisted to catch my attention. A new friend in the last few months since she'd started dating Dad, I was glad to see her. Deenie might be about the same age as Glenda, my oldest sister and Carly's mother.

I liked Deenie, because Louise didn't of course, but also because I didn't care if she wore her clothes a bit too tight and didn't have a supermodel body. She was smart, insightful, and funny. An added bonus is that she kept an open mind about everyone. She even seemed to still like Louise.

Deenie grinned, showing her uneven front teeth, and flashed me a thumbs up.

I returned her smile but hers dribbled off her face before she saw mine. I whipped my head toward where she looked as Dad walked in. Well, stumble might be more like it. He held a longneck bottle of Bud dangling between his fingers and had his arm draped around the shoulders of a woman I'd never seen.

Since I was still the law around here and open containers in the courthouse were frowned upon, as was public drunkenness, I jerked upright and rushed toward the door to intercept him.

"Howdy, Katie!" He waved with the hand not holding the beer and nearly choked the woman.

She didn't seem to mind, probably because, judging from her glazed eyes, she was in no better shape than Dad.

I planted a hand on his shoulder and with not so gentle guidance, steered him and his date from the room, down the hallway, and out the back door into the dark night. The air spiked goosebumps after the stuffy meeting room and maybe I didn't completely hate the excuse to leave.

Dad pulled his arm from around the woman, and she wobbled, letting loose a high-pitched giggle. He grinned at me. "That didn't look like much of a party in there."

I barely recognized the man I knew as Dad. All through my childhood he'd been the stable one. Even though he worked as a conductor on the BNSF Railroad and was gone for thirty-six to forty-eight hours every couple of days, his calm influence had guided us all. He'd taught us to care for each other and to not neglect neighborly gestures. Because of him, we never missed a funeral, wedding, anniversary, or birthday party. He was related to nearly everyone by blood or marriage, or even proximity, and took the concept of family seriously.

In the last two years since Mom abdicated being our matriarch, he'd reverted to what his sister Twyla told me he'd been like in his youth. Partying, running around with women, and generally shirking all responsibility except showing up to work, mostly sober.

I snatched the nearly empty bottle from his hands and tossed it into the Dumpster. "It's a recall, Dad, not a rodeo."

Not a tall man, Dad had always been wiry and tough. Now in his late sixties, and with his rambunctious lifestyle, he looked less vital than I'd ever seen him. All the mirth evaporated, and it seemed like the muscles in his face melted. "I'm sorry as hell about this recall, Katie. Seems like you've had a string of bad luck lately." He paused. "We all have."

Pulling the keys from my pocket, I hit the button and unlocked the cruiser. "Luck had nothing to do with the recall. Louise filed deliberately."

He dropped his gaze to his boots. "Because Marguerite left us."

"That's right, *Miriam* ran away. Not me." Wow. It sounded way more bitter than I'd expected. I probably needed to deal with that, something I'd been telling myself for quite a while and yet had not come to terms with.

I opened the back door and held my arm out to indicate he and the woman should get in.

For the first time, it seemed, she took stock of her surroundings. "Are you arresting us?"

"I'm driving you to Dad's trailer where you can—" I almost said, "sleep it off," but choked on it. "Sober up."

Dad tilted his head in a way that said it made sense to him. He placed a chivalrous hand on the small of her back and ushered her into the back seat, sliding in beside her. "Katie's always had a good head on her shoulders."

He grunted and I waited for him to pull his legs in before I shut the door. "She saves us all and that's why Louise got so mad at her when Marguerite left us. We expected her to fix it and it couldn't be fixed."

I slammed the door with more vehemence than necessary. Since when was it my job to make sure the planet spun on its axis? I never applied for the position and I sure as shootin' wasn't getting paid for it.

By the time I'd dropped Dad off and watched to see him and his friend safely inside—without him ever telling me her name or even where she was from—and got back to the meeting room, the vote tallying was well underway.

Someone had wheeled an old-time chalkboard into position behind Ethel and Betty, and Clyde Butterbaugh stood with chalk in hand, marking slashes. Betty pulled the ballots from the box and spread them out. Ethel read aloud, Garth and Betty's daughter scribbled, and Clyde scraped his chalk under yes or no.

I zeroed in on the chalkboard and added the bundles of fives. Sixty for yes, I should be recalled. Sixty-two for no. Yippee. I was winning.

Zoe gave me a thumbs up from where she still rocked her baby near the back wall. Deenie tried for an encouraging smile, but it looked as wilted as I figured her heart felt. She seemed to really like Dad and his behavior tonight would feel like a punch to her gut.

"Yes," Ethel intoned. "Yes." That made it a tie and probably not many votes left.

Betty unfolded and slid a ballot to Ethel. "Yes." One more, "No."

Sarah and Robert. Douglas. Susan and Carly. That would have created a margin. If I'd done even a bit of campaigning, I could have recruited Newt and Earl, and maybe even a few more. I'd been glum about the whole affair but hadn't honestly considered I could lose.

Betty made a great show of holding up a single bit of paper. "This is the last one."

Dahlia twisted in her chair to look at me. From the satisfied smirk, she must have anticipated a win.

I looked her in the eye with all the confidence I could muster. It must have been a good psych because she swiveled around quickly.

Before this whole sheriff business started for me, I'd been surrounded by my brothers and sisters. More than I'd wanted, really. They called and texted. At any of the frequent gatherings of our tiny community, the Fox clan created a nuclear bubble. Michael and Douglas, the twins, were always pulling some kind of prank or causing mischief, even in their thirties, but they barely spoke to each other these days. Because of me.

Maybe I actually wanted to lose the election. It could be the start of our family coming together again. I would be out from under the burden of being sheriff. Might get a job with regular hours or at least time off without being called in because of the risk of an emergency. Everything could settle down and the Foxes would go back to living, if not a peaceful life, at least our normal level of chaos.

Yes. Losing might be the best thing.

Betty smoothed the ballot and slid it to Ethel.

Maybe trying to create suspense, though Ethel had no flair for theatrics so it might be she was trying to focus her eyes, she hesitated.

Everyone seemed to be holding their breath. Or maybe it was only me. My vision tunneled to where I could only see Ethel at the end of what seemed like a long hallway.

She cleared her throat. "Yes."

4

Turns out, I didn't want to lose the recall election. Ethel's last "yes" shot between my ribs and directly into my heart, making it summersault into my throat.

The only lucky thing that had happened to me all day—if you didn't count no human fatalities at Garrett's accident earlier, which I should but didn't have the gratitude for right then—was that I was standing in the doorway, so it only took a second to spin on my boots and beat a full retreat.

The back door banged open and ejected me into the night. Assuming people would spill out quickly since it was after eight o'clock, which meant a late night for most of these folks who went to bed and rose with the sun, I strode away. It took only a few steps before I lost all my restraint and ran.

I pounded down the alley beside the courthouse and through the gap between Dutch's and the UCC Jumble Shop. The Long Branch was still open and since I didn't want to sprint past the windows and risk someone seeing me in my shame, I crossed the empty highway and went down the railroad right of way.

Normally, I'd find someplace quiet and retreat until I gained some perspective or at least settled myself down. But tonight, maybe for the first time ever, I craved confrontation. I had no interest in being reasonable since this recall business was insane from the start.

It hardly felt like my feet hit the ground as I flew across the tracks and up the embankment on the other side, heading for the dark house. I stormed through the side yard on a cracked walkway that led to the safe place of our childhoods. It had stopped being a sanctuary long ago. I burst through the kitchen door, some tiny bit of me expecting to see the red appliances and polka dots from Mom's retro kitchen. And always that sliver of hope Mom would be sitting at the picnic table that served as our dining set, drinking tea, willing to listen to my latest heartbreak.

Of course, that wasn't what greeted me.

Louise had redecorated. While the picnic table still took up its usual spot along the back wall facing the big front window, she'd painted the whole place a cheery yellow and replaced the appliances with buffed silver from the scratch and dent store in Rapid City. A nightlight above the stove gave off scant light and the whole house slumbered.

Since Louise's family had moved in, the smells of home had gradually shifted. Instead of paint, turpentine, and the earthy odor of clay that rose from Mom's basement studio, now the scents of baking and large meals cooked daily lingered in the air.

I stood in the middle of the kitchen, door open to the night, fury building in my core like molten rock. I'd been trying to get some traction on my life for the last three years since I'd discovered Ted and Roxy were having an affair and not only had the rug been pulled from my life, but the subflooring and even the foundation were gone. And now, I had no idea where I'd go from here.

A car pulled in the side alley that served as Fox family parking. Headlights washed in from the door and snapped off. I didn't move while the slap of flipflops, maybe a herd of them, ran up the walk and into the door.

Carly rushed me. She'd barely thrown herself into my arms when Susan hit right behind her. "I'm so, so, so sorry."

We'd never know if their timely arrival had saved Louise's life or if I would have curbed my murderous intent before acting on it.

I disentangled myself from the two of them. Susan, a younger and definitely hipper version of me, stepped back. Her long, wavy brown hair was now a series of bright colors like a rainbow fountain exploded from her head. In her baggy Husker basketball shorts and tight tank top, she launched into a Susan-spiel. "Those pieces of shit rolled in toe jam and stuffed with hairballs. What the fuck do they think they're doing? I can't believe they did this to you."

Carly, so much different than Susan, with her straight blonde hair, her Spandex volleyball shorts and Husker T-shirt, waited for Susan to drop a few more F bombs before she reached in to give me another hug. "This is truly shitty."

I wanted to say something pithy. Maybe shrug it off and joke about it. But when I opened my mouth, my throat closed, and I had to suck in everything to keep from bawling.

Carly reached behind her and snapped on the kitchen light. Even though this was Louise's home now, with her husband and their five kids, habit made everyone feel this was still Fox Central and we belonged here. "The silver lining is that now you can help out at the Bar J. We're starting to ship cattle and Rope really isn't up to it."

Susan, the Fox with the deepest sense of justice, let out a huff. "I can't believe you turned this around to your advantage."

Carly drew her head back in an "oh yeah?" gesture. "I don't see what's to gain by sitting around and moaning. The best way through a bad situation is action."

Carly's words seemed wise to me. But then, I'd had a strong part in raising that kid while her mother had been sick with cancer and after she'd passed.

Susan gave no indication of backing down. She flicked that rainbow over her shoulders. "Give her five minutes to feel bad and then let her figure out if she even wants to be a rancher. She could probably go back to school and get a degree that she could actually use."

So much going on here. Susan and Carly fighting wasn't a big deal. With less than two years separating them, they'd grown up best friends, even if Susan was Carly's aunt. Their fighting was a part of how they loved each other, as fiercely as I loved my brothers and sisters.

Most of my siblings anyway, because right then I couldn't feature being friendly with Louise, who had thrown a Molotov cocktail into my life. And speaking of the culprit, we turned to the sound of slippers scuffing to the kitchen door.

Louise blinked, like a 'possum in a searchlight. She sounded confused. "What?"

On the other hand, I had crystal clarity. "Are you kidding me? You uproot my life and then go to bed early because it's not a big deal to you?"

In her pink terrycloth robe over pajamas, and probably Mom under-pants and bra because Louise would need armor from any sensual sensa-tion, her gaze wandered from me to Susan and Carly. She seemed to put it all together about the time her twelve-year-old daughter, Esther bopped into the kitchen, her eyes bright and curious.

Esther launched herself at Susan and Carly, hugging them and squealing with delight. She grabbed a fistful of Susan's hair. "I love this! Will you do it to mine?" A little color wouldn't hurt Esther's tween awkwardness.

Faced with that kind of threat to her daughter, Louise sprang to life. "She will do no such thing. You march yourself right back to bed."

Esther, one of my favorites, came back without hesitating. "I have a stomachache and I feel hot. I might be coming down with something."

That flipped a switch in Louise, and she hurried over to place a hand on Esther's forehead. "You do feel warm."

Well, yeah. Esther slept upstairs and even if the evening had cooled off, all the heat from the afternoon would slither upstairs and breathe down on the beds. Louise should know that. We'd spent so many sweltering nights tossing in the double beds up there.

Susan and Carly shared a conspiratorial glance with Esther.

Susan jumped into the game, pushing all of Louise's buttons. "Mom was never good when we were sick. If it was bad enough to interrupt her work, she'd usually give us some homeopathic tincture and send us back upstairs to that hot bedroom."

Louise hustled Esther to the picnic table and sat her down. "Drink some ice water first and we'll see if that brings down your temperature. If not, we'll get the Children's Tylenol." She rushed to the cupboard for a glass. "Are you hungry? I can make some pudding."

Carly's mouth twitched and she looked away, I was sure to keep from laughing.

Esther winked at Susan and said, "I don't want to eat. I think maybe the goulash you made for supper hit me wrong." Now she was just being mean.

Louise paused on her way to the fridge for ice. "I didn't have garlic, so I added extra onions and peppers. I'm so sorry."

Up until she'd filed the recall, I enjoyed teasing Louise as much as the rest of them. Now, if I couldn't punch her in the nose, I didn't want to talk to her. Even so, I got stuck on Susan bringing up Mom as if she were still a part of our family. She wasn't any more welcome in my life than Louise.

Norm, Louise's husband, shuffled into the kitchen in a plaid robe, his thinning hair in a pyramid at the top of his head. He nodded to each of us in turn. He mumbled, "The Foxes are returning to the den," surprising me by his wit, something he wasn't known for.

He paused and considered Esther. "Suppose it was only a matter of time before you joined them." With that, he exited, and we heard him shamble back down the hall to the bedroom and a click as he closed the door.

"Honestly, Louise," Carly said. "What the hell?"

Louise put a warning in her eyes and hitched her head toward Esther, clearly telling Carly to watch her language.

Susan plopped down next to Esther and repeated, "I mean, really? What the hell? What did you hope to gain by the recall?"

Carly grabbed the cookie jar from the counter and set it on the table. "And how could you not even care enough to stay up for the results?" She moved around the kitchen as if it belonged to all of us.

While Louise set the water in front of Esther, Carly grabbed the old Tupperware tumblers Louise had nabbed when Grandma Ardith went to the home. She set the stack of four on the table and opened the fridge. "Got any iced tea?"

Louise didn't turn. "There's Kool Aid." It would be some off brand that she'd mix with half the required sugar.

Emboldened because she had backup, Esther spoke up. "She couldn't sleep so Daddy made her take a pill because she's 'spose to drive for the twins' football game tomorrow in Bryant."

The only school buses in Grand County were used for high school and junior high athletics. For everything else, the parents were on their own.

Louise gasped. "Esther. That isn't for everyone to know. You aren't even supposed to know that."

Susan separated the cups. "Better living through chemicals, Louise."

Carly agreed. "No shame."

I stood in the middle of the kitchen, no longer needing to murder Louise but still wanting to do something to her. Maybe pull her hair or box her ears.

Susan and Carly didn't seem to mind the idea of the diluted drink. Carly poured, not bothering with ice. She shoved a half-filled glass to the end of the table for me.

Louise joined them, sliding in next to Esther. No one sat at the head of the table, where Mom used to sit. "Filing the recall was the hardest thing I've ever done. But I'm not sorry I did it." She took the lid off the jar and fished out a chocolate chip cookie the size of a discus and took a bite.

"I could make you sorry." I mumbled it and maybe Carly was the only one who heard. Her eyes twinkled as though I'd been joking.

Carly set cups in front of the rest, and Susan pulled two cookies out of the jar and handed one to Carly. Even if I wanted a cookie, which I didn't because my stomach was already a sticky web of tension, I'm not sure I could have brought myself to touch the jar. It was one of Mom's creations. Made extra big especially for Louise's cookies.

I packed my words with potent sarcasm and aimed them at Louise. "I'm happy it's all worked out for you." I reached for the pink tumbler, the color no one ever wanted.

Carly whipped her phone from her shorts pocket and started punching it.

Louise, about the size of Susan and Carly put together but with twice the flesh and half the bones, blinked as if chasing away the last of her sleepiness. "The point wasn't to punish you. It's to *save* you. As long as you were sheriff, you were going to keep pitting yourself against the family."

Susan's mouth opened in disbelief. "What are you talking about?"

Louise was serious enough to put down her cookie. "If she hadn't been sheriff she'd have helped Jeremy and Michael before they ever got into real trouble. They couldn't come to her when they needed her because it would make everything complicated with all the legal."

There was a round of scoffs, which Carly broke up by mumbling into her phone.

Louise raised a hand to continue. "And if you hadn't been sheriff, you wouldn't have investigated and found out Mom's past and she wouldn't have run from you. If that hadn't happened, we wouldn't be having all these problems."

That was about the most convoluted logic I'd ever heard. "We wouldn't be having problems if you hadn't filed a recall against me. And now I'm out of a job and would rather skin you alive than talk to you."

"And yet, here you sit at her kitchen table." The commanding voice of my oldest sister shot out from Carly's phone.

I slapped a palm on my forehead. "Diane." Of course, Carly had called her. "I am not sitting at her table now or ever again." Might as well get all of us in on this. I took in the whole table. "Anyone want to call the brothers?"

Carly propped the phone against the cookie jar so we could see Diane. It might be late by Sandhills standards, but Diane's evening was probably getting started, so it was no surprise she wore a full face of makeup, jewelry and a button-up blouse. I don't think she slept more than four hours on a good night and probably woke up looking ready to step into a board room.

Ever practical, Diane said, "I don't have time to gather the brothers and they wouldn't have anything useful to say anyway. I've got an overseas call in ten minutes so let's get down to it."

Susan popped her empty cup on the table and reached for the pitcher. "And we've got to get on the road."

Louise, who had resumed eating her cookie, spoke around the crumbs. "You can't drive back to Lincoln tonight."

"Carly's going to drive since she doesn't have class until ten. I have to be at work at eight." She paused while she refilled her glass. "Carly thinks Kate should be ranch manager at the Bar J. I think she should go back to school." She pointed at Louise. "You got her unemployed, what do you think she should do?"

Louise studied me, and before she could speak, I shot at her, "You don't get a say."

She interrupted me before I finished the sentence. "You should get your vet tech certification and work for Heath Scranton. I'm sure if you two were around each other more you'd grow close and eventually marry. It's a perfect opportunity for you."

We all stared at her. I wondered if she'd finally had a total psychotic break.

"Bullshit," Diane shouted. It lost impact coming from the small screen of Carly's phone. Still, we gave her our attention. "You should come to Denver. Live with me and help out with the kids. I can hook you up with an internship at the bank and you could launch your career from there."

Carly jumped in, "She doesn't want to live in Denver. The traffic would kill her and if she did that, you'd have to fire your nanny."

"Don't let Kimmy and Karl hear you call her a nanny," Diane said.

Louise: "She belongs here with family who can surround her with love. The vet tech job is perfect."

I gave a sarcastic grunt. "Love. Right."

Susan: "She was on the Dean's list as an undergrad and would only need a couple of years to get her master's in psych. And Carly and I are in Lincoln."

Carly: "If she doesn't come out to the Bar J, I'm going to have to put it in an environmental easement and I really don't want to do that."

The argument swirled around and around like a whirlwind of useless energy. I quit listening and stared at the pink plastic Tupperware tumbler, not able to lift it to my lips. Who knows how long I sat amid the clutter of opinions gathering like dust around my feet before I stood up.

Diane was the first to notice. "Where are you going?"

"If you won't let me kill Louise, I'm going home."

Louise pried herself from the picnic table. "You can't go. We haven't decided anything, yet."

Carly jumped up, followed by Susan. They crowded by the door. Carly said, "Just think about the Bar J. I could really use the help."

Susan slapped Carly's arm. "Back off. Give her time to make a decision." To me she said, "You've got time, right? I mean, you have savings?"

Sure. Wealthy as all get-out, as county sheriffs are. My funds would last me a month. But I was grateful my bungalow was paid for.

From the phone, Diane shouted at me, "I've got to go, but call me tomorrow. I'll get some options gathered for you."

Louise stood in her shapeless robe, a stern look on her sleep-lined face. "You forgive me." It wasn't a question.

I let my gaze rest on her a moment. "I don't think so."

Esther, who had the good sense to have stayed quiet the whole time, caught my eye from where she still sat at the picnic table. She formed her hands in a heart gesture and blew me a kiss. It gave me a glimmer of hope.

I shut the door behind me. Despite the cluster of family who supported me, and that didn't count Louise, there were only two people I wanted to talk to right then.

One had run to Canada, taking my childhood with her.

The other lived in a skyscraper in Chicago and held my future hostage.

The decision whether to drown myself in a pool of self-pity, drink myself into a stupor, or scream obscenities into the stillness of the night was taken out of my hands when my phone rang.

5

When I saw Sarah flipping me off on my phone screen—her profile picture —my heart leapt into my throat. Maybe she was in labor, and everything was going great, and I'd need to meet her and Robert on their way to the hospital to take Brie, our agreed-upon plan. Or maybe she was in labor, and it wasn't going well, and I'd need to act. Or maybe she'd heard about the recall and was calling to find out who I wanted her to murder first.

There was a pause and a hint of a grunt after I answered, not assuring me this was good news. Then Sarah said, "Labor's started."

I sprang into a run, half surprised not to see my cruiser. It was still parked behind the courthouse. "On my way."

"Wait."

I trotted away from Louise's house toward the railroad tracks, not getting any more news from the phone connection. If I knew Sarah, her silence meant she gritted her teeth as she stared straight into the eyes of a painful contraction.

The night had cooled even more, and the town felt still and silent, that secret quiet that felt like a blanket over the world. My feet swished through the weeds as I pounded down the steep hill toward the tracks.

"Roxy's on her way to get Brrrrrrrrr-ie." It sounded like a cross between a bear growl and strangled chicken.

She'd called Roxy before me? I conceded this night might not be all about me and my losses, but did Sarah have to hand off my best friend duty to my ex-husband's new wife? It felt like she buried a hatchet in my chest and twisted it.

I shouldn't question the choices of a woman in labor, especially since the first time Sarah had a baby it hadn't been all that pleasant. But I heard something like a whine escape me. "Roxy? I thought our plan was for me to keep Brie."

A sound like a rattlesnake warning came through the line and I let her breathe through the contraction. "I'm about ready to let loose with a string of words inappropriate for our daughter. If you don't drive faster, we'll have to mortgage the ranch to pay for her therapy." Obviously, that wasn't for me, but aimed at Robert.

From beside her, Robert said, "Hang on, headlights up ahead. Looks like Roxy's rig."

Sarah panted and it sounded suspiciously like each exhale started with an f. I kept rushing toward the courthouse and my cruiser. Even if she'd handed my role as babysitter to Roxy, I wasn't about to sit on my thumbs doing nothing. But I felt as unwanted and useless as if she'd recalled me along with the county.

A ding of a pickup door opening on the other end and Robert's soothing voice talking to Brie indicated they'd pulled over and were making the child exchange.

I tried to sound hopeful, not as if my feelings had been stomped on by a herd of stampeding buffalo. "How're you holding up?"

Sarah made a sound like a balloon releasing air through a pinched valve, only throaty enough it could be coming from the bowels of hell. When it seemed impossible she could keep going, she sucked in a whoosh of air. A door slammed closed, and the dinging stopped. "I'm fine for a woman whose vagina is being pried open by a baby rhinoceros with six-inch claws. Sorry about the election."

I hiked up the right-of-way to the highway. Main Street was empty now, except for Tuff's pickup in front of the Long Branch. He'd probably hitched a ride home after too many beers. Or he'd hooked up with someone and, if so, I didn't care to know about it.

Sarah had heard about the election and even in the midst of her own crisis, she'd thought about me. She hadn't favored Roxy; she was trying to give me time to recover from my loss. That felt slightly better. "Don't worry about it. I'm okay and on my way to get Brie." At least I hadn't said "save" Brie from Roxy.

"N-n-n-n-ooooo." Again, she restrained the moan and made demonic static instead.

I continued across the highway and up Main Street toward the dark courthouse.

Rustling and grunting sounded as if there was a battle on the other end, and then Robert spoke. But not to me. "Would you just concentrate on labor and try to breathe like they taught us."

"US?!" Uh-oh. She might be hitting transition. "I don't see you trying to poop out an Edward Scissorhands who is shredding your vital organs. So, drive the damned pickup and let me talk to Kate."

There was another tussle of some kind and then Robert spoke to me. "You need to go down to the Blume place."

Apparently, that was for me. "Where Garrett and Tony are living?" Maybe Sarah wanted me to tell Garrett she was in labor, and he didn't have a landline and their phones didn't work out there. Except I knew they had a landline.

Sarah hadn't been lying when she said she was ready to release the cursing. Not only was she calling the new baby words that would warp the child's self-esteem in perpetuity, she spared a few choice ones for Robert, giving me an image of his anatomy I'd never seen while we were kids.

Robert sounded resigned. "We'll be at the hospital in thirty minutes. You can cuss your doctor then. She's used to it."

"She isn't the one who got me here." And away she went again.

Robert came back to me. "Tony called while we were loading up Brie and getting ready to leave the ranch. He said Garrett hadn't come home."

It was nearly ten o'clock. By Sandhills standards, that was the deep, dark of night. "Where is he?"

"Damn it! This doesn't feel right!" Sarah let out a squeal that went straight to my gut.

I started running toward my cruiser. "What's happening?"

It sounded like Robert dropped the phone. "How is it not right?"

"Oh my God." She spoke with a combination of terror-filled agony I'd never heard from her before. "Look at all the blood."

That clinched it for me. I jumped into the cruiser and took off on the sixty-mile drive to the hospital in Broken Butte, not bothering to let Poupon out for a break. I doubt he cared since he barely opened his eyes from where he slept in the backseat.

With worry as my front seat companion, I gunned the cruiser, figuring Robert and Sarah had about a half hour jump on me. The phone had gone silent, whether that was because it got crushed underfoot or if Robert had retrieved it and turned it off, I could only guess. And guessing was the last thing I wanted to do because in my state of mind, I'd go to the dark side pretty quickly.

Fifteen minutes later the phone rang, and if I hadn't been belted in, I'd have hit the ceiling. I jabbed it on, praying it was Robert telling me all was well. Instead, Heath Scranton greeted me. "I was just out at Derby's for an emergency foaling and Amanda told me about the recall. I'm really sorry."

Heath was the new vet—new because he'd only been in Grand County for three years—and we were friends. "The citizens have spoken."

He clicked his tongue. "That's not true. Most people probably figured it wouldn't be close, so they didn't vote. What are you going to do now?"

The question of the hour. "I'm on my way to the hospital because Sarah's in labor."

"Oh, gee. Wish her luck for me."

We ended the call quickly, but before I took a breath, it rang again. For this late in the Sandhills, two calls set a record. This time Barbie Drake, the postmistress, gave me condolences and then said, "I heard something in the back alley. Maybe a cat, maybe hoodlums. You know how they get wild at the start of the school year—the hoodlums, not the cats. Could you drive around and maybe scare them home?"

The good citizens had voted me out. Performing non-life-threatening patrolling didn't appeal to me. "I'm out of town. I'll call dispatch and they can send Ted over from Bryant."

Barbie jumped in. "Oh. Don't do that. It's not worth that much trouble."

I grumbled an if-you're-sure kind of answer and cut her off. Before anyone else interrupted me, I contacted dispatch and switched calls to them. I'd only done that a handful of times in my tenure as sheriff. But I had no guilt about it tonight.

I didn't catch up to Robert and Sarah on the way to Broken Butte and in forty-five minutes I whipped around to the back of the hospital. Robert's pickup was parked under the awning at the emergency room entrance. Garish light bled from the wide doors that whisked open as I parked and hurried toward them.

Robert stormed out, keys in hand. He paused when I rushed to him. "They're prepping her in case she needs a C-section."

"How is she?" Good? Bad? At least she was alive and under care.

Robert ran a hand through his hair. "She's cursing like a rock star on TV and vowing they aren't going to do the surgery. She thinks she's going to push that little bugger out on her own."

"What do you think she should do?"

Worry lodged deep in his eyes, but he looked resigned. "I think this baby is like her mother and this is the first of a battle of wills that will plague me the rest of my life."

That sounded like Sarah and didn't necessarily mean she was as strong as she made out to be. "Poor you. But maybe tonight it's more about Sarah."

He shook his head. "Obviously, I haven't said any of that. I've been all, 'You're doing great. It's going to be fine. I won't let them cut you open.'"

If I had to go through a harrowing experience, I'd be glad to have Robert with me. Maybe not as unruffled as Dad used to be, Robert would always come through steady and strong. "What about the blood?"

His face was drawn and pasty with worry, but a hint of a smile lifted his expression. "Turns out that wasn't blood. Ellie had given Brie one of those awful cherry pie things from Fredrickson's and Brie dropped it in the seat of the pickup. It's a mess, for darned sure, but not blood."

"Can I see Sarah?" I started for the door.

He opened the pickup door. "Not if you value your life. She thinks you're going out to get Tony and if she finds out otherwise, you're likely to get shot. They told me I have to move my rig and I'm going right back inside. I'll let you know how it goes."

I hated to leave Sarah, even if Robert would take care of her. "I thought they took Garrett to the hospital in Ogallala and Tony was with Ellie and Alden."

Robert seemed impatient but explained. "Belinda Carson is a nurse down there and her shift ended at six, I guess. Since she was on her way home, she said she'd give Garrett a ride."

Belinda and her husband lived in Bryant. He worked on a ranch up that way, and she commuted to the hospital a couple of times a week. Swinging by the Blume would have been on her way. "He got conked on the head pretty hard. They were sure he was okay to be released?"

He'd had enough. "I don't know, Kate. I'm not a damned doctor."

I wasn't done with him, yet. "Why didn't Tony call Alden and Ellie?"

Robert pulled himself inside the pickup. "If you had a choice between them and Sarah, who would you choose? Sarah didn't want to call Alden and Ellie because they go to bed super early. And she didn't want to add more stress on Ellie by letting them know she's in labor. Ellie doesn't hold up well on a good day."

Sarah filtered her life for Ellie, only telling her mother the highs, never letting her in on the challenges. And always hiding anything Ellie might judge as low class or coarse. It had always been that way and Kate and Robert knew the rules.

Robert inserted the key. "Plus, after what happened today and Alden getting all up in Garrett's face, Sarah didn't want to get him in any more trouble."

It surprised me Sarah would protect Garrett. She had a bear-sized resentment for him returning to the ranch and trying to take over. "Trouble? The man is in his forties. Isn't that a little old to worry about making Mom and Dad mad?"

Robert closed his eyes. "Look, I've had a really long day and it's shaping up to be a hell of a night. Can you just do this Sarah's way and save me that battle, at least?"

If we were normal people and not affection averse, I'd probably have hugged him and told him it would all be okay. "I'll take care of Tony. But if you let anything happen to Sarah, I'm coming after you with a dull knife and a vengeance."

That he didn't bite back let me know the weight of his worry.

6

Alden and Ellie owned three good-sized ranches. They lived at the home place, where Alden's great granddad had put up a soddy and made a living by collecting the stray cattle who had wandered off from cattle drives from Texas to Montana and hidden out in the Sandhills. It now had a two-story house built by Alden's granddad and the wife he'd wooed from Boston. Surrounded by towering blue spruce, it might be one of the finest places in the Sandhills.

Robert and Sarah lived on a three-thousand-acre place south of the headquarters. Their house was a Sears and Roebuck prefab stucco that had arrived in pieces on the train and was constructed in the early thirties. For the last ten years, Robert and Sarah had been slowly taking over the operation, moving Alden toward more modern ways of ranching.

A few months ago, Sarah's brother Garrett and nephew Tony had shown up for Haney's branding without wife and mother Sheila. Everyone assumed they'd spend a few days here and go back to Arizona. But the two of them had stuck around. Why his sudden move and what happened to Sheila, apparently Garrett didn't feel the need to explain. But Garrett and Tony had cleaned up the old ranch house at the third and most remote place. Everyone called it the Blume, after the original homesteaders who'd sold it to Alden's grandfather.

Since then, Garrett had been a burr under Robert and Sarah's saddle. Tony, a kid who might or might not be a bad seed, had been exiled from my sister Louise's home and her nine-year-old twins had been banned from playing with him. That being a direct result of him nearly burning the town down last July.

So off I drove to take possession of the junior reprobate. Unless Garrett showed up by the time I arrived. I thought about calling the landline, but only after I'd taken off. I didn't have the number and didn't want to disturb Robert and Sarah. Calling Alden and Ellie would defeat the whole purpose of me helping out, so Poupon and I settled in for the hour drive to Hodgekiss and another twenty to the Blume.

Like Harold and his purple crayon, a book I'd read to every niece and nephew so many times it was burned into my brain, the moon followed us. It didn't feel compelled to give me a life path, though. I was too stuck in feeling rejection to climb my way to any plan, so I spent the majority of the drive feeling sorry for myself. I couldn't even muster the gumption to listen to music and made do with the lonely murmur of tires on the road.

I hadn't been to the Blume for so many years I thought I might have trouble finding the house. I'd helped the Haneys round up cattle there as a teen. Turns out I didn't need to worry since the ranch headquarters looked like the Vegas strip in the dark sky of the Sandhills. Light shone from every window in the one-story red brick ranch house that squatted at the end of a tree-lined gravel road. The kitchen and living room had double-paned windows with no openings, like a store front. The other windows were small rectangles toward the tops of the rooms. The yard light created shadows around the burn barrel, empty chicken house, an old pickup and some farm implements. The barn and corrals beyond were dark.

I parked in front and let Poupon out. It'd been some time since he'd stretched his legs, so he had some business to attend to. It didn't require my supervision, so I walked across the grass and up the two steps to the concrete patio. I rapped on the door and turned the knob, pushing open the door and sticking my head inside. "Tony, Sarah—" I jerked back, hit the ground, and shouted, "Holy crap! Put that down!" I hoped Tony didn't have the nerve, know-how, or fear to fire the shotgun he'd aimed at the door.

When I still didn't hear anything, I shouted, "It's Kate Fox. Are you okay?"

The gun crashed to the floor and footsteps ran to the door. "Why the hell didn't you call and tell me you were coming? I thought you were a robber or something."

Well, now, that was pretty tough talk for a ten-year-old. When Poupon stuck his wet nose on my cheek I brushed him away and stood up. "Sorry about that. But handling guns is dangerous if you don't know what you're doing."

He leaned out the door, silhouetted in the light from the living room. "I do know what I'm doing and that's why it isn't loaded."

I brushed myself off. "I take it your dad isn't home yet?"

He opened the door wider for me and Poupon. Despite the house being old enough to collect social security if it were a person, the inside looked shiny and new. A polished tiger-wood floor, butterscotch leather furniture with a mid-century modern décor, artwork on the walls that didn't look like they came from Target, all worked together to make me feel as if I'd stepped into a swanky home in, say, Scottsdale, and not a ranch house in the Sandhills.

A game console sat on the couch where it appeared Tony had been stationed until he'd moved to a dining chair—a three-legged contraption of blond wood that seemed more decoration than furniture.

Tony stomped into the room and plopped down on the couch. He glared at me as if I was responsible for Garrett's disappearance. "He was here when Grandma brought me home and Dad was all, 'I'm sick of this place.' And, 'We're packing our shit and going back to Arizona.' And I'm all like, 'Great if you really mean it, dude.' 'Cause, like, he's said that before and I know it's all bullshit."

My ears hurt to hear a kid his age talking like that. But I'm not the vocabulary sheriff and mentioning it would take me one step closer to being like Louise, a leap it made me queasy to think about.

Poupon didn't make eye contact with me as he wandered over to Tony and hopped on the couch next to him. I started to give him the usual line about no dogs on the furniture, but Tony dropped a hand on Poupon's head and started petting him. I figured it might help Tony calm down enough he wouldn't be cursing and reaching for guns, unloaded or not.

My guess was that Garrett had gone to Ogallala or North Platte to tie one on. I didn't know Garrett enough to say this with any certainty, and what I did know made me reluctant to think he'd leave Tony on his own like this, but Garrett had a lousy day. I knew he'd also had a pretty crappy few months. So, maybe he'd had enough and needed a time out. Not the most adult way to handle life, but perhaps better than getting dead drunk and maybe taking out his frustration on Tony.

My head felt too heavy for my neck and my eyelids fought to stay open, so I dropped into a chair with enough wood and angles there'd be no chance I'd get comfortable enough to fall asleep. "Where do you think your dad is?"

Tony played with Poupon's ear while the goofy dog let his eyes close in a bliss I envied. "How should I know? I mean, Grandma dropped me off right after supper and Dad said he just got back from the hospital. He went outside to talk to Grandma, and I figured they were going to dis Gramps because that's what they always do but they don't want me to hear it."

Gramps, huh? I wondered if Tony called Alden that to his face. He'd never seemed like the Gramps type to me. There was a reason we called him King Alden.

"Where did he go after that?"

Tony kept his focus on the dog. "I don't know, man. I was playing *Red Dead Redemption*, and, like, you got to ride your horse around and shit and it takes a lot of concentration. I lost track of time."

If this is what happened without Internet, what would it be like if they had wi-fi? Would Tony be sucked into the void?

Since Garrett's pickup had been wrecked, I asked, "What would he be driving? Does he have a car or maybe a ranch pickup?"

"We left the Lexus for Mom in Arizona. There's an old blue beater that he lets me drive sometimes. I guess maybe that."

I glanced at my phone for the time. After one. "Okay. You get to bed. I'll sleep on the couch, and I'll bet by morning your dad will be home."

"What if he's not?" Tony stood up and Poupon opened his eyes.

And what if Sarah's labor is horrible and something happens to her or the baby? What if I don't get another job? What if Dad won't straighten out his life? And what if they'd released Garrett too soon and he was out in some pasture seizing from a concussion? Dang, I'd about had it with this whole stupid day. But here was a worried ten-year-old with the vocabulary of a drunk sailor looking at me as if I had any answers at all. "He's somewhere and we'll find him."

Tony gave me a skeptical frown then turned to Poupon. "Come on. You're sleeping with me."

I couldn't blame my deputy for choosing a bed and leaving me with the couch. But that didn't stop me from regretting my own bed since getting comfortable on the stylish, but hard couch, especially in my uniform, was like a cow sitting on a rabbit. It could happen, but it wasn't likely.

I must have gotten at least a little sleep since I woke with a start, my mouth feeling like the mummy's tomb, a crick in my neck, and a few terrified seconds when I couldn't remember where I was.

The sun had opened one eye, enough to turn the ranch yard gray on the other side of the window. I debated a minute before I pulled out my phone to call Robert, remembered there was no service out here and found the landline. Then I had to look up the number on my phone so I could poke it into the cordless headset. So many scenarios played out in my head, from the baby being born and everything shiny and new, to Sarah still in labor, to the unspeakable, and in any of those, a phone interruption wouldn't be welcomed. On the other hand, I couldn't *not* call.

It rang a few times before Robert answered, sounding like a cartoon character who'd been run over by a truck and was still flattened on the road. "We're still here. She's still in labor. The baby's heartbeat is strong, so Sarah is being stubborn and not letting them do the C-section."

Sarah didn't sound nearly as rubbed raw as Robert when she hollered from the background. "Is that Kate? Let me talk to her."

"Doc said you need to rest between contractions." He'd lost a bit of that patience from the night before.

"I don't give a good goddamn what she says. That's my Kate and I want to talk to her. Now." And that was my Sarah, all the banners flying.

He didn't need me to tell him. "You might as well let her talk to me, she won't give up until you do."

"Yeah."

The exchange took only a second and she barked out, "Did Garrett show up?"

That's not what I wanted to talk about. "No. How are you? Sure you want to keep at this? Wouldn't it be less stress for the baby to have the C-section?"

"I know what's best for this baby and it's for her to shoot out of me the way nature intended. And it's going to happen that way. So you and Robert can go to hell and have drinks with the damned doctor. Now, what about Garrett?"

Guess she put me in my place.

If there was a real danger to her or the baby, they could always knock her out and take it. Of course, dealing with her when she woke up might take chainmail and swords. The best I could do for her would be to give her the report she demanded. "He's not home yet. When Tony gets up, I'll take him to Ellie and Alden's and call Trey to get a search going. Do you know the make and model of whatever he'd be driving?"

With a low hiss of a woman refusing to surrender to pain, she said, "2007 blue Ford F150. Can you keep Tony with you? I don't want Mom and Dad to know Garrett's AWOL."

She knew I wouldn't say no. And I knew she wouldn't ask if it didn't matter to her. So, whether I wanted to keep Tony or not, he was riding shotgun with me until we found Garrett. "Since when have you been Garrett's champion? Last I knew, you wanted to string him up, gut him, and slice him for jerky."

It took a moment to pant through a contraction, then she said, "When we were loading the heifers yesterday, he started to talk to me behind the trailer. He was all worried. I don't know why. He said something about Sheila, how he was really concerned and then Dad started yelling at him and he shut up. But there's something big going on."

"And you don't want Alden to know?"

"It might have to do with Dad. I know Garrett's a pain in the ass and I'm really mad at him. But acting like this isn't like him at all. And that wreck was because he was on his phone or something." She broke off and let out a string of curse words that probably short circuited the heart monitor.

Sure, hormonal surges could make pregnant women act out of character, but this sudden concern and maybe even affection for Garrett seemed off point for her. Still, I'd do what she asked. "Okay. Tony's with me. I'll see about finding Garrett." And try to figure out what to do about the recall. Probably not try to fix Dad. And maybe work at getting over wanting to maim Louise.

Robert came back on the line, and I assumed Sarah was done with me for now. "Will you call Roxy and let her know we're still at it? Maybe let the brothers and sisters know but please, God, tell them not to call and I'll get the word out when the baby's here."

Sarah in the background: "Oh, this baby is here. It's all up in here. It's so here I'm about to grab it with a grappling hook and pull it out."

Robert's voice still sounded like he could stand to be reinflated. "I know you're not a praying woman, but maybe say one for me, anyway."

Sarah's response blistered my ears but maybe Robert wore a Kevlar suit. "You?! The prayers need to be coming my way, buddy. All of them."

I hadn't wanted to add stress to Sarah, but I could ask Robert. "How worried should I be about Garrett? Is him not coming home normal?"

A few footsteps took him out of earshot of Sarah's grunts and curses, so I assumed he slipped outside. "He's got a self-centered streak wider than the Mississippi during spring runoff. But he takes good care of Tony. So, yeah, I think his disappearance is weird. But you're going to have to take this one. I've got my hands full here."

I wished him luck and hung up.

The click of Poupon's feet heralded Tony and his blurry-eyed entrance into the kitchen. "Is Dad home?"

I tried to sound cheerful. "Not yet. We'll get some breakfast and, while you dress, I'll send out an alert to see if he's in Ogallala or North Platte." His thick hair was a nest of tangles and he still had a little boy smell of sweat. He surprised me by asking, "How's Sarah?"

I gave him a pass for not calling her Aunt Sarah because it warmed my heart that he'd thought about her. "She's still in labor."

He glanced at the wall behind me, no emotion on his face. I'd seen Sarah do the same thing with the exact blank expression. She did it when she wouldn't admit something bothered her. It made me want to assure him. "It's not unusual for labor to last this long and I'm sure it's fine."

His shoulders relaxed a little and with a casualness I thought might be false, he rubbed Poupon's head and said, "Yeah. Who would be in a rush to have another baby around? All they do is piss and cry."

He sure had some stickers on his stem, but what was the point of calling him to the carpet for rough vocabulary? He wasn't my kid to raise. "Can you let Poupon outside?"

He clattered to the front door because boys—even barefoot boys—aren't capable of doing anything without noise.

It surprised me that the fridge and pantry were well stocked. I found milk, eggs, butter, and everything else needed for pancakes. It seemed like the ultimate comfort food and if Tony didn't need it, I darned-sure did.

He took Poupon outside and, from the window, I witnessed my usually uninvolved companion dog romp on the grass with Tony. He only tolerated the person who filled his bowl with kibble, but loved May Keller, Ethel Bender, Beau Conner, and now, apparently, Tony Haney. No accounting for taste, as Grandma Ardith liked to say.

I found the coffee and while Tony and Poupon romped in the wet grass, the house filled up with the soothing smells of breakfast.

When Tony tromped back inside, he plopped down at the oval table in one of those three-legged chairs and gave the meal a skeptical appraisal. "Dad says sugary stuff and lots of carbs in the morning is a bunch of empty calories and will make you hungry all day. We usually have yogurt or chia pudding."

Yeah, I'd noticed the oat milk and low-fat this and that. "Admirably healthy." I slathered butter on my pancake. "But every now and then, it's good to check out the trashy side."

He lifted his chin and gave me a thoughtful expression. "As long as you went to all the trouble I might as well have one."

I pushed the syrup his way and didn't say anything when he poured enough on his plate the pancake looked like an island.

After we ate, I called the state patrol and gave them the pickup and Garrett's description. Just to be thorough, I called the hospitals in Ogallala and North Platte and checked in with the sheriff departments in both of those counties. No trace of Garrett, which was a relief.

Teeth brushed, clean jeans and T-shirt, Tony joined me outside. "I get to ride in front this time."

Two months ago, due to weird circumstances which seemed to happen to me more than they should, I'd been forced to drag Tony around with me on an emergency call. Since he'd been—again, a Grandma Ardith saying— a little pill that day, I'd made him ride locked in the back of my cruiser. "If you promise not to touch the siren or lights, you can ride up front." Also, Poupon had already taken up position in the back.

A slight haze rose from the ground letting off the scent of damp grass and dirt, giving me that particular fall morning feel that reminded me of early volleyball practice and marching through the streets of Hodgekiss getting ready for band day competition. This time of year always smacked of new beginnings and the opportunities being a grade older might open up. That optimistic bump still survived underneath the imploding bomb of my life.

I rolled the windows down to the cool air.

Tony rolled his up. "Where are we going?"

That was a debate I'd had with myself. No point in heading south to Ogallala or North Platte since officers were already on the lookout for Garrett. Tony wouldn't know of any favorite drinking spots on the ranch in case Garrett had gone out to tie one on and fallen asleep. My best plan was to go to my house on Stryker Lake where I could shower and change and, by then, hope something had happened.

Instead, I got a call from Vicki Snyder, the editor, reporter, ad salesperson, and office manager of the weekly paper, *The Grand County Tribune*. "Listen, Kate. I didn't get a chance to tell you last night how sorry I am. Ethel's gone too far this time."

The grasses on the hills were sliding from summer to fall and covered the prairie with golds, reds, and soft green. You'd hardly notice the breeze if you stood outside, but it caused a gentle ripple. For some, a lake lapping on the shore or a creek trickling brought comfort. For me, the empty hills of grass, like an ocean of life, calmed my soul.

From this point of Zen, I said, "Ethel didn't file the recall. She only did her job but I'm sure she'll be happy to have Ted back."

Vicki snorted. "The only person happy to have Ted back is Dahlia. I have to send the paper to the printer this afternoon so can I get a quote or two from you about the election. Maybe some idea what's next for you?"

Tempting as it might be to call Louise a misguided troll with fantasies fueled by sugary baked goods, I said, "No comment on this one. I'll have some time to figure it out. The commissioners will need to meet at some point and decide on an appointment. Until then, I'll remain in office." The three commissioners, Jack Carson, Clyde Butterbaugh, and Buster Duran weren't known to be fireballs. After the disaster with Commissioner Clete Rasmussen, in which I'd played a big part days after being sworn in, Grand County had opted for commissioners who wouldn't shake things up and would hopefully do as little as possible.

"Apparently, Butterbaugh's daughter is having a baby in Spearfish any time and Clyde wants to get this decided before they head up there. Now's your chance to make a parting shot before the commissioners meet and appoint Ted."

Three years ago, Ted had been shot and accused of murdering Roxy's then father-in-law. I'd ended up having to suss out the real killer and then I'd run for sheriff, beating Ted in a landslide of Fox relatives or folks who secretly hated Dahlia or thought Ted was incompetent, or often all of those reasons. I'd hoped Ted would fade into the background of my life, a has-been like your first car that you loved but were relieved when you traded off for one that didn't break down on every road trip. The exception being, of course, my 1973 Ranchero I called Elvis, which would remain the love of my life.

But when two of the sheriffs in our co-op of four had ended up losing their jobs and their freedom, Ted had been appointed sheriff in Chester County and I'd had to work with him. Not only that, but my family had some kind of unwritten code that once family always family. (Of course, that had been suspended in my case.) But Ted and Roxy were on hand for most Fox gatherings.

And now, here we were, full circle with Ted getting his job back.

I suppose I could let the Chester County commissioners know I was in the market for a job. But that was a step so low even I wouldn't take it.

Vicki's mind might have been looping in the same path. "What are your plans?"

I hesitated.

"Off the record of course," she said. "I only ask because I sat next to Sid last night and he's worn out. He said at least twice that he needs a manager for Frog Creek. I know it might be weird, but it just seems like you fit out there." She hurried to add, "Not with Ted, for the love of God. But, well, it's a thought."

A thought that wasn't new for me.

The house at the Blume sat about five miles from the one-lane oil strip connecting two east-west rural highways. North about ten miles was Sarah and Robert's place, sometimes called the Groskopf, for the people who'd first settled there. But mostly, we didn't call it anything. From there, it was another five miles to the highway where a left took you seven miles to Hodgekiss, and a right turn headed you ten miles to Bryant. Basically, the Blume sat far from anything, the kind of location I'd love.

After I'd disconnected, Tony didn't venture any comment, which indicated how worried he must feel. Every other time I'd been around him, Tony had a wisecrack for everything.

We drove across the valley and toward the oil strip and I tried to engage him. "School starts next week, right? It's always later at the country schools so you get more time off than townies."

He kept his eyes on the prairie outside the window. "I guess. I don't see the use in my starting when we'll be going home soon."

I supposed that was Tony's wishful thinking, since Garrett's home sure looked like he planned to stick around. "There's a new teacher, I hear. And I think there will be six or seven kids. So that means you'll get to do a lot of fun things. Experiments and field trips."

He whipped his head to glare at me. "It's a fricking one-room school like

Little House on the Prairie and I'm going to be the oldest. This is bullshit. And Dad knows it. That's why we're not staying."

Though I tried to put the shine on a dirty penny, I doubted I'd have been any more thrilled with a one-room school than Tony. Trying to come up with a spin that might brighten the situation, I let my gaze wander to the right, where a sandy path veered into what looked like an alfalfa field. A center pivot irrigation sprinkler was visible with its big tires on the ruts. A flash of blue caught my eye.

I hit the brakes, bumped out of the sandy road, and pulled close to the fence line to make a U-turn.

"What the heck?" At least Tony hadn't cursed this time.

"I might have spotted your dad's pickup. That's what they call the east pivot, right?" I maneuvered around and back to where the trail led to the alfalfa field, a sea of bright green hidden by a three-wire fence choked with years' worth of tumbleweeds and tall grass.

"Yeah. You can hear the sprinkler from the house." Tony scooted to the windshield and scanned the area, his face drawn together in worry. When he saw the same blue I'd seen, he bounced in his seat. "That's it. Dad's pickup."

I stopped the car and grabbed his arm as he reached for his door. "Whoa. You stay here while I check it out."

He jerked his arm away, making his thick hair flop on his forehead. "No way. That's my dad."

I squeezed tight. "Exactly." I held his gaze, his eyes large and mink-brown and exactly like Sarah's. I knew her so well; it made me almost think I could read Tony's mind.

Smart, like his father and aunt, he must be turning over possibilities of why his father would have been less than five miles from the house and not make it home. A war fought behind his eyes that I figured pitted his need to know against his reluctance to see something he couldn't erase. It was a battle well beyond what a ten-year-old should be able to handle. And yet, he held steady while coming to his conclusion.

I squeezed his arm. "Trust me."

He inhaled and sat back. "Okay." I couldn't guess at the maturity and restraint it took for him to come to that. No way I could have been that self-possessed at that age. I might need to rethink my opinion of this little guy. He'd been such a pain all summer, getting my nephews into trouble, back-talking to everyone, tossing out smirks and snark without limit.

Poupon sat up in the backseat. He shook his head and gazed around, probably to see if we'd stopped someplace that might provide him with a Slim Jim.

I climbed out of the cruiser and strode toward the break in the grass that took me into the alfalfa field and the pickup parked at the pivot. The optimistic bubble of early fall fizzled with a buzz of nerves. Whatever I'd find wouldn't be good.

The Zimmatic irrigation system had to be at least thirty years old. It had one long arm, about the length of a football field, with sprinkler heads every few feet pointed to the ground. This contraption was tethered to the center point and rotated around a massive circle. Every ten yards or so, fat tires cut ruts in concentric circles from the center. Metal ribs rose in arcs from each tire to support the pipe that carried water to the sprinkler heads. An electrical control box was attached to each of these towers. We didn't have pivots on Frog Creek, so I wasn't an expert, but I did know fuses popped and wires burned and repairs to the towers seemed an almost full-time job in the summer. The last tower was anchored into the ground in the very center of the field. This is where the master electrical panel and switches were located and where the well pumped the water.

Garrett's old blue beater was parked about four towers, slightly less than a football field, away from the center. He'd driven out there, flattening the alfalfa in two tire tracks and then smashed more alfalfa when he turned the truck around to point the hood back toward the road. I'd never have been so cavalier with the pricy forage. I'd have walked out and, if needed, dragged a ladder to reach the tower. But, as Sarah often complained, Garrett had a lazy streak. The pivot wasn't moving, which meant it was probably broken down since the third cutting hadn't been completed and they should still be putting water on the field.

My hope was that Garrett had brought his Jack Daniels—or in his case something fancier that a Scottsdale attorney would drink—out here to drown his sorrows. With any luck, he'd had too much, passed out, and today would suffer nothing worse than a hangover and humiliation.

Not that I pegged Garrett as the suicide type, but I gulped at the fear he'd come out here for a conversation with his rifle. I'd seen stranger things happen, all of them grisly.

I trotted up the trail to the pivot, glad I wasn't lugging my utility belt along with gun, cuffs, and all the equipment that made it feel like a hundred pounds. Dread was heavy enough.

The haze had already lifted from the ground and bright sunshine lit up the verdant alfalfa, now knee high with at least ten percent of the field showing purple blooms, meaning it was ready for the final cutting. All of this information swirled in my brain trying to keep out the anxiety of what I'd find when I finally reached that blue pickup.

A meadowlark sang so sweetly like she tried to convince me nothing bad could happen in this fresh meadow on this new day. I'd been around the hills and up and over a few ridges enough to know that bad things can happen in the brightest sunshine.

When I got closer I shouted, "Garrett?"

Nothing moved. The meadowlark stopped singing, and the sun slipped behind a cloud at the same time a breeze spiked a chill up the back of my neck.

I yelled again every few steps, with nothing to create an echo so his name puffed into the morning air.

My stomach swirled in a sickening heap of syrup and pancake, Garrett's advice about beginning the day with protein instead of sugar made sense. Hope and hope and hope for a drunk. Deepening dread for anything else. I made my feet keep on their pace even though I'd much rather stop advancing and, even better, flee the other way.

I reached the hood of the pickup. "Garrett." The driver's door was open. No dinging because that annoying wire would have been cut years ago.

I took a few more quick steps, determined not to flinch at what I might find inside the cab. I'd seen a suicide victim blown apart by a gun to the head. It's not an image you ever get over. I could imagine a drunk choking on vomit or a drug overdose. I prayed not to find any of those things. But the cab was empty.

One moment of relief before I stepped back and scanned the area around the pickup. When I spotted the boots on the ground beyond the bed of the pickup, toes pointing up, all the jitters flowed back in, stronger and with a deeper current.

I skirted the open pickup door and followed the sight. Boots, jeans that started at the ankles, then knees, then hips, where an untucked button-up took me the rest of the way to what yesterday had been a remarkably handsome face. A face so much like my best friend's that I loved him on that fact alone.

But now that face was a hideous mask with eyes open and staring, eyes that used to be mink-brown and intelligent, now a shocking and vivid red. His mouth in a frozen grimace the Joker couldn't match. His arms splayed out, fingers of both hands curled as if clutching at life, fingertips blackened. A slight scent of cooked meat hit me, maybe imagination, maybe the real consequence of an electrocuted body.

7

Oh. No.

It took me a matter of seconds to put together the puddle of water underneath Garrett, the leak that must have come from a bad gasket in the pump. The steel pipes, wrench tossed several feet away. He'd been working on the irrigation sprinkler. But why hadn't he shut the power off?

Power. I whipped my head around to locate the panel.

Tony was running toward us, Poupon on his heels. They'd made it halfway from the road to the pickup.

I raised my arms. "Stop. Go back."

He kept coming. "Is it Dad? Is he here? Is he okay?"

This was a sight no son should see. I took off to intercept him and had to clutch his arm and tug him to slow him down. I grabbed his shoulders and leaned into him. He was tall for his age and at my five foot three inches, I only bested him by a couple of inches. "I'm sorry. So sorry. Your dad had an accident."

Tony wrenched from side to side, hair flying. His beautiful eyes glimmered in panic. "No. He didn't. What's the matter? I want to see him."

It took some brute strength to push him back down the road. Poupon bounded around us, barking and letting us know he was in the game. "It's not safe. I need to cut the power. This isn't something you want to see. Believe me. He wouldn't want you to remember him like this."

Tony went limp. His breath hitched in his chest, and he blinked rapidly. "Are you...? He's not? I don't...."

I hugged him then, even with his arms limp at his sides. What else could I do? "I'm sorry. So sorry." Suddenly, I hated that word. It couldn't fix anything. It was small and ugly and wholly inadequate to hold a young boy's grief and fear.

Tony seemed like a computer powering down. He moved but without purpose. He didn't speak or take in the world around him. We plodded back to the car, and I drove us to the oil strip and a few miles toward town until I had a signal and could call. I left Tony in the car and walked several feet away.

Instead of calling dispatch, I used Trey Ridnour's private number. He was a state trooper stationed in Ogallala and I knew he'd arrive sooner than anyone. With my iffy status of likely being replaced by this afternoon, I figured the details of the death would best be handled by the state patrol. Besides, sheriff wasn't my job anymore. Or it wouldn't be as soon as Ted was sworn in.

As with any unattended death, this would need to be assumed suspicious and investigated. Crossing t's and dotting i's, because not long ago, my assumption of accidental death nearly led to more murder.

Trey said he'd be there in an hour. I called the Grand County coroner who lived in Broken Butte, and it sounded as if I'd woken him from his mid-morning nap. Ben Wolford might not be as old as May Keller, but he wasn't far behind. He gave me permission to call the death, typical for our county. One more call to the emergency crew lead, Eunice Fleenor, who would collect more EMTs and bring an ambulance. No hurry on that chore.

If I doused him in bronze Tony couldn't look any more like a statue. He stared out the windshield without movement, without tears.

The next calls would be tougher. If it had been a stranger, I would have bowed out and let the state patrol take care of it. I was done being sheriff. But I wasn't done being a friend.

I weighed whether to call Robert and came down against it. Right now, he and Sarah needed their focus on birthing their baby. It was a harsh truth that Garrett wouldn't get any deader. With that in mind, I decided to wait until Trey arrived and then drive Tony to Alden and Ellie's. No one should get the news of their son's death over the phone if it can be avoided. Even if having to be the bearer would be more uncomfortable for me.

Death tugged at me, making me heavy with its finality. I wanted to deny and turn away, but I drove us back to the road near the pivot and left Tony in the car while I hoofed it to the electrical panel and cut off all the juice.

When I returned, I opened the doors of the cruiser to the warming day and coaxed Tony into the backseat with Poupon. In a move I'll always be grateful for, Poupon laid his head in Tony's lap, giving the kid more comfort than anything else at that moment.

In well less than the hour Trey had predicted, he barreled up the lane with two other state patrol cars behind him. Good that he brought reinforcements to process the scene. He braked hard and jumped out, not bothering with his Smoky Bear hat. "Man, Kate. This is harsh. I heard about yesterday and I'm sorry."

There was that turd of a word. It felt like a hard acorn stuck in my gullet to have to respond but Trey had always been on my side, and I knew he felt bad about me losing my job. "I admit it surprised me."

He was tall, with a broad face and blond hair, and a general sense of kindness about him. "What are you going to do now?"

That's a question that was getting old fast. "Right now, I'm going to take Tony to his grandparents and tell them their son is dead."

Trey winced. "That's spoiled mayonnaise on a shit sandwich. I'm so—"

I cut him off before he could drop that mouse pellet word again. "The deceased is Garrett Haney. He and his son live a couple of miles up the lane here. Looks like he was repairing the pivot and didn't get the power off. I snipped the wires after I found him."

The other two officers, a young woman who looked fresh out of college and a man in his forties, joined us before I finished.

"Ambulance should be showing up in the next twenty minutes," I said. "You've got this?"

They nodded and turned back to their cars. No reason to walk all that way to the scene when they could drive, especially if you didn't care about squashing the alfalfa.

The next forty-five minutes felt like swimming through shattered glass as the cruiser carried us over the country roads to Alden and Ellie's house. Tony sat in the back seat a green tinge on his face, the only movement his fingers tangling in Poupon's fluff. Every now and then he shuddered and Poupon would lift a paw and drop it in Tony's lap. I didn't have anything to give him. All the platitudes in the world couldn't cut into his wall of disbelief.

When we pulled up in front of the two-story house, painted a pristine white and surrounded by towering blue spruce, I braced myself for the worst. Ellie, who had never been one to take charge and who always seemed attached to Garrett in a way that irked Sarah, would probably crumble. Who could guess Alden's response. And in the middle of it all, their grandson, who now had no home until we located his mother and she came to retrieve him.

I opened the back door and Tony slowly creaked his head to me. He looked puzzled, and then glanced around and seemed to recognize the place. Poupon edged outside and Tony followed.

Since it was close to noon, it didn't surprise me that Alden swung open the screen and walked out on the front porch. Yesterday aside, Alden usually had an air of confidence and good cheer like a politician. And like most politicians, it always felt put on. His attention generally shifted quickly, and he'd forget about you like a puff of dandelion seeds blown into the wind.

He seemed a little nervous beyond that store-bought smile. But when your grandson is brought home in the back of a sheriff's car, that would be appropriate. "Katie Fox. What brings you out here?"

Tony only took a few steps across the grass and stopped.

I placed a hand on his shoulder blade, and it felt sharp and fragile. With a gentle nudge we walked to the porch together.

Alden's smile dribbled off and his focus shifted from Tony to me. "Want to tell me what's going on here?"

Tony slumped onto a step, and I left him there while I continued up to meet Alden on the porch. I hated to use that piece of crap word but couldn't find another. "I'm sorry. There was an accident on your east pivot. Garrett must have been repairing it and didn't cut the power first."

Alden's face blossomed into an unnatural shade of purple. Maybe a stroke and the Haney patriarchy would be decimated. "He knows better than that. Stupid move. Always trying to cut corners. Damn it. I suppose he's back at the hospital. And we're going to babysit again because of his numbskull move."

Ellie pushed through the screen behind us.

My heart sank to my toes, taking my backbone with it. I'd hoped to tell Alden and have him break the news to Ellie.

He glanced over his shoulder at her approach.

How he couldn't read the clues of Tony's behavior and my solemnness, I didn't know. But he blustered on. "That dimwitted son of yours short circuited himself and probably busted the pivot so bad it'll cost us a fortune to fix. And now we've got Tony again."

Ellie's mouth dropped open a half inch and she turned to me. "Garrett is hurt?"

Part of me wished Ted was already sheriff and doing this, but the other part was glad Ellie and Alden would get the news from someone close to them. "I'm sorry." Damn word. I expected to say the usual, that your son has been killed. Or he didn't make it. What came out was, "We lost Garrett." My throat closed up and tears suddenly gushed from my eyes.

Completely unexpected. I didn't sob, but only because I choked it back and swiped at the tears. I'd been in professional mode since I'd found him, but standing here, on the front porch where Sarah and I had spent countless hours having picnics as grade schoolers, playing millions of card games of Nertz as junior high kids, sleeping out and talking boys and dreams as high schoolers, listening to Sarah complain about her older brother, spying on him and teasing him, it suddenly felt like family.

And I knew the pain of losing family.

I understood that, as much as she griped about him, Sarah loved Garrett. And that these two people in front of me, not my family but weirdly connected by my closeness to Sarah, would be devastated by the news. The wall of my job disintegrated, and I became one of the "we" that had lost him.

I'd assumed Ellie would be the one to fall apart. But Alden's legs buckled as if his bones melted. He sank to the porch with a thud.

"Alden!" Ellie knelt and put her arms around him. "It's okay. Be careful. Your heart."

Okay? When the unthinkable happens, words come out that make no sense. I felt helpless as Alden fisted his hands and beat on the porch. "No. No. This isn't happening." It had the feel of a Shakespeare tragedy, or a summer melodrama on the stage at Fort Robinson.

I can't tell how long this first phase of disbelief took and the dawning of the truth began to sink in. Eventually, I was able to gather Alden, Ellie, and Tony and move them inside. I poured ice water and seated them in the living room. I called Hal and Bertie Rasmussen, neighbors who I knew to be good friends and I waited until they arrived.

Exhausted and hungry, I left the Haneys' place. Still no news from Sarah and Robert, but I had a few missed messages from Carly, Susan, and two from Vicki Snyder.

I didn't need to answer to know the commissioners had done their job and Ted was back.

8

Clouds began to form and weak afternoon sun shot through the windshield as I drove to town. My plan was to stop at the Long Branch and have Uncle Bud cook me a medium rare hamburger. Unable to resist any longer, I called Robert. No answer.

That wouldn't do. My next call was to the hospital where I asked for Aunt Tudy. She was Dad's cousin by way of some marriages and maybe a divorce or two. Even Ted, my ex, couldn't get that connection straight, no matter how often I'd explained it to him.

Aunt Tudy picked up the line as I parked in front of the Long Branch. "I swear, Kate, there's other sick folks in this place besides Sarah, who isn't sick but having a baby for pity's sake."

I took that greeting to mean Sarah was not in imminent danger and more brothers and sisters had been checking in. "Sorry," I winced, realizing how often I used that word. "I've been working so I haven't talked to anyone. How are Sarah and Robert doing?"

I imagined her pinching the bridge of her nose, as she often did. "A mortal would have given in six hours ago. But Sarah is getting weaker, so my guess is they're going to make the call any minute. For now, they're letting her carry on. Like she'd allow any different."

Sarah wouldn't have any energy leftover to deal with losing her brother.

Then the push-pull of hormones after delivering a baby wasn't going to help. Again, I wondered about having Aunt Tudy ask Robert to call and stuck with my previous decision. I thanked her and reached for the door handle and froze.

If this day could have gotten any worse, this was the way. It felt as if I'd swallowed a ball of burrs soaked in Tabasco. A fancy Super cab Ford F250 pulling a stock trailer loaded with furniture parked on the opposite side of the highway from me. Ted at the wheel. Roxy beside him and, no doubt, Brie and Beau in the backseat. My grand luck to run into them moving their household to Frog Creek and celebrating Ted's new-old position as Grand County sheriff.

I reinserted the key in the ignition, intending to settle for gas station pizza from Fredrickson's, but I hadn't moved quickly enough. Roxy bounded from the cab of the pickup and raced across the empty highway toward me. I didn't wish for a passing vehicle to hit her so much as slow her down. But, as Grandma Ardith was fond of saying: Wish in one hand, shit in the other and see which one fills first. Of course, she switched out her vocabulary to "poop" if Dad was around. He didn't tolerate cursing from his mother any more than he did from us kids.

I let Roxy bang on my window a second before I lowered it. She wore tight Wranglers, faded—with real wear, not purchased that way—and a stretched-out T-shirt with some of the blinged "Cowgirl Way" missing so it looked like clouds covered the stars. I'd never seen her in tennis shoes, but she wore them today. Bless my soul, Roxy was doing manual labor. "I just talked to Aunt Tudy."

I bristled because Tudy wasn't Roxy's relative in any way, but I didn't comment.

Roxy continued. "She said they're prepping Sarah for the C-section."

Now I was steamed. I'd just talked to Aunt Tudy, so how would Roxy have the scoop? Sarah must be worn out or no doctor would have had a chance.

I'd about had it with Roxy wedging herself into my life. Okay, she was welcome to Ted. And I wouldn't fight her over Louise. "I'm on my way to Broken Butte now." I said it as if I'd been planning all along when I'd only decided in that moment.

"Oh. Really?" She sounded disappointed. "'Cause I was going to ask if you could keep Brie since we're moving stuff out to Frog Creek."

Because your husband is taking my job, nitwit. "Sorry." I felt just fine dropping the little ball of stink that had followed me around all day. I let it sit there and billow out, doing its job.

She pouted. "You don't have kids, but you probably know how impossible it is to get anything done with a little one underfoot and having Beau is already hard enough. I was actually going to see if you'd take them both. Just for a few hours. Maybe it would take your mind off things. I mean, I didn't tell you I'm sorry about the recall and everything."

Ugh. She'd spit that word right back at me. Obviously, she hadn't heard about Garrett yet. It'd be all over town soon, which was another reason I should get to Broken Butte and tell Sarah before someone else did.

Roxy leaned in, casting a glance at the pickup as if not wanting to be overheard. Ted had both toddlers by the hand and was making his way toward us. Roxy spoke quickly. "You know how complicated this sheriff situation is. I mean, Ted is my husband, but you're my best friend. I know you understand."

I had Sarah as a best friend. Roxy settled for me, a person who fought queasiness every time we spoke. Karmic justice delivered.

Roxy pulled her head away and gave Ted a serious nod. "She says she won't watch the kids."

Ted stopped mid-stride and set his jaw, as if wanting to force me into it. He didn't raise his voice, but I swear I read his lips saying, "It's not like she's got something else to do."

"Kay-Kay-Kay!" Little Beau, my buddy, tugged Ted's hand, trying to make a break for me. Brie, who also loved me, got into the act, and pulled against him.

At that moment, Clyde Butterbaugh's Chevy pickup turned left from Main onto the highway, making Ted drag both kids to the curb. Clyde raised one finger off the steering wheel and flashed a wide grin as he drove past. He was followed by Jack Carson in his dusty Ford. He allowed us a grave nod. And finally, Buster Duran brought up the tail end of the commissioners, though he turned east and didn't need to acknowledge us at all.

It would be hard to describe the look on Ted's face as he watched them drive away and turned to me. Sort of a victory smirk but sprinkled with guilt and seasoned with a pinch of compassion. But mostly like he held back an explosion of confetti and fireworks. He knew the men—always men—leaving Hodgekiss meant the commissioners had made their decision.

I hadn't expected to be ousted so quickly. Truly, I hadn't expected to be voted out at all. That's the kind of hit no ego needs. I didn't have time to even order the cake for my pity party before four little arms circled my legs and high-pitched squeals pierced our ears. I squatted down to their level, mostly because it took me out of eye contact with Ted and Roxy. "Have you been having fun together?"

Brie started in with her breathless two-year old enthusiasm. "Mom and Dad and they...my bed...."

Beau, nearly three weeks older and wiser, yelled louder. "And us. So. So. So. Big."

Who knows the beginning, middle, and end to their story, but they were excited about it. I tried to support that. "Wow. You have been busy."

Roxy nudged Ted. "Isn't she great with kids? It's so sad she won't have any of her own."

It showed a deep well of restraint that I didn't snap back any number of comebacks. Let her believe her life choices were the envy of all.

My phone vibrated in my pocket, and I straightened up to answer. Sarah's bird flipped at me, and I punched quickly and turned away from Ted and Roxy, walking down the sidewalk.

"Olivia has arrived." She sounded worn to a nubbin, but clear and cheerful. "She held out a good long time but when they started prepping me for the C-section, I showed her who's boss. When she finally gave in, she hurried right on out."

My throat closed up. Another niece. Another human to love and welcome into our lives. "Olivia. Got it." Obviously named for Olivia Colman, Academy Award Best Actress. Keeping alive the naming custom that Mom and Dad started.

"I'll let Robert tell you the gory details. Wanted you to know she's here. I won. Now they're going to refill my blood tank and I'm going to sleep."

I hesitated a moment. Should I tell her about Garrett? Would it taint this memory for her? If I didn't tell her, she might not forgive me.

She took the decision out of my hands with her straightforward attitude. "What is Garrett's trouble?"

I wanted to be as upfront as she was, but I stumbled. "How, he. Well..."

She gave an aside, I supposed to Robert, "In a second. I need to talk to Kate." To me, she said, "Tell me."

Hearing it from me would be best. "I'm sorry. I found him on the east pivot. Electrocuted by the sprinkler."

The only sounds for several seconds were the clanking and rumbling that must be Robert and the birthing staff. Finally, she came back on, her voice stronger. "Can you locate Sheila? I don't know where she is, and Mom and Dad won't bother with her."

I may not be sheriff anymore, but I could still work on finding someone. "Of course."

She grunted. "If you have trouble, you can ask Dad where she might be. He was down in Scottsdale right before the branding. I know they had some words, but I didn't ask about it."

Robert spoke in the background. "Hang up. They've cleaned up Olivia and she's ready to eat."

She didn't speak to him, but I imagined her stern frown that said she'd hang up when she damned-well was ready to hang up. "I suppose Tony is with Mom and Dad and that's probably fine until I get out tomorrow, then he can come stay with us."

"The hell he can." That was Robert. "I'm not having that hoodlum around my kids. And there's no way they're letting you out tomorrow. You've lost too much blood."

Maybe she held a finger up to silence him. Maybe she ignored him. Robert wasn't a pushover but, more times than not, Sarah got her way. I stopped short of offering to let Tony stay with me. If needed, I could always volunteer later.

"Are you okay?" I asked, wanting to take the burden of her brother's death away from her for a few hours at least.

She didn't let a crack into her voice. "Probably not. But right now, I need to concentrate on our new little girl. I'm throwing this Garrett situation on your shoulders because I know you'll handle it for me. We share adjoining kingdoms, Kate. You rule the Land of Denial and I'm Queen of Compart-mentalization. We're both screwed up but taking care of business."

I loved her more than I could say. At least way more than she'd willingly hear me confess. "Kiss Olivia for me. Tell Robert I said to be nice to you. Call me if you need anything."

Rustling on her end made me think she was settling the baby. "Can you check up on Brie and make sure Roxy remembers she's got her?"

I whipped around to see Ted, Roxy and the toddlers entering the Long Branch. "I have them in sight now. Brie and Beau are making do the best they can."

9

The best place to start my search for Sheila was with Tony. I didn't really crave the thirty-minute drive back out there again. But first, Poupon and I needed to eat, and I'd make a quick trip to my house to clean up.

Not even the lure of Uncle Bud's hamburger could make sharing space with Ted palatable. I opted for a quick stop at Fredrickson's for lunch. Poupon roused himself and stood in the back seat, focus on the front doors, tail wagging. Forget about bells and treats, Pavlov's principles worked on Poupon with Fredrickson's and Slim Jims. He was salivating all over the back seat in anticipation.

Newt and Earl's Monte Carlos were parked out front. Since Poupon made Newt nervous and the afternoon had topped out at about seventy-five, with a slight breeze, I rolled down the windows and assured Poupon I'd bring him a Slim Jim. He was disappointed, but he'd get over it as soon as he had that greasy goodness in his mouth.

A black Cadillac with Arizona plates was parked on the other side of the Monte Carlos. It's not unheard of for travelers to pass through the Sandhills but there really isn't any big draw unless it's deer hunting season or you had some relatives here. Birders occasionally came here on purpose, but Hodgekiss really wasn't on the road to anywhere.

The bell on the door jingled when I walked in and the man standing at the counter turned. He wore khakis and a polo shirt, the relaxed kind of uniform of a city guy. I might not have paid much attention to him, except he took in every aspect of my appearance, from my boots, up my uniform, to my curly hair. It didn't take long because I'm pretty short. But it was enough time for me to feel awkward and to notice his dark skin and black Van Dyke beard and a snake tattoo on his neck. He had the stance and bulk of a wrestler and the awareness of a hawk.

Norm was ringing up a bottle of iced tea and a snack of hummus and breadsticks. I'd wager Fredrickson's sold ten to one Cheetos to hummus snacks. Another indication that guy wasn't from around here, as if we needed one.

Norm, being Norm, tried to make conversation with the guy. "Where you heading to?"

The man grunted with an annoyed grimace.

It didn't deter Norm's polite curiosity. "Have you been on the road a while?"

He made a sound like a snarl as he collected his receipt and turned to leave, giving me another intense survey while he passed. Tension wafted off him and I had the impression he'd like to sock someone in the kisser, as Grandma Ardith would say.

After the door closed, I made a comical face at Norm. "That's one friendly guy."

Newt popped up from behind the emergency grocery aisle. Maybe he'd been shopping for Miracle Whip or bread on a lower shelf or maybe he'd been hiding. "We seen that guy down in Ogallala day before yesterday."

Earl came out of the bathroom. He smelled of soap and I said a silent thank you to Blanche Johnson who might not have driven home the point that regular bathing was necessary, but had evidently taught them to wash their hands after using the facilities. "Is that the weaselly guy in the caddy?"

Newt made his way by the candy bars to me. "We think he's a G man."

Earl agreed. "Or a mob hitman. Either one."

Norm laughed. "Get out. He's some kind of businessman. Check out his credit card."

Norm stabbed at the cash register, and it dinged open. He pulled out a receipt and passed it to me.

"Evergreen Enterprises. Gregory Fisher." I handed it back to Norm. To tease the brothers, I said, "Could be an alias. Evergreen Enterprises is pretty generic. Maybe a front for the mob."

Earl elbowed Newt. "See?"

Inspired by the Van Dyke stranger, I picked up a hummus snack and Poupon's Slim Jim, the extra-long one, and placed them on the counter along with a cold soda. Lunch of champions and the unemployed.

Newt and Earl followed me out, but Newt stopped short when he saw Poupon's head thrusting from the back of the cruiser in anticipation of his treat. Normally stoic and even haughty, the promise of a Slim Jim brought out his primitive inner wolf. I unwrapped the meat stick and broke off a chunk, handing it to the slobbering beast through the window.

Poupon fed, I slid behind the wheel, peeled the top off the package and dipped a crunchy bread stick into the hummus.

Sheila Haney. I'd met her a few times when Garrett brought her to the Sandhills for brandings or a holiday. Sarah had no use for the woman, but I couldn't give an opinion one way or the other. What I knew was that she was a realtor in Scottsdale who concentrated on high end properties. Not expensive in the way we knew, where a new manufactured home with a basement meant the height of luxury. But in the "don't bother asking me to list it if we can't slap a price tag of multiple millions on it." She wore designer jeans and heels for her dressed-down days on the ranch. Which meant she spent no time in the branding corral or on horseback. Sheila didn't cook. What I remembered is that she spent a lot of time locked away on her laptop working or settled into a corner with a book.

Maybe I did have an opinion about her, but it wasn't based on conversations. It's possible she had a great sense of humor and was insightful and interesting. The feeling I got from her is that she thought all of us Sandhillers weren't worthy of her notice.

We pulled up to my little cabin on Stryker Lake and I took a moment to admire the ducks floating serenely in the mild afternoon while clouds drifted in the blue sky. I watered my sorry excuse for a garden, showered, and dressed in jeans and a T-shirt. No need to smother in the unattractive polyester uniform. Another silver lining.

I opted for the sheriff cruiser, though. Since I didn't have official notice that I'd been replaced, I might as well let Poupon ride in luxury in his favorite spot stretched out in the back seat.

On the way back to the Haneys, I called Trey to get any updates on Garrett. "It's definitely electrocution. The investigators assume that thunderstorm you had last week blew a fuse and Garrett got sloppy and didn't turn it off to repair it." He paused as if remembering the scene. "Man, four-hundred and eighty volts is one hell of a lightning bolt. Probably stopped his heart immediately."

That didn't sound right. "Garrett wasn't stupid. He'd know to shut it off before he messed with it."

Trey made a humming noise. "Yeah, that's what I thought. But the only other possibility is someone turning the power on while he was working on it."

Center pivot irrigation systems were massive and not something to mess around with, but Garrett would have known to take care. "His sister said he was upset about something, maybe scared. It might bear looking into."

He clicked his tongue. "That could explain being distracted and forgetting safety." He paused. "I know you don't like easy answers, but sometimes hoof beats are horses."

And sometimes they are zebras. But I kept that to myself. Not my case. The investigators knew their job.

"Here's an interesting thing, though. They aren't sure about Garrett changing the fuse because the one in the sprinkler didn't look burnt out."

That jangled in my head. More details that didn't make sense.

"Have you notified next of kin?" Maybe Trey had taken care of finding Sheila and I wouldn't have to.

"I thought you talked to his parents. And the kid. Is there someone else?"

"He's got a wife, but they're separated, maybe divorced. I'm trying to track her down. Thanks for the update."

He spoke quickly. "So, um. The state patrol is always looking for qualified people. I don't know what you've got in mind for the future, but we, I, could use a good hand here."

"Oh." That's an idea I hadn't considered. "I'll keep that in mind."

I drove the rest of the way considering doubling down on my law enforcement experience. It would pay the bills. I would probably have to relocate but could still stay in rural areas. I stuck it on the list with managing Carly's ranch, going back to school, letting Diane plan my future, and, let's not forget, Frog Creek. Although hooking up with Heath Scranton was definitely off the table.

Hal and Bertie Rasmussen's pickup was parked in front of the house, and I pulled in next to it. The afternoon was dwindling and clouds lumbered across the sky, maybe bringing in another storm. Last week's had seemed unfair. Hail and thunder and lightning were part of the summer threat around here. But September had a foot in autumn. An early snow squall wasn't unheard of, but hail wasn't expected. Often, we'd get a cold rain where we'd justify our first chili and cinnamon rolls of the season. But no one asked me my weather preferences, so I took the weird weather and was grateful I didn't live where rising sea levels targeted my house.

Stepping out of the cruiser, the breeze carried a hint of briskness and a reminder that the first frost was looming. The grass was still thick and green with only a couple of yellow leaves from an old cottonwood.

I climbed the porch steps for the second time that day and knocked on the screen. Bertie opened almost immediately, no doubt having heard me arrive. Bushy dark hair showing two inches of stark white roots, Bertie pushed open the screen door to let me in. "Oh, you poor thing. It's been a bad day for you. First the recall and then finding Garrett like that. I'm so—"

I broke in before she could say it. "How is it going here?" I was kind of surprised there weren't people gathering, that I didn't smell the coffee brewing.

Bertie whispered. "This isn't good. They haven't even called the pastor yet."

My footfalls thudded on the carpeted hallway as if the house was a tomb as I made my way to the kitchen.

Hal leaned against the counter with his arms folded, looking as glum as a kid in detention. "Hey, Kate. Sorry to hear about the election. Me and Bertie wanted to make it in to vote but we had a bull get out and the day went to hell."

Sorry as all get-out. "Thanks."

"What are you going to do now? I heard they need some help at the sale barn in North Platte." He probably would rather make conversation with me than deal with the Haneys.

I acknowledged that with a nod, then turned to Alden and Ellie who sat facing each other at the table. Alden's face looked mottled, a sickly yellow and purple mixture, and his eyes were dry and red. Ellie held a tissue and dabbed at the corners of her eyes.

Alden pushed back from the table and his old-man belly stuck out. "I suppose you've got some theory why a full-grown man who's been around center pivots all his life, would forget to turn it off before he worked on it."

Ellie gave him a pleading look. "He had a head injury, dear. He must not have been thinking correctly."

He tapped on the table with an open palm. "He never thought clearly as far as this ranch is concerned. It's a certainty that if I left this operation to him, he'd have destroyed it in a generation."

Ellie squeaked and sopped her eyes again. "You know, those pivots have been a problem from day one. You were forever working on them. And always cursing them. And then you got Garrett after it. I never understood their benefits."

I might agree with her about the worth of the pivots. They cost a lot to maintain and, as she said, it seemed they were always breaking down. But alfalfa was better feed than prairie hay, and in a drought year, it made all the difference. Although, if fields went fallow, there was almost zero chance they'd regrow indigenous vegetation. People complained about draining the aquifer, but the Sandhills sat on the deepest part of the Ogallala Aquafer—one of the largest in the world—on sand so porous water trickled right back down.

Ellie's mouth turned up in a sad smile. "Garrett never liked them, either. He had big plans. Was talking about making another golf course. Those upscale resort places like Creekside Golf Club. He said there was room out here for more than one. I think that's a good idea."

Alden sniffed. "That's bullshit. This is a ranch and that's my legacy. I'd not let Garrett destroy that. At least we don't have to worry about that nonsense anymore. This is safe for Tony, now."

What about the daughter who'd given her life to the ranch? "Sarah and

Robert are really making a name for themselves in purebred genetics. They're glad to be raising their children at the ranch."

Ellie stared at her coffee. "I'm not sure that's a wonderful thing. Children raised in this kind of isolated place may not fully be able to venture out into the real world. You take Garrett, for example. For all intents and purposes, he was a successful lawyer in an impressive setting. But look at this, he eventually became overwhelmed and had to retreat. I don't think Tony will be like that. As long as he doesn't stay out here."

Alden pointed a finger at Ellie. "That's where you're wrong. It's leaving that ruined Garrett. Made him forget his roots and goddamn forget how to fix a pivot. Tony will stay put out here."

This might be an opportunity to get some information on Sheila. "I would imagine he'd live with his mother. Do—"

Alden erupted, the feet of his chair squealing on the floor as he pushed back. "Over my dead body. If that twit was a heifer she'd have been shipped to the sale barn by now. She's not a fit mother."

Ellie sniffed and turned to me. "She's not a quality person."

"Still, I need to notify her." Maybe I wouldn't explain her legal rights as Tony's next of kin in case it set them off. "Do you have a contact number? Or maybe know where she might be found?"

Alden looked as if he'd swallowed something bitter. "Why would I know anything about her?"

"Sarah said you'd been to Scottsdale last May before Sheila disappeared. I wondered if she'd said anything to you."

Alden stood and stomped out of the room. "Don't bother trying to find her. She's not an option."

I turned to Ellie, who stared out the window at the gathering clouds. "Is Tony around? I'd like to talk to him."

Ellie frowned. "I don't think that's a good idea. He's upstairs watching movies. I don't want you to upset him again."

Bertie winced like it was painful to interfere, then she spoke gently. "Ellie, honey, he's been alone for a long time His daddy has just passed, don't you think he might want to talk to someone?"

Ellie seemed unplugged from reality, like she skimmed the surface without getting her feet wet. "Okay, I suppose. But try not to bring up Garrett. He is very upset about his father going away."

Going away? Had she convinced herself Garrett wasn't dead? Ellie might be slipping gears. "I'll go see if Tony needs anything."

"See if he'd like hamburgers for supper or if he'd rather have tomato soup and grilled cheese?" Ellie winked at Bertie. "You know he's getting to that stage where he's always hungry."

Bertie gave a wan smile. "Honey, don't you think we ought to talk about making some arrangements? Call Pastor Steve? I'll help you with that."

It was unusual the word hadn't spread about Garrett's accident. But no one in the state patrol lived around here so they wouldn't pass it on. I hadn't said anything. Obviously, Hal and Bertie were respecting the Haneys' privacy. From Bertie's concern, I didn't think that would last long.

I found Tony in the TV room upstairs, what used to be Sarah's bedroom. He huddled in the corner of the couch staring at an old Spiderman video. He wore gym shorts and a yellow Sun Devils T-shirt, his bare feet curled under him. He'd lost that green cast but still looked pale, and dark circles hung under those eyes so much like Sarah and Garrett's. It didn't appear as though he'd cried, and that made me ache for the anguish dammed inside of him. He didn't move when I sat down next to him. My opening move wasn't impressive. "How's it going?"

He stared at the movie. "Fine."

Maybe it would be good to force him out of his own head. "I think your grandmother is going to start planning your dad's service soon. Is there something you'd like to include? Something maybe you want to be sure they say about him?"

Tony's eyes filled but he blinked it away. "Not really. He was a good lawyer. He liked to golf."

No mention of being a good dad. "Think about it. I can help you write some thoughts if you'd like."

He swallowed and the tears didn't fall. "Nah."

I reached for the remote sitting next to him and turned the volume down. Turning the movie off seemed too abrupt. "We need to talk about your mother."

He kept his eyes on the screen. "What about her?"

I spoke in a quiet voice. "We have to contact her. She'll need to come get you to live with her now."

He dropped his gaze to his fisted hands. His tone was like brittle shale. "She doesn't want me. She wouldn't care about Dad."

That ripped my heart apart. "Maybe there was some tension before, but this is serious. She's your mother and needs to know."

He didn't say anything for a few moments. I didn't know if he was stubborn or fighting for control.

"Can you give me her phone number?" I urged him.

He finally turned to me. "Oh yeah. I can give it to you, but it won't do you any good."

"Why is that?'

A flash of pain struck like lightning across his face, replacing the studied look of boredom he normally practiced. "She didn't take her phone when she left." His voice cracked. "I don't even know what I did."

And now I felt completely shredded inside for this kid who felt like he didn't have an anchor. "I'm sure you didn't do anything wrong."

He sounded strained, as if holding everything in hurt his throat. "Then why would she ignore me all of a sudden? I mean, that sucks."

"I promised your Aunt Sarah I'd find your mother, and you know what happens if you don't do what Sarah wants."

He gave me a weak smile. "How is she doing?"

It surprised me he thought to ask. "You've got a new niece. Her name is Olivia."

A tiny twinkle lit his eyes. "Cool. It's good that Brie has a sister. I wish I had a brother, or I'd even settle for a sister."

I had siblings to spare. But there isn't one of them I'd give away. Okay, I'd pay to have someone take Louise. I couldn't imagine life without those ties. "So, maybe a little help with finding your mom?"

"I don't know where she is, okay?"

Maybe if we backed up. "Why did you and your dad move back here without her?"

He jerked to his feet and stomped to the other side of the coffee table. "How should I know? I'm just the kid. They acted like I wasn't part of the family. My job was to do whatever they said and go wherever they wanted.

All I know is that they were fighting a lot. And then one day Mom doesn't come home."

"How long ago was this?"

He pushed a hand through his hair. "Long time, like a couple of weeks before school got out. And then Dad is all like, 'If I got to be the parent now, then we're going to Nebraska.' And I know that was because he wanted Grandma and Gramps to take over raising me. But, hell, I'm past needing someone to raise me."

He probably believed that. "Still, it's good to have someone looking out for you. You need to finish grade school, and maybe even college before you'll be ready to go out on your own. I don't suppose you can get a credit card for a few years, yet."

He paused in his pacing and glared at me. "Okay. But I don't need, like, Grandma tucking me in at night. Or Gramps giving me lessons in the value of hard work."

"Do you know what your parents were fighting about?"

He did another lap around the room and dropped to the floor. I didn't speak for a few seconds while he stared in his lap, and he gathered something inside to push out. He spoke with his chin on his chest. "Some guy named Cole."

Oh, man. Sheila was having an affair. No wonder Garrett had left. I knew how that kind of betrayal could explode your life and you might need to escape.

"I'm sorry." Ugh. That word again.

"She was after Dad about Cole and how he should accept him, and Dad was mad and said if she loved him so much she should be with him. And then she said stuff about Dad never being around and she was sick of being a single parent. And I don't know what the hell she was even talking about because I tried not to make things hard for her. I mean, I got straight As so she never had to go to the school. And I got my own lunch and didn't ask her to make me dinner or anything." He started to cry then. Big, wrenching, little boy sobs. Enough to gut me.

I sat next to him on the floor and wished I'd brought Poupon inside. I had an urge to pull him to me but if this kid carried Sarah's DNA, a hug would only make it worse. "You're a kid. It's a parent's job to take care of you and love you. You didn't make your mom leave you."

He wiped at the tears, but they kept falling. "Dad told her he wouldn't do what she wanted, and she should leave. So, she did but I don't think he believed she would. And then Dad told me we were coming here for the branding but then we never went home."

He punched his calves. "And now Dad's dead and Mom doesn't want me and I'm going to be stuck living out here forever. With Grandma and Gramps. And they are the worst."

At that point, I couldn't help putting my arm around his shoulders and tugging him into me. He didn't fight and after a moment, the braces that had held him loosened and he leaned into me. He gave one little hiccup, held his breath, then let loose and bawled.

I didn't know what would stop a mother from contacting her ten-year-old son for three months. I tried to maintain an open mind, though I thought even alley cats kept better track of their kittens. "I'll find your mother. Until then, someone will take care of you."

We sat like that for quite a while before he pulled away and swiped his face with the hem of his T-shirt.

I couldn't bear the thought of leaving this hurting boy with Alden and Ellie. "Sarah might be home tomorrow, and I think she's going to have you stay with them until I can find your mother. If you'd like, I can talk to your grandmother, and you can stay with me and Poupon tonight."

He sniffed. "I think I should stay here. Like you said, if Dad is going to have a funeral or whatever, I want to make sure they don't do something stupid."

He might be right.

"And they kind of need me. Grandma is weird, like she isn't understanding what happened. And Gramps keeps yelling that Dad was an idiot for not turning off the power when the pivot was struck by lightning. But the pivot wasn't struck by lightning. It wasn't even busted. It was working when Grandma took me home. But then, Gramps told Dad it wasn't, and he had to fix it."

That didn't track with the investigators saying lightning had probably damaged it. This whole situation gave me a bad taste.

10

Since it was still daylight-saving time, Arizona was an hour earlier than Nebraska. That would give me time to make a call before, I assumed, Garrett's law firm would close for the evening. Even if he hadn't been to the office in three or four months, they'd surely have contact numbers still on file. Unfortunately, it meant I'd have to go the courthouse before Betty and Ethel began their evening race for the front door. With any luck, Poupon and I could sneak up the back stairs and to my office without being noticed.

I let Poupon in and eased closed the door. His claws clicked on the linoleum, but I kept my footfalls silent. We'd nearly made it to my office when Betty popped from her office. "I thought I heard you come in." She scuttled to me. "This whole business has been a disgrace. You didn't deserve what's happened to you."

It looked like she had every intention of hugging me and maybe even shedding a tear or two, so I backed up, nearly falling over Poupon.

In an unprecedented move, Ethel spewed from her office at five minutes to five, slammed the door and turned the key. She must have seen the surprised look on my face because she sniffed in irritation. "I'm taking some comp time. After being here at all hours last night and having to take notes at the commissioners' meeting, I'm pooped."

She stomped past us on her way to the front door. I'd have thought she'd be plum delighted to have her Teddy back as sheriff. Maybe Ethel wasn't cut out to be happy.

She didn't make a clean getaway, though. May Keller reached for the glass door at the same time as Ethel.

Small but scrappy, May held her ground, blocking Ethel from leaving. "Hold on there, cowgirl. I got a question about the property line betwixt my Lamb pasture and Joshua Stevens' land."

Ethel, who'd switched out the scuffs she wore at work, rocked from one foot to the other on ankles that were always swollen. "You'll have to come back another day. We're closed."

May made a great show of checking the oversized men's watch strapped to her scrawny wrist. "Appears as though I got four more minutes before five."

Ethel's nostrils flared as she readied to charge. "May Keller. You are the orneriest cuss in the county, and I don't have the patience for you today." With that, she barreled on and if May hadn't jumped out of the way, she'd have been flattened.

I might have expected May to be sputtering mad, but she let loose with a cackle to rival any hen after laying an egg. "I about didn't make it in time. I knew she'd be fit to be tied today after what the commissioners pulled. I'd've been here five minutes ago but I ran into Newt and Earl and them damned boys wanted to tell me about that flibbertigibbet they got down in North Platte."

Betty tittered and put a hand to her mouth. "Ethel got her comeuppance, that's for sure."

The door opened behind May, and we all turned to see Zoe Cantrel walk in, baby strapped to her chest. She flipped her long hair over her shoulder and nodded a hello to us. Long and lean, it didn't appear she carried any leftover baby weight. She spoke to me, "I saw the sheriff rig outside and hoped to catch you."

I spread my hands out. "I'm here. What can I do for you?"

She looked puzzled. "Well. I'm not really sure but I thought maybe we could figure it out together."

That had me stumped. I looked at Betty, who stared back with an expectant expression. Then I glanced at May.

She paused a second, then let out another of those egg-laying cackles. "She don't know! This day is getting better and better."

Zoe grinned.

Betty patted my shoulder. "Oh, honey. I thought someone would have told you about Ted."

May made a *pfft* at Betty. "This ain't got nothing to do with Ted, unless you count that the birdbrain commissioners finally figured out Ted's got mush for brains. And I got to tell you, with those three men, it surprised the stuffin' out of me that they did it."

I still didn't understand, and it must have been apparent from my expression.

Zoe squared her shoulders. "They appointed me to fill your position."

It took a second or two for that to sink in and when it did, a grin spread across my face. That was the best news I'd heard in a week of Sundays. Maybe since, well—I had to really think about it—Carly being found after so long. At any rate, it was darned good news. And not only because that meant Ted didn't get the job and had humiliated himself by assuming he would. It would only make it better if he'd already resigned in Chester County and if he'd have to beg for his job back.

But choosing Zoe was a smart move. She had ambition and drive. I'd known her since before she, Susan, and Carly had been toddlers and formed their tight triumvirate. She was courageous, loyal, intelligent, and even-tempered. I admit to being disappointed she'd married so young, not that I didn't like her husband. I didn't want her to go the route of so many women out here, to put themselves and their ambitions second to their husband's.

Betty's expression was sympathetic. "Of course, you're still sheriff until Zoe is sworn in. And that might be a while because Butterbaugh's daughter went into labor and he's gone."

After three years, I'd settled into being sheriff and took my responsibility to heart. But now that I'd been voted out, every duty would be torture.

Zoe was unsentimental. "I'd never have thought to run for sheriff until you got elected. And you've done such a great job, I can't believe you were recalled. But, I thought, there's no reason I can't do this. And Grand County can get used to seeing a woman in uniform."

May Keller coughed and fingered the cigarettes in her pocket. She'd already been inside longer than her smokeless limit. "Hell, yes. You can do it, cookie. I've always thought you three girls could run the world if you got organized."

Zoe's face brightened even more, and her hand circled automatically on her baby's back. "Aw, coming from you, that means a lot. Gram says you were liberated before there was even a women's lib movement."

While May preened a bit, Betty eyed the baby. "How are you going to manage with a little one?"

Zoe drew her head back and looked at the sleeping child. "She's got a dad on the ranch and can be with him most of the time. And when that won't work, Blaine's folks said they'd take her."

"They're all okay with this?" Betty acted as if it was unheard of.

Zoe looked puzzled by the question. "Why not? An outside income helps everybody."

May nodded and Betty looked frustrated with the answer. She mumbled about locking up and retreated to her office.

May left without saying goodbye, lighting up before the door closed behind her.

Zoe and I made a plan to meet the next afternoon and go over the duties and the equipment.

I got to my—Zoe's—office with time ticking down. A quick search gave me Dougherty, Fleishman, Haney and Associates' number and a bright woman's voice repeated the string of names ending with, "How may I help you?"

I started with what would soon be untrue. "I'm Kate Fox, sheriff in Grand County, Nebraska. I'm trying to locate the wife of one of your partners. Sheila Haney, married to Garrett Haney. I'm hoping you have some information on where she might be."

The woman paused so long I'd have wondered if she'd hung up except I heard murmured conversation away from the phone. She finally came back on. "Mr. Haney is no longer with the firm. So, I'm afraid we can't help you."

"Wait. Can I speak to another partner?"

She sounded doubtful. "Oh. I'm not sure if anyone is available. I can take your number and have someone call you."

That wouldn't get me anywhere. I hated to do it this way, but this gatekeeper was trained to protect her bosses' time. "I'm afraid I have some sad news. Garrett Haney passed away yesterday, and I need to notify his wife."

There was a squeak and intake of breath. "Um. Let me transfer you to our HR manager, Becca Monroe."

Becca sounded all business, speaking so rapidly I had to focus, or it would sound like Russian. With such an abrupt manner, I didn't expect her reaction when I told her about Garrett. Her voice shook and then she broke into obvious tears. "How did it happen?"

Not being sheriff would spare me more of this kind of torture. I gave a quick overview while she sniffed and huffed in sobs.

"Where did you say this happened?" she asked, sounding more in control.

"In an alfalfa field."

"No. I mean, you said you are in Nebraska? Why would Garrett be there?"

"Grand County. It's where the handle connects to the pan if states actually had panhandles. Garrett's family ranch is here."

"Garrett grew up on a ranch? In Nebraska? And he went back there?"

I waited for more questions, and she came up with one. "How long has he been there?"

He and Tony had shown up at the branding in early June. "About three months."

"Really. That would make sense."

"Garrett didn't tell you where he'd gone? He said he'd resigned and planned on staying at the ranch permanently."

She *huhed* in the back of her throat. "Well, that's news to me. I doubt he told the rest of the partners anything about it, either."

"So, what? He just stopped coming to work?"

"Something like that...."

The silence billowed and I finally popped it. "Can you give me a little more than that to go on? I've got a ten-year-old boy whose father just died, and he needs his mother."

"Gotcha."

"Does his employment file have an emergency contact that maybe would have her number?" I doubted that would do any good since Tony said she'd left her phone.

Computer clicking sounded and then Becca came on. "There's a cell number for his wife. And then a second number for her office. I know she's a realtor." She read those off.

I jotted them down. "I know I'm asking you to step outside of professional bounds, but do you know if was there a problem with the two of them or maybe at the firm? I mean, why would Garrett leave so suddenly?"

"I really shouldn't say. But Garrett and I were friends and...." She stopped, probably trying to control her emotion. Her voice sounded like paper crinkling when she started again. "I can't believe he's really gone. I've been so angry at him for disappearing like he did. I mean, we were close, or at least I thought we were. It's going to take me some time to wrap my head around him being from Nebraska. He seemed so sophisticated. I assumed he was from the east coast or Chicago or something. Never Nebraska."

Okay, okay. Maybe the rural west didn't have a reputation for being suave and cutting edge, but we weren't without brains and worth. Seriously, how good of friends could they be if she didn't know the basics of where he grew up? Unless he was ashamed of his upbringing and kept it secret. "Would anyone at the firm have been in contact with Garrett?"

She sounded annoyed. "No one had a clue where he'd gone. But he didn't volunteer much. For instance, if I didn't know, I doubt anyone else knew he was from Nebraska."

I wanted to get her back on track. "Do you have any idea why Garrett might have moved so abruptly?"

"His wife was really nagging him. Like, constantly."

"What about?"

Becca huffed out in irritation. "A lot of wives or husbands don't understand how it is at this level of business for a law firm. It's not nine to five for the lawyers. We have demanding clients and there is a lot at stake for some of them. It's not unusual for our partners to work seventy-or eighty-hour weeks. The reason they have sofas in their offices isn't for the clients' comfort, I'm telling you. Some of the lawyers spend a night or two here every week."

"And Sheila didn't like that?"

Becca lowered her voice, though I didn't believe there was anyone else in her office, but because she knew she was flat out gossiping and it wasn't appropriate. "Garrett told me she was riding him about spending more time with their little boy. From what he said, Sheila enjoyed his income and prestige, but she didn't want to be stuck with their son all the time. It's like she used Garrett for her money plan, but she didn't want to do her part to earn it."

That sounded catty and harsh to me. "I thought Sheila had a high-end boutique real estate business."

Becca scoffed. "Hardly. Garrett said it was more a hobby than a job. She probably sold a house every several months, so yeah, not really a big hitter."

I did some quick math and thought a couple of multi-million-dollar house sales per year might yield an income a Sandhiller could live on for a decade. But by Scottsdale standards, it might not amount to much. "If they were having conflict, do you think she left him?"

Becca huffed in derision. "Not unless she found another sugar daddy. But I can tell you, all her pinging at Garrett took a toll. He made a huge gaff and I know that weighed on him."

Her voice hitched again and she gave way to sobs. I waited for her to get control. "I'm sorry." She sniffed. "I shouldn't be telling you any of this. It's just, I really liked Garrett. He always took the time to talk to me, not like the other partners. He was...." She drew in a shaky breath. "So kind. So...handsome and alive."

In the time Garrett had been in the Sandhills, whatever his worry, it seemed to become heavier and heavier, making him drawn and twitchy, not at all the kind, handsome man Becca might be thinking of. "What was Garrett's mistake?"

She made a clicking noise with her tongue. "Now that I really can't say. That's confidential and would need a subpoena. But it wasn't too long after that Garrett disappeared. I thought it might be because he is such a perfectionist he couldn't face the failure. But then, when we didn't hear from him, I really started to worry the client might have threatened him or something. The partners took over his cases and put out that he was taking time off. Burn out is real here, so they were giving him a break before deciding anything." Her voice caught as if she suddenly remembered. "And to find out he died in a farm accident. It's, well, it's a lot."

I didn't correct her that it was a ranch accident. Most urbanites don't discern the difference between farm and ranch, a vast distinction in rural America.

I left Becca with my number and asked her to call me if she remembered anything that could help me locate Sheila.

I leaned back in my office chair and took in Poupon sprawled on his side. He stretched out on the overpriced memory foam bed I'd provided for his comfort, well, in an attempt to keep him off my chair. He only used the darned thing after I tugged him out of my chair and sat down myself.

I jotted down a few notes on where to go next in my Sheila search, starting by looking up her real estate business.

On a whim, I pulled up the Dougherty, Fleishman, Haney and Associates website, which I already had open. Before I got too far, my phone rang, and I snatched it up to see Carly's impish grin on the screen.

After quick hellos, I said, "You made it back to Lincoln in time for Susan to get to work?"

She brushed that aside. "No problem. I heard about Garrett Haney. That's some messed up shit. I feel bad for Tony."

We spoke briefly about the incident, and I told her about searching for Sheila. She didn't linger on that subject and got to her point. "Listen, I need you to help me out tomorrow if you can."

Interesting way to put it. She needed me to do something, but then she set it down gently, so I wouldn't feel forced. Diplomatic, even if I saw through it. "What do you need?"

"Rope's arthritis is acting up. He says he can't ride very long. But we've got a truck coming tomorrow for about thirty head and we need to round up the pasture and get them loaded. Please say you can help."

I needed to find Sheila, but that might mean a few phone calls. It was too late to get much done tonight and I supposed the calls could wait until later in the morning. I'd probably be back to town by ten or eleven, an hour earlier in Arizona. "Yes. I can do that."

She gave me the few details I needed and came back with a series of thank yous. She didn't mention me working for her full time, though I knew this was the camel's nose under the tent.

11

The sun peeked over the eastern hills, lighting up the scattered clouds in shades from the softest peach to calming baby blue. The bite in the air fore-shadowed fall, but in another couple of hours, we'd swear summer still reigned. As a good Sandhiller always does, I'd checked the weather and knew we'd probably have some rain later on. The horse Rope had saddled for me was solid and had some giddy-up to her. They'd named her Honey and that's what her coat reminded me of. She responded well to herding the thirty or so culled cows we rounded up in the forty-acre pasture.

Poupon and I had made it to the Bar J before light. He preferred to lounge on the front porch of Carly's old ranch house. It had been her grandfather's and his parents' and anchored the headquarters with the barn, cookhouse, calving lot, feed bins and fuel tanks. Roxy's monstrosity of a new build loomed fifty yards away. If Carly had her way and I decided to manage the Bar J, it's possible I'd move in there. Though I'd prefer the more modest older home, it might be fun to live in luxury for a change.

The plan was to bring the cattle into the corner of the pasture not far from headquarters where a set of pens and a cattle chute were located. The stock trailer, pulled by a semi-truck was scheduled to arrive shortly. Rope waited at the pens and, with the help of his trusty blue heeler, Barney, we'd corral them, then push them up the chute and into the trailer. Simple plan. And so far, everything was moving along nicely.

The morning couldn't have been any lovelier. The cows meandered as if they hadn't a care in the world. They were well fed and rested, and Honey and Barney weren't concerning them. Meadowlarks trilled and a king fisher tried to warn me from a nest. Dew still covered the long stems of the grass that was in various stages of turning from green to gold. The smell of damp grass crushed under hooves made everything feel fresh, a balm to my scraped ego.

We'd gathered the corners of the pasture and pushed the herd to the east fence line. If we'd have any trouble with them at all, it would be when they realized we were taking them to the pen. Most of the time, if there wasn't something to agitate them, they'd traipse along congenially. Sometimes, one critter might remember she'd had a nasty experience in a pen, and she'd balk. That could cause others to revolt and since we didn't have many hands—just me and Barney—an outbreak would be a disaster.

Rope, an appropriate name for a man who'd spent his life as the Bar J ranch manager and was as lean and worn as an old lariat, had thrown open the pen's wire gate and stood twenty feet to the side in case a cow had a mind to skip entering and wandered off. Barney and I kept well back from the last cow. We wanted to be a presence to keep them moving forward, but not so much to make them nervous.

When my phone rang, I debated about answering, but seeing my brother Douglas's face on the I.D. made it safe. "If I'd had any idea the vote would be close, I'd sure have made it into town."

Douglas, Michael's twin, was always a soft landing for me. "I know you would. Don't feel bad."

"What are you going to do now?"

Honey and I plodded after the cows and let Barney do the work. "I've got some options." None of them good.

The waft of wind preceded his words, letting me know he was outside. "I could use a hand out here. Not for a career, sure, but if you need a few months to transition to something else."

A warmth spread in my chest. "I know you don't need any help. You're pulling that out of some budget that you could use for something better than charity."

His pause was confirmation. "Actually, it was money I'd designated for donations."

"Thanks, but no. Something like that could get you fired for fraud." I should know, nepotism was one of the claims leveled against me.

"Okay. I'll keep my ears open for anything else. Gotta go. We're studying the digestion of sheep, and I can't resist that open sided stomach view."

He hadn't changed since he was seven and offered me his favorite G.I. Joe when Danny Duncan broke my heart sophomore year.

A motor sounded in the distance. The truck must be getting close. It would be good to have the cows penned up before it got here.

The first cow edged to the gate and lowered her head. She hesitated. Not a big deal, just making sure it all looked okay.

The sound of the engine got louder more quickly than I thought it ought to. Was the driver gunning it? We hadn't expected the truck for another half hour, so the driver being in a rush wasn't necessary.

The cow in the lead pulled her head up and her tail whipped to the side. The three behind her raised their ears. Not one of them took another step into the corral. Rope flapped his arms and made a *shshsht, shshsht* sound to encourage them.

The roar of the engine suddenly increased, and I realized it wasn't the sound of a truck at all. It boxed my ears and wasn't coming from down the road but...from up in the air.

I glanced up in time to see something I hadn't expected to ever see on a Sandhills prairie. A helicopter popped over the eastern ridge, the silhouette against the rising sun not only spooking the cows, but normally unruffled Honey, Barney, and maybe even Rope.

It hovered, causing a windstorm to pummel everything with sand and bits of weeds and chaff, pelting my skin. Honey lost her battle for control and began with a series of jumps with all four hooves off the ground. I tightened my knees and grabbed the saddle horn, squeezing into her.

Barney let loose with a series of barks and ran toward Rope, forgetting all about the cows.

Rope seemed to be the only one concerned about the herd, but on foot, and with his arthritis, he couldn't do much except wave his arms and yell.

I had my hands full with Honey. She'd given in to full on panic and reared back, pawing the air. I was impressive, staying on for that ride twice before she managed to throw me off on the third go-round.

By then, the helicopter had picked out a spot on the hay meadow in front of Carly's house and had planted itself. The engine began powering down and the hurricane around us subsided.

Honey, now feeling remorse, stood next to me, head up, ears alert, still on edge.

Rope let out a string of cursing that surprised me with its depth and breadth—and I'd seen Rope collide with trauma most of us wouldn't have weathered.

The cows, of course, had backed up and scattered. All we saw were their tails as they raced over the hills and, no doubt, into the corners of the pasture. We'd be lucky if they didn't stampede through the fence.

Luckily, I'd landed on my rear and didn't believe I'd broken anything but my pride. I pulled my hand up and winced at the cactus spine sticking from my palm. Pinching it between my thumb and forefinger, I gave it a yank, feeling the frustration build inside like lava rising up the cone of a volcano. The spine broke off, leaving a sliver in my palm that burned, but not nearly as hot as my rage.

I leapt to my feet, the tinge in my backside making me pause only a second before I grabbed Honey's reins. She hopped a bit when I thrust my boot into the stirrup, but I growled and took the slack from the reins to let her know I was in charge. That seemed to calm her a bit and I swung into the saddle.

By this time, the door of the helicopter had opened, and a man and woman hopped out. He leaned in and dragged out two suitcases, then slammed the door, giving it a pat like sending a horse out to pasture. I couldn't believe it when the couple bent down and scuttled under the rotors, moving quickly while the helicopter started in with a whine and roar and the blades increased.

Despite my authority and effort to keep her calm, Honey gave in to her panic and again reared and hopped like a champion bronc. I might have stayed on, but decided to make a controlled landing and slid my toes from the stirrups and pushed off. This time, instead of landing in a heap, both feet hit the sand and though I didn't stick the landing and toppled onto my knees, I saved my rear and possibly a broken bone or two.

I grabbed her reins as the helicopter rose. She reared and I avoided her hooves. If I'd thought I was mad before, now I felt like my head might explode. The cows were long gone by now. Not only would I need to round them up in their riled state—something that might be impossible—all this running and fear would burn pounds off them. That was money out of Carly's pocket.

Without waiting for Honey to calm down, I grabbed the horn and yanked myself into the saddle, squeezing my knees tight and giving a firm tug on the reins to wheel her around to gallop toward the couple.

It didn't matter who had caused this catastrophe, I wanted to draw and quarter them. But in this instance, the outrage ratchetted way past eleven because the person at the center of not only disrupting the morning's work, but my whole danged life, raised his hand and waved in greeting.

Damn it.

Glenn Baxter.

12

If you take a whole life of thirty-two years where you'd thought you felt love before, and suddenly, you meet someone whose soul swallows yours whole, and you realize there's a level of connection you'd never dreamed existed, and before you can begin to explore what that means, you blow it all up because you were too fearful and stupid to understand what you had, you're left with a hole that sometimes scabs over, and then unexpectedly breaks open into a sucking wound. And sometimes, all that hurt and frustration boils into fury.

That rage is what propelled me as I galloped across the pasture toward Glenn Baxter.

He and a woman stood holding their suitcases in the middle of the hay meadow, recently mowed and stacked and now a field of eight-inch-high sharp stalks. She seemed perfectly fine with a wild woman galloping at her full speed.

Baxter had lowered his hand and at least had the wherewithal to figure out I was not coming in friendship. He took a slight step to put him in front of the woman, maybe protecting her from my charge. How gallant.

I started yelling before I got close. "What the heck do you think you're doing? You made a mess of the whole thing." Maybe I was talking about the cattle. Maybe I wasn't. How could I gauge anything with my insides engulfed in flames that might have been lit from rage or desire or total emotional annihilation?

When I was about ten feet away, I pulled back on the reins and Honey slid to a stop in such an impressive way dust rose from her hooves. A rodeo queen couldn't have looked any better.

I sprang from the saddle and landed on the run, Honey's reins clutched in my fist. Probably a good thing because it might keep me from throwing a punch.

Baxter, not a super tall man, but taller than me, matched my temper. His handsome face, eyes so much like a lion's, looked braced for battle. "It's not as if we knew you'd be out here playing cowboy." He raised his arm and coughed twice into the crook of his elbow.

The woman moved out from behind Baxter. She was slender and fit, in the way someone with a personal trainer looked. I'd seen her once before but from a distance. Now, with her long, sleek, dark hair and olive skin, and her tight-fitting jeans and a white V-necked T-shirt, it felt like a blow to see how stunning she was.

She gave him a surprised look. Even that came off so super-model beautiful it stabbed my gut. "Oh Glenn, we obviously arrived at a terrible time." She closed the space between us and held her free hand to me. "I'm Aria Fontaine. Sorry we created such havoc. If you've got a spare horse, I'd be happy to help you round them up again."

What? Her offer came at me like a cool breeze on a sunny day. It definitely shifted the wind on my wildfire. "I can do it. But the truck's going to be here any minute and they're not going to be happy to wait." I found it hard to be angry with her.

But not difficult to turn it back on Baxter. I whipped to him. "What are you thinking landing a helicopter out here? What are you even doing here?" I felt like I was sputtering, not able to tell him what I really wanted to, which was more like, "Seeing you here, with her, is like getting a blast of oxygen and then being strangled." I literally gasped for air.

He put a hand on the small of Aria's back and directed her across the stubbled field. "We're staying a few days to assess the ranch. Carly's going to put it in an environmental easement and I'm helping out."

I lunged to the side to block his path, making Honey step with me. My skin felt scorched from the inside out. "Oh, no you're not. Carly's not putting this in an easement where she won't be able to work it for years. You're trying to manipulate her."

He snorted. "When has anyone been able to manipulate that girl? She's more stubborn than you are."

Aria had approached Honey with her hand out, palm down, letting Honey smell her. She started to caress that satiny spot on the nose, the softest thing on the planet, and spoke to us in a low, quiet voice. "Carly's got her own mind and she's smart. I don't see how that makes her stubborn. Besides, you shouldn't say stubborn like it's a bad thing."

Aria knew Carly? And also, the last thing I wanted to do was like this woman and here she was, already making me warm to her.

My heart was still thundering and my hand stung, my rear hurt and now, the impact of the fall seemed to be tightening the muscles in my back. All of it hardly a blip compared to the wild rampage of every emotion from lust to disgust, from love to hate. "Go on to the house and relax," I spit at Baxter. "I've got to get these heifers rounded up and then I'll talk to Carly about this easement nonsense." And give her hell about setting me and Baxter up for this encounter.

I whirled around to locate Rope and see if he could still help out. He draped his arm over the top panel of the steel gate and stood with one foot resting on the other, looking like a scarecrow with only half of its stuffing. He needed to be resting someplace, not manning a gate and loading cattle.

Aria followed my gaze. "He doesn't look well. You're going to need our help."

I'd be damned if I'd let that happen. "It's fine. The truck driver will help me load once I bring them in."

Baxter turned his back and started for the big house, Roxy's fancy digs. But when he looked over his shoulder and saw Aria wasn't following him, he came back. "Let's get settled. Carly said we could use the ranch pickup while we're here and I'll give you a tour."

Aria glanced down at her cowboy boots. They weren't the working kind, with their soft leather, colorful tooling, and two-inch stacked heels. She plopped her suitcase on the ground and squatted next to it. "We scattered that herd all over the pasture. The least we can do is help."

Baxter sighed. "Kate doesn't want our help. She's got it under control."

I tried not to think about the only other time I'd seen this woman. It was two years ago on a Chicago sidewalk. I'd been staring at Baxter's building. Encased in steel and glass, it towered over everything, and I had imagined Baxter in his office on the top floor. I'd been swimming in a sour sea of heartbreak and regret, wondering what life might have been like if I hadn't betrayed Baxter and if he hadn't turned his back on me, refusing to forgive. If I was honest, it was a film I still played over and over at least twice each week.

Suddenly, Baxter had emerged from the revolving door, popping out on the sidewalk. For a second I'd thought maybe our souls had connected in some fantastical romantic way and he'd felt me out there. My foolish heart wished him to come to me and the misunderstandings would be washed away, and we'd ride away together into the sunset, a big red heart closing on our silhouettes. Exactly how it never happens in real life.

Instead, I'd seen Baxter's face light up when he noticed a woman, Aria, hurrying toward him. Their casual kiss had seared me. I had never forgotten her red dress and the way she'd so confidently owned the street, probably all of Chicago, and maybe even the world.

Crouched down, Aria rummaged in her bag and whipped out a pair of cracked and worn ropers. These weren't the fancy boots of a city slicker. The soles were scuffed, the leather needed polishing, and the toe box had that just-right broken-in look. Even more surprising, without showing the least squeamishness, Aria plonked onto the ground in her perfect jeans, pulled her foot around and tugged on her fashion boot. "I know you've got more than one horse on this place. Bring one in for me and we'll get to work."

Baxter looked down at his running shoes. "I guess you'd better saddle two."

Aria had succeeded in changing one boot and was working on the other. She threw her head back and laughed. "Now that's funny. You'd be more trouble than help. Take our bags to the house and then tell that old man to go sit down." She issued orders as if used to others hopping to it. And yet, it didn't seem entitled, simply confident.

Neither Baxter nor I made a move. We both watched Aria finish with her boots, stuff the dress boots into her bag and stand up. She brushed her back end and I shifted to see if Baxter appreciated the view.

He was glaring at me.

I held up my hands. "What?"

"Every time you show up there's always a problem." He bent over to grab Aria's bag from the ground.

Baxter had a way of pushing every button I had, even if they'd been shut off for years. "I'm not the one who flew in like an alien invasion. I'm supposed to be working here."

Aria surveyed the ranch yard and nodded at the barn. "Right. You kids quit your bickering. We've got cattle to round up."

She strode across the field.

I scowled against the image of Baxter opening his arms to me, pulling me close, kissing me with all the passion and longing I felt for him. Instead, I whipped away and climbed on Honey, trotting her to the barn to find a horse for Aria.

Obviously, Aria had ridden before, either that, or she'd bought ropers at a vintage shop. But the way she took charge and the manner in which she'd introduced herself to Honey convinced me she had some experience. Still, I picked a mild-mannered horse, Fog, named for her soft gray coat.

I had her haltered and tied next to the tack room when Aria entered the barn. "She's pretty. I hope not too spirited. It's been a while since I've ridden."

I grabbed a brush and whisked the dried grass and dirt from Fog's back. "Are you a seasoned rider?"

She stepped around me into the tack room. "I grew up on a farm in New York. Well, I spent a lot of weekends there, anyway. Mostly I did dressage, but I spent a few summers working on dude ranches in Wyoming when I was in college. They were working ranches, so we did quite a bit of cattle work." With her hands on her slim hips, she eyed the saddles lined up on pegs in the tack room. "Which one of these should I use?"

I pointed to Carly's and grabbed a saddle blanket. I positioned it on Fog's back.

She hefted the saddle and walked out of the tack room, giving it a swing to gain momentum and settling it squarely on Fog. She got to work tightening the cinch and flipping the stirrups down.

We were saddled and back in the pasture in short order. Baxter wasn't anywhere around so I assumed he'd gone to the house.

True to her word, Aria knew how to round up a pasture. She took a diagonal to the northeast corner, and I headed to the northwest. I sent Barney with Aria and he happily trotted off, confident his day would be filled with what he loved to do most.

The cows weren't cooperative, and Honey worked hard getting them headed in the right direction. I had about twenty head and I hoped Aria had located the other twelve. Maybe Honey wouldn't be listed as a cutting horse, but she whipped from side to side with the slightest direction from me, sometimes as little as me leaning or applying pressure from my knees.

Sure, having to do this all over again was annoying. But normally, I'd be as happy herding cattle as Barney would be. The day couldn't be any nicer with sunshine, a light breeze, the birds still chiming in and the soft smell of the grass slightly damp from dew.

All of that Sandhills goodness bounced off of me. I hated to admit how rattled I was to see Baxter. He'd shown up unexpectedly several weeks ago in Hodgekiss with Carly and sent me into such a tailspin I was still reeling. For over two years I'd worked to get him out of my head and my heart. For the most part, I could hold the memory of him behind a levee. But every now and then, that barrier struck a leak and then the whole thing crumbled, leaving me as devastated as if he'd walked away from me the day before.

Now he'd landed in my world again. He'd invaded my sanctuary. Not only that, but he'd brought a woman. They were obviously in love. And unlike how I felt about Roxy, when she hooked up again with Ted, I couldn't hate Aria.

All of that led back to Mom and my need to let that pain go as well. The losses in my life kept piling up. First my oldest sister, Glenda, who'd been more of a mother to me than Mom. Ted, though that didn't count as such a loss since I was better off without him. Carly had gone missing as a kid, but she'd been recovered all grown up, just in time for me to lose Louise and probably Michael and Jeremy. I didn't know if I could forgive any of them for the big-time loss of my job. Now I needed to rethink my whole darned life.

So, what had started off as a pleasant favor for Carly on a glorious morning, had ended up in a cluster with the cattle and morphed into digging into all my problems. By the time my herd met up with Aria's in a stew of hair, mooing, and scuffling hooves in the sand, I felt like I'd been thrown into a coffee grinder and switched to fine.

The earlier roundup had been a slow walk to quietly push the cows toward the pens. Now, it was a constant battle with Honey flying to and fro at the back of the herd to keep them from doubling back and Aria on Fog running alongside to round up any cows that broke out.

Aria bounced in the saddle but that could be because she was rusty and out of practice with the rhythm of the horse. She seemed fearless and competent, holding the reins with authority and keeping her balance without gripping the saddle horn. We didn't have much time for conversation.

By the time we topped the last hill, the truck was backed up to the loading chute and ready. Rope held the steel gate open. To my surprise, Baxter stood to the side about fifty yards out, exactly as he should, to form a loose funnel to direct the herd into the pen. Rope had probably given him directions, but not many because Rope was a surly man of few words. And his history with Baxter wasn't friendly.

As we neared the gate, the herd created a sort of whirlpool with those about to enter the pen balking and turning back. They kept up a chorus of moos and grunts, snorting and slapping their tails. Aria and I kept the pressure on the back of the herd with Barney nipping at heels and tails, narrowly missing kicks. His tongue lolled and he looked like he couldn't quit laughing. Poupon would never work this hard. He was probably lounging on the front porch, content to avoid any effort except getting comfortable for his next nap.

If Ted had been here, he'd have whooped and hollered, pushed the herd too hard in his impatience to get them into the pen. Aria seemed to have the same strategy I did, keep quiet, make going into the pen the easiest choice for them. We stopped a moment, our horses breathing into the quiet, punctuated by the moos of the cows and their hooves scraping the sand.

Aria sucked in a contented breath. "My God this is beautiful country."

I admired the sweeping hills. "I think so."

"This is exactly what I needed. I'm so cooped up in Chicago. It's a rare day if I get a walk by the river. And then, there's the noise and the smells. Out here, there's literally no smell."

Maybe not to her, but I detected the peppery tang of sunflowers and the juicy scent of trampled prairie grass. "What do you do in Chicago?" I wanted to know. I didn't want to know. I didn't want to imagine what she did that interested Baxter. Didn't want to know how much better she was than I was in every way.

She watched the cows ahead of us. "I manage my family's foundation. It's a bullshit job."

See? She managed finances of a fortune. If I spent more than fifty dollars on a new dress I panicked. "How so?"

She shrugged. "My job is to give away money to worthy causes. But not too much. And I manage investments to make sure the coffers keep replenishing after my sisters' clothes, vacations, remodels." She paused and emphasized the last word with a finger in the air. "And I'm not only talking about their houses."

"That sounds like a lot." And as far outside my understanding as swimming was to a cat.

"It's a balancing act to make sure I keep everyone happy. My two sisters are always worried I'm going to throw away their fortune and if they speak to me at all, it's to accuse me of embezzlement or mismanagement."

"Family can be difficult."

She grinned at me, and one dimple in her right cheek looked too adorable for words. Of course, Baxter would love to kiss that divot. "Your family seems really devoted to each other," she said.

What did she know about the Foxes?

I must have shown my surprise because she laughed. "Glenn talks to Carly quite a bit. He's been advising her on the ranch and investments and probably life. She's full of family stories about all the aunts, uncles, and cousins. It sounds like fun to be part of something like that. I've heard your name mentioned. I didn't know Glenn actually knew you, but from the way you reacted to each other, I assume you've had a run in or two. Probably over Carly. You were her guardian, right?"

"Yeah." But that's the tip of the pizza of what Baxter and I were to each other. For almost two years we spoke on the phone daily and he became such a part of my life that being without him still felt like a cold wind blowing right through me. I was glad when she kept talking.

"Glenn wants to be helpful to Carly. But I don't think he really understands the love someone has for land." She threw her arm out to indicate the hills. "This is amazing. I've flown over the west, and I spent all that time in Wyoming, but I've never seen a place like this. We landed Glenn's jet in North Platte and took the helicopter here, and I got a good sense of the vastness of this place. You're lucky to be here. And surrounded by family."

"Sometimes I think our family is overly involved with each other. I wouldn't envy it too much."

She waved that away, the dimple still visible but the light dimmed in her eyes. "Any kind of family that could share a joke or eat a meal together without someone stalking off would be a change from mine. I hate to say sitting on three generations of increasing fortune takes away the closeness and security of family relationships, but in our case, it seemed to drive a wedge."

We urged our horses a few steps closer to the cows. "I'd think not having to worry about money would keep everyone relaxed and make it easier to spend time together."

"I'm sure you've seen those shows like *Succession*? Well, that's more what it's like. So, yeah, living out here like you do, with a giant loving family, seems like heaven."

It took several minutes for the cows to swirl in a bovine stew, but one cow stumbled through the gate. Suddenly free from the crush of the herd, she trotted a few more steps into the opening.

When those behind her became aware of her escape from the confusion, they followed. Cows aren't all that smart so there wasn't a lot of thought behind their group decision to shove through the gate.

We were nearly out of the woods when one cagey cow decided to change direction. Just before she crossed the threshold into the corral, she swung to the side and bolted. Though Honey was fleet, the cow caught us unaware.

She took off for freedom with a singleness of purpose. Rope shouted something. I probably did, too. Aria tugged Fog around to chase, but that old cow had the lead on both of us.

From his position well back from the main action, Baxter started on a run to intercept the cow. Maybe he wasn't a born cowboy and hadn't spent time around cattle, but he wasn't stupid and he'd seen the goal. If he hurried, he might spook her and turn her back to the herd.

I kicked Honey into a gallop to help. It would be a feat if Baxter got to her in time and turned her in the right direction.

Running across a pasture full of bunch grass and weeds, cactus and critter holes isn't the same as jogging in Grant Park. But Baxter put effort into it. He should slow and wave his arms, shout a *hyaa* or whoop. Instead, he kept going as if he could shove her out of her path.

I'd made it far enough away from the corral so I could swoop around and get in front of her before she made it over the hill. "Okay," I shouted at Baxter. "Let her go."

Either he didn't hear me, or he didn't care. He kept going. Like maybe he had a vision of himself as a bull fighter and my hollering was simply the roar of the crowd.

I figured the cow would see Baxter and swerve away from him, which would put her between me and the pen, and I could direct her toward her compatriots. They didn't care she went rogue, but she'd see and hear them and, hopefully, rethink joining them for security's sake.

But she didn't seem to notice Baxter, maybe because he was more intent on running than making himself seen and heard. Baxter wasn't slowing down, and they seemed on a collision course. I'd given him credit for some cow sense, but now I revoked it all. The fool didn't understand she was over a thousand pounds of panic, and he didn't stand a chance.

I'd seen cows collide with people. Broken ribs, shattered occipital bones, jaws that needed to be wired. Earl Macomber had internal bleeding no one knew about until three hours later when he keeled over dead. Tana Fleenor's knee had been shattered so badly she needed a cane for the rest of her life. Fear zinged through my veins at the thought of Baxter's broken body.

"Stop!" I screamed.

And then, he did. Gopher hole, bind weed, any number of hazards might have led to him flying forward, hands splayed, chin out. It was a Superman plant of epic proportions.

I pulled on Honey's reins, and she stopped almost immediately. It felt like I willed my breath into Baxter as my whole focus zeroed in on him, watching for any movement to tell me he was okay.

He lifted his head and our eyes connected. When they say an emotion washes in, that's exactly what they mean. The relief was like a cool wave over me, soothing my panic. I whipped my head around to locate the escapee but not before I caught the lift of Baxter's lips in a smile.

Like we shared a private joke. No room for anyone else.

While I charged after the cow to coax her back, Aria was holding the rest in the pen until Rope swung the gate closed.

That ringy beast ran to the northeast corner of the pasture before I turned her toward the loading pen. By the time we trudged to the gate, the cow was now exhausted and giving up on life, willing to go where Honey and I directed. The trucker and Rope waited to let her in.

While Rope followed her up the chute and they closed the trailer door, I dismounted and waited for Rope. He limped down the wooden loading chute and rested against the fence, face pale and dark circles under his eyes. "That was some rodeo today. Surprised we got 'em loaded up."

"It's not every day a helicopter lands on the meadow, I guess."

Rope pushed himself from the fence. "Happens more often than you'd think." He started to amble away then turned back. "That girl ain't bad help. Darned sure better than the dude. He'll be hobbled for a while, though."

Carly's old ranch pickup rumbled away from the headquarters toward us. Rope dipped his head in that direction and headed toward the cookhouse, where he'd lived for the better part of fifty years.

I led Honey to the side of the road and the pickup stopped near me. Aria rolled down the window of the driver's side and raised her voice to be heard above the diesel engine. "I unsaddled Fog and gave her a bit of grain.

Sorry for making extra work, but thanks for letting me get out there. It felt good."

Coughing came from the passenger side, reminding me that with Baxter's lung ailment, running around a pasture probably wasn't the best thing to do.

I leaned around her to peer into the cab. Baxter sat propped against the door, one leg stretched out on the bench seat, his mouth held in a straight line. "Are you okay?"

His voice sounded like a bucket full of sand. "Fine." He held a cough back, so he jerked a little.

Aria let out a clicking sound. "I think he might have broken his ankle. At the very least, it's sprained. I wanted to call the ambulance, but Rope said it would be better to drive him to Broken Butte myself."

I nodded in agreement. "Can take them some time to round up EMTs since it's all volunteer."

Aria cast a sympathetic glance at Baxter. "I've had a little emergency medical training. I thought at one time I'd like to be a first responder. It looks like it's not life threatening. But I'll bet it smarts. So, we'd better get going."

I jumped back from the pickup. "Sure."

She rolled up the window and continued down the road but what I saw was her hand reaching to Baxter and their firm clasp. Fingers entwined. What I wouldn't give to be the one feeling his grip.

13

Honey and Fog brushed and turned out, cattle on their way to the sale barn, I collected Poupon and drove back to town. About five miles from Hodgekiss, my phone rang. I swiped it on. "Sher—" I stopped and started again. "Hello." Since I was voted out, I couldn't answer with the title.

Ralph Crumpton's creaky voice filtered to me. "Morning, Sheriff. I got this problem here. My cat's stuck in the crawl space of the basement and she's putting up a ruckus. Can you come up and get her out?"

My first reaction was to have him call Zoe. But she wasn't sworn in, yet. And besides, Ralph didn't care if I was sheriff or not. He probably didn't care a whole lot if his cat was rescued, knowing that she'd get herself out sooner or later. Ralph's wife of seventy years had passed away a few months ago and, sometimes, he just wanted to talk to someone. Since the citizens of Grand County paid my salary, and Ralph was one of those, I had no problem showing up when he called. Truthfully, being sheriff wasn't the reason I helped out Ralph, even if the title gave him an excuse to call me. "I'll be there in five minutes."

On my way my phone rang again. A quick glance showed my newly found Aunt Deb, my mother's sister from Chicago. I put her on speaker.

Her sincere sadness laced through her Midwest accent. "Louise told me about the vote. Honey, I'm so sorry."

I grumbled. "Thanks. But Louise isn't sorry at all."

"Sisters." That word carried love, frustration, pain, so much weight we both knew. "What are your plans?"

I cruised into Hodgekiss and turned up the first street. "I'm considering options."

"While you think about it, you're sure welcome to come see me in Chicago. We'd love to have you."

That caused a lump in my throat. I would think about that, but I wasn't sure I could stand to be in the same city as Baxter and he wasn't likely to hang out here long. "That's kind of you."

She accepted the thanks and paused, making me wonder what else she had on her mind. After an "um" and smack of her lips, she said, "You haven't heard anything from your mother, have you?"

I choked. The last thing I wanted was to hear from her. Or maybe it was what I wanted more than anything. "That's not likely to happen."

"Yeah. That's what I think." But she didn't sound like that's what she thought.

"Is something going on?"

Again, it took her a second. "I didn't tell Louise but Mom's been talking about Miriam coming to see her."

"Doesn't your mother have dementia?" Technically my grandmother, but that connection was never formed.

"Well, yes. It's just...." She trailed off and I waited, curious to know where she was going with this. "I assumed Mom was confused. But then, I found some of her favorite candies in her apartment. She's not supposed to have sugar, so I watch it carefully. She doesn't have friends who visit and I'm sure the staff wouldn't give them to her. When I asked where they came from, she said Miriam brought them."

As far as mysteries go, it didn't rank with who killed Garrett. "She may not remember someone coming by. It's not Mom, though. She wouldn't risk coming back into the country."

"I'm sure you're right." Again, she didn't sound sure.

We visited a little more about the beauty of Chicago in the fall and signed off. Not for the first time I almost wished Deb had been my mother instead of her sister.

By the time Poupon and I arrived at Ralph's, the tabby was curled in Ralph's threadbare recliner. I always brought Poupon with me because Ralph liked the fluffer, though his cat kept a close eye on him. Acknowledging the cat was beneath Poupon's dignity so it all worked out.

I accepted the offered Werther's candy and waited while Ralph made over his good buddy, Poupon. As long as I was there, Ralph wondered, would I mind lugging a box of paperbacks from his basement and dropping them at the Jumble Shop?

That task completed, a few minutes of conversation about how the rain this summer compared to the summer of 1969, and a promise to tell Dad howdy from him, and I loaded Poupon and waved one last time as Ralph stood on his porch and watched me drive away.

Maybe I'd leave Zoe a list of seniors who regularly called for assistance on everything from changing a light bulb to unsticking a windowpane.

I hadn't made much headway with locating Sheila. Maybe I could get a little research done before Zoe arrived for our scheduled meeting.

I parked the cruiser in back and slipped into the courthouse, hoping Poupon and I could make it to my office undiscovered. No such luck.

The pass-through in Betty's office clanked open and Betty scurried out. "Oh, Kate. I'm glad to see you."

I stopped and Poupon took a few more paces, his focus on Ethel's office door. If dogs could pray, he'd bow his head for her to appear with the inevitable scrap of steak or bit of string cheese.

Betty's sad expression made it seem she might shed a tear or two on my behalf. "I can't believe you won't be showing up here every day with your sunny smile and your willingness to help out anywhere you're needed."

It's the kind of attitude mourners take on at a funeral, showering the deceased with false praise even if the dead guy had been a slimy buzzard. It kind of made me feel corpsey and maybe starting to go ripe.

"Zoe said to tell you she'd be a few minutes late." Betty leaned in. "Do you think she's going to work out? I honestly don't see how she can raise a baby and be sheriff."

I shrugged. "Ted seems to be making it work."

Betty opened her mouth to respond, probably to say something about Ted having a wife to take care of Beau, then maybe she realized Zoe had a husband. She closed her mouth. Change came slowly to Grand County, especially for women like Betty who hadn't altered her hair style in forty years. "Okay, then. There's coffee if you'd like to talk. This has to be hard. Your family turning on you like this."

In the three years I'd been sheriff, I'd never had coffee with Betty. Now didn't seem like a good time to break that streak.

"Thanks, Betty. But I need to take care of a few things. Maybe some other time."

I felt bad the way she brightened up as if I'd asked her to the prom.

In the office, Poupon started for my chair. "Oh, no." I pointed to his bed, and I swore he shot me a dirty look before flopping down with a sigh of the truly oppressed.

I fired up Bessy, my ancient PC and waited for her to grind and whir. Maybe Zoe would have more luck finding room in the budget for a new computer. When Bessy was finally ready to work, I searched for Sheila's real estate business in Scottsdale.

Footsteps made me look up to see Zoe enter the office. She wore jeans and a plain brown T-shirt. With a flat belly, muscular arms and long legs, she looked fit enough to run a marathon. She'd captured her long sandy-colored hair into a French braid down her back. "Sorry I'm late. Blaine had a tractor break down and it put him behind to take Ivy."

I waved her off. "Don't worry about it. Most of the time, it's a loose schedule. Just so you can be on call if there's an emergency."

She moved into the office, now crowded with the three of us. It would probably be best if I relocated Poupon and his luxury bed.

Zoe was the perfect mix of Carly and Susan. While Carly crackled with energy and came up with harebrained schemes, Susan followed rules and often came across as owly. Zoe had Carly's fearlessness without her reckless nature. Like Susan, Zoe had respect for rules, but didn't mind bending or breaking them for a good cause.

For instance, one summer when the girls were in high school, they wanted to see The Black Keys at Red Rocks outside of Denver. Of course, parents and guardians shut that plan down. Carly decided they would say they were camping out by the river on Zoe's family ranch, then they'd drive the five hours to the concert and make it home before sunrise the next day.

When Susan argued they should simply inform their parents they were going and duke it out, Zoe was the one who agreed they ought to sneak out, but make sure someone responsible knew where they were going. They ended up letting Douglas in on it and promising to check in. By all accounts, which we heard a few years later, it had been a caper worthy of the risk.

Zoe leaned over to see the screen. "What are you doing?"

I punched away on the keys. By now, Zoe would have heard about Garrett's accident. "I'm trying to find Garrett's wife. Tony doesn't know where she is, and I need to notify her of Garrett's death." I pointed to a wooden chair I'd commandeered from the commissioners' room. "I'm not sure what I'm doing but I thought I'd start with her real estate business."

While Zoe dragged the chair around, the legs scraping on the floor, and settled in next to me to squint at the screen, I found Sheila Haney and pulled up her website.

"Whoa," Zoe said. "Look at her listings." She stabbed a finger at the screen. "That one. Four million dollars? It only has four bedrooms. It ought to have twenty for that price. But man, look at the infinity pool."

That house wasn't the only property that had our jaws gaping. Gated communities, city views, mountains, pools, and landscaping worthy of five-star resorts. We ooed and ahhed over acreages in the desert with bridle trails, tennis courts, and more fountains with statues and tile than I'd expect at an Italian castle.

I called the number listed and got about what I expected, an automated voice telling me the mailbox I'd been trying to reach was full. Cross off her personal phone and business phone.

"Now what do we do?" Zoe asked.

I thought a moment. One of the pages was dedicated to previous sales and testimonials of satisfied customers. I took down the name of the owner of the last gargantuan home sold. "Maybe we can find this Angela and see if she can tell us anything about Sheila."

"How are we going to do that?"

I googled the Scottsdale police. "We call in reinforcements."

She listened while I wound my way from the staffer who answered the phone to an investigator.

A man picked up with a clipped tone. "Tim Morris, what do you need?"

I explained who I was and why I was looking for Sheila Haney. I gave him Angela's name and the neighborhood of the house she'd sold recently. "Can you run a search for home sales last March with this information and find her name and contact information?"

Maybe I'd expected irritation or a flat-out refusal. He surprised me with a quick and upbeat response. "Sure. I've got some contacts. Might not take too long."

Zoe and I spent the next hour going over protocols, deadlines, budgets, and forms. The boring parts of the job. She'd already enrolled in the training in Grand Island and said her husband and parents were on board for childcare. Classes started in three weeks. Until she completed the 16-week course, she wouldn't be able to perform so much as a traffic stop. She could patrol and keep an eye on things, help out Ralph and others, and show up in uniform at ball games and such, but anything official would be handled by the state patrol or by the sheriffs in adjoining counties. Not an ideal situation, but that's how it'd been for me and even for Ted when he'd started. We're a law-abiding bunch in the Sandhills, so it usually didn't create a lot of problems.

"How about lunch? Long Branch okay?"

She hesitated. "I brought mine. If we're going to save enough to get our ranching outfit going, we're on a strict budget."

Can't argue with that ethic. "My treat."

She looked doubtful.

"Come on. I'm not going to take you out every day. This is your welcome dinner." I felt generous, although I knew I should start conserving, too. Since I had no prospects for a new income source soon, I needed to corral my pennies.

Most of the tables in the bar side had been shoved together to accommodate the senior lunch crowd who met three days a week. About ten folks gathered in there, eating hot beef sandwiches and mashed potatoes and gravy. Looked like a big helping of green beans on the side, along with packaged dinner rolls. Bud had probably made a pan of apple crisp for dessert. Not a bad deal since it was subsidized for the seniors.

Twyla stomped past us as we made our way to a booth on the restaurant side. Senior lunch always put her in foul temper. She thrust her order pad and pen at me. "Get your order to Bud. I don't have time to mess with anything but these danged old folks." She took a falsetto tone. "I need more coffee. We need more ranch dressing." She glared at me. "Ranch dressing? Are you kidding me? We're having beef sandwiches and spuds. Where the hell do they think they need more ranch dressing?"

She didn't wait for an answer but stomped into the kitchen, grousing to Bud.

Zoe's eyes twinkled down at me. "Hate to be a bother. I'll have a chicken strip basket."

I jotted that down and added my burger and fries. While Zoe claimed one of the red fiberglass booths next to a window overlooking the highway, I poured us a couple of drinks from the fountain.

We chatted about their ranch and when they planned on weaning and circled around to the perennial deputy situation. In the four-county sheriff co-op, we shared a deputy so every sheriff could have one planned weekend off a month. We hadn't been able to score a deputy for three years since two of our troop had landed into legal hot water and our deputy, Kyle Red Owl, had been appointed in one of the counties and Ted had landed in the other.

Twyla hollered at me from the cash register by the front door. "Come get your dinner."

Zoe and I jumped up and refilled our drinks, picked up our plates, and grabbed the ketchup before settling in to our lunch. As far as I'm concerned, a hamburger a day would suit me fine. And there wasn't much to compare to Bud's. Juicy, warm, all the fixin's. We kept up an easy conversation about Susan and Carly, moving from one topic to another.

In mid-question, Zoe stopped talking and her sharp eyes lasered on something behind me.

I twisted in time to see Louise, a takeout bag in her hand, the grease already starting to darken it. My stomach dropped and I straightened to face Zoe, as if Louise wasn't there.

Ignoring her didn't seem to have any effect. She planted herself at the head of our booth with a satisfied grin. "I'm so glad to see you're making the transition. Look at you," she said to Zoe. "You already seem official. I know you're going to be fantastic."

I dipped a fry in ketchup and pretended Louise wasn't there, while keeping track of her from the corner of my eye.

Zoe didn't return Louise's gushing grin. "I'll be lucky if I'm half the sheriff Kate is."

Louise took a step back and tutted. "Of course. But it wasn't an appropriate position for someone related to almost everyone in the county."

Zoe's closed-mouth smile didn't give Louise any leeway. "Blaine and I have a lot of family around, too. I don't expect it's going to be a problem. And I have Kate's example of professionalism to follow."

Louise's head tilted in a prissy way, as if she'd been insulted. "I only wanted to congratulate you and let you know we're rooting for you."

Zoe looked up, chicken strip clutched in her fingers. "I'm really sorry about that thing with Ruthie. Freshman year can be tricky, but that's really a bad deal."

Louise's eyes started to blink, and her mouth dropped open. "What thing with Ruthie?"

Ruthie, Louise's oldest daughter, was in her first year at the University of Nebraska. (Go Big Red) She was a lot like Louise, someone who knew right from wrong and wanted to make sure the world adhered to her principles. I'm sure they were thinking of her when they coined the phrase "fun-hater." But I loved her anyway and felt bad for the dose of reality she was sure to receive at college. I hoped it wasn't too serious.

Zoe shifted her eyes to her plate as if regretful she'd said anything. "Oh, I'm sure it's nothing. Never mind."

Louise spun away, her footsteps thudding in the noisy restaurant. She didn't pause to say goodbye.

I set down my burger. "What's going on with Ruthie?"

Zoe took a bite of her chicken and spoke around it. "Nothing as far as I know."

We finished, I tallied our ticket, left Twyla a tip, and met Zoe outside in an afternoon shaping up like yesterday, with sun in the morning and clouds filling in. Vivid blue mixed with the fluffy white, not looking threatening, but making sure we didn't take sunshine for granted.

We climbed Main Street on the way back to the courthouse. "So, what's with Louise filing the recall against you?"

A tiny fist punched my gut. "My theory is that when we found out about Mom's past and she took off, Louise got thrown off-kilter in a worse way than most of us. She's always been a control freak, but this time, it pushed her too far. She wanted to control everything, including me."

Zoe soaked that up. "Wow. I know what you mean about the controlling thing. When Carly lived with her, before you got to be her guardian, I heard plenty. But what she did to you is messed up."

I shrugged. "It's a theory."

Zoe pulled out her phone. "I'm going to check up on Ivy. See if Blaine has it under control."

Before Blaine answered, my phone buzzed, and I slipped it out of my pocket to see the number of the Scottsdale cop. Tim Morris hadn't wasted time. After hellos, he said, "Angela Romero. Not hard to identify. She's bought and sold several times in the last few years, upgrading every time she divorces one guy and marries up."

"That's a lot of information in a short amount of time. I'm impressed."

He didn't chuckle but I thought I heard a smile in his voice. "Scottsdale isn't that big, and you hit my sweet spot. My wife is a realtor and she happened to know about our delightful Angela. That woman runs through realtors like she does husbands. For a while, they're her bosom buddy and then they're out the door. Lots of drama with that one."

"Our lucky day," I said.

"My wife primarily handles commercial property but others in her company have had dealings with Angela Romero. She's got a reputation as quite the shark."

"Did you ask your wife if she knew Sheila Haney?"

"I did. She'd heard of her but no one in my wife's office knew her." He recited her number and I thanked him. "You say the woman disappeared in May? Got a description and any information on her? We can keep an eye out for her. Is she in any danger, do you think?"

"I have no reason to think that." At least, no more reason than I had to wonder about Garrett's death.

14

Bits and pieces from the last two days balled up in my head. Tony saying the pivot hadn't been struck by lightning. Becca saying she worried about Garrett's client. Trey saying there was no fuse burned out on the pivot. And now Sheila missing.

Was there more to Garrett's death than an accident?

Zoe and I both ended our calls and clumped up the back stairs of the courthouse. We made it to the office and rousted Poupon from my chair.

Zoe folded into her chair and flipped her braid behind her shoulder. "Blaine is doing great. I knew he would. They checked windmills and Ivy loves the pickup." She leaned back. "I probably should feel bad about leaving Ivy, but it's nice to be an adult for a while."

At twenty-four, she hadn't had a lot of experience being an adult. But in my opinion, Zoe showed more maturity than most people her age and was probably more considerate and thoughtful than the majority of people of any age.

I told her about Tim Morris's call. "Well?" she said.

"Let's see if she answers." I gave it a shot and dialed. The phone rang three times and rolled over to voicemail. "This is Sheriff Kate Fox from Grand County, Nebraska. I'm trying to locate Angela Romero who sold a house in Scottsdale, Arizona, in March. If you're Ms. Romero, your help can be vital in an ongoing investigation." I asked her to contact me and gave my number, as if she couldn't simply hit reply.

Zoe sat back and gave me an expectant smirk. "And now?"

"Now I guess we talk about—" My phone rang, and I snatched it, noting the Arizona number. Zoe grinned when I gave her a thumbs up and put it on speaker.

She sounded more irritated than curious or cooperative. "This is Angela. You said you needed information about an investigation? In Nebraska? I've never been there."

I tried to give heft to my voice so she wouldn't make me out as a scammer. "We're trying to locate a missing person and hoped you might have some information that can help us."

There was silence. "I'm not sure I should say anything without an attorney."

Well, now. People in Scottsdale with bazillion-dollar homes might have more to protect than us Sandhillers, but she seemed paranoid. "This isn't a criminal investigation. There's been a death and we need to notify next of kin."

She shot back. "I have no idea how I can help you or how you even got my number. With someone in my position, it's important to guard my privacy."

She was starting to frost my tomatoes. I spoke with the force and authority of my position as sheriff. "I'm not a telemarketer." I let that sit a second. "This is an important investigation involving a minor child. The Scottsdale PD helped me locate you through the sale of your home in March."

She gasped. "A child is missing? From my old neighborhood? You'd think this city wouldn't have that kind of problem. I blame the Mexican cartels. They have the money to live in Scottsdale but they're animals."

Zoe and I exchanged a "what the heck?" look and let her go on.

"That is exactly why I moved to this new area. That old place had a gate, but they weren't serious about keeping out the bad element. This one is walled off and the security is top-notch. But to let a child go missing is beyond the pale."

At least I had her attention. "The child in question is the son of the realtor who sold your home in Paradise Island. Sheila Haney."

Her voice squeezed tight, as if she practiced at being devastated. "Oh my god. Tony is dead? He was such a sweetheart. For a child, I mean." Maybe she heard herself sound so exaggerated because she brought it back to a more normal tone. "I didn't really know him, though. I'm not much of a kid person, you understand."

Zoe made a gagging motion.

Good thing I didn't need to like this woman to get information from her. "Tony is fine. It's his father, Sheila's husband, who has passed."

She let out a huff. "Well, that's another thing all together. What happened? Murder? Suicide?"

Zoe held out her hands in an expression of, "Do you believe this?"

Serious and professional. "It was an accident. But we're having trouble locating Sheila. Do you have any idea where she could be?"

Angela paused. "Why would you think I'd know anything? She was only my real estate agent."

If she wanted me to work for everything, I guess I would. "Tony thought he remembered his mother saying how much she admired and liked you. That she considered you a friend."

Zoe's face questioned me, and I shook my head to explain that Tony hadn't said anything.

I didn't need to know what Angela looked like—though I pictured a scrawny, leathery over-tan woman in her fifties dripping in sterling silver and turquoise—I could hear the preening in her voice. "Sheila said that? I felt that connection too. Which is why I was astounded when she ghosted me."

Darn. Zoe's wide brown eyes showed disappointment and she faked a finger click to indicate a near miss.

"When was this?"

She hmmed, like she was calculating. "I'd say maybe three or four months ago." She inhaled. "Wait, it was in late May. I remember because Hal and I were throwing a garden party and Sheila and I had gone shopping for the perfect dress. Well, I didn't find one for me." Maybe she felt she had to explain but I shared Zoe's eye roll. "I'm hard to fit because I'm so petite if there's not a tailor on hand I'm out of luck. So mostly I just have my clothes custom made."

Probably not from Etsy.

"But Sheila is a more standard size. We found this baby blue sheath with ruffles around the neck to draw attention away from..." she paused. "Well, Sheila needed the emphasis off other parts of her body."

Zoe dropped her head back and stared at the ceiling.

It made sense Sheila would ghost this woman. It would take more than the commission from a four-million-dollar sale to get me in the same room with her. "And that's when you lost touch?"

"She didn't show up to the party. No call. No email or text. Not even flowers or an apology." We could hear her level of affront.

"What do you think happened?" If someone told me I needed to draw attention from my butt by wearing ruffles around my neck I'm pretty sure I'd vanish from their lives.

If I had to guess, I'd say Angela looked around to make sure no one was listening, then leaned into her phone to confide her malicious gossip. "If you hadn't said her husband just died in an accident, I'd guess that maybe he killed her. He seemed like that weak victim who finally gets tired of being pushed around and lashes out, you know the type? Like maybe he'd been spoiled by an overbearing mother or abused by a brutish father. Sheila was definitely afraid of someone, and I thought it might be him."

That startled me. Angela might have more insight than she knew. Zoe focused on my face, and I wondered if she'd read my reaction.

Angela nattered on. "But since this development, I'm thinking maybe someone else got to her. There was a lot going on in their lives and when you get into something so deep, well, it can get dangerous. But I don't honestly think someone put a hit on her. Not really."

Zoe's mouth formed a little o of interest.

"Back up a minute. Sheila was afraid of someone?" Sheesh, Angela was a lot of work.

"Well, yes. Maybe I should start with the fact that her husband, Garrett, oh my, what an entitled snowflake."

Zoe raised her eyebrows at me.

Finally, Angela seemed to warm to the topic. "Supposedly, he's a real hot shot attorney at one of the better firms in the city. But Sheila said he was burned out." She put a distinctive sneering tone in the last two words. "For fuck's sake. That firm has the wealthiest and most influential clients in the country. You get to that level, you don't quit. This is between you and me?"

She paused and I realized she expected an answer. "Of course. I'm a sheriff." As if that had anything to do with it.

"Sheila told me he had clients wanting to groom him to run for office. I'm not one to sugarcoat things and I told Sheila, a firm like that, with clients like that? Honey, if he played nice, he could easily be slotted into the state's highest offices. They'd start getting him placed strategically and within a few years, he'd be poised for the big time. Come on, you've seen him. He's a looker." She paused as if remembering the reason for our call. When she started, she sounded a bit more subdued. "Or, well, he was And he's Republican. In this state, with those kinds of friends, who like a bit of quid pro quo, he was sitting pretty."

Zoe and I stared at each other in disbelief. I wanted to be clear on what she'd said. "You mean, Sheila wanted Garrett to start getting on track to run for public office? And his clients would help elect him for favors he might do for them once he was in office?"

Angela shot back like a mother scolding a child. "What did I just say?"

"You think Sheila was scared?"

"Sweetie, I think Sheila was pissed about it first. Here she is, sitting on a gold mine and all her hubby has to do is agree, maybe put in some long hours here and there, kiss some gold-plated ass, and she's first lady of Arizona, with a husband young enough and handsome enough, that the sky's the limit."

We'd hit a mine I hadn't known we'd aimed for. "But Garrett didn't want to do that?"

Angela sounded irritated. "Who knows what he wanted? I never met him. I know Sheila had about enough of the whole game. She'd had the obligatory baby for the optics. And played mommy for years. And I'm not saying she didn't like the kid or whatever. It sounded to me as if she liked him just fine. But she'd given up a lot to hitch herself to Garrett and help him up the ladder. When she was younger, she was gorgeous—I saw the pictures— and she's smart and ambitious so she could have had anyone. And then, for him to wimp out like that, well, let's just say, I wouldn't be surprised if she had a new game plan. I know I would have."

"What do you mean?"

She seemed to forget her earlier restraint about giving away personal information and let out a sly chuckle. "You're a sheriff, a macho career, so don't take offense to this. I'm a feminist from the beginning. But here's the truth. Some women are born to be doctors or lawyers, accountants, what have you. Anything they want, just like men, obviously. But some women, and I'm talking about women like me and Sheila, were born to be wives of great men. Our talent is to partner with someone who shows potential and do what it takes to make them rise. Don't fool yourself, it's a challenging career worthy of all the skill and savvy of any other. Like the CEO of a corporation with an eye to every detail. Sometimes, our investment doesn't pan out and we need to move on to the next position. I've done it a few times. It's unfortunate, and sometimes there's heartbreak. But we're not children, and ambition is a fire that needs fuel."

"Sheila left Garrett for a more successful man?" It tasted sour when I said it.

Angela made a *ummp* sort of squeak that I took to mean "probably, why not, I would do it."

Zoe's eyes looked like dinner plates and she mouthed, "Wow."

"Is she having an affair with the client, the one who wanted to groom Garrett for office?"

Angela let out a disbelieving guffaw. "Oh, he's way out of her league."

Bottom line, it, Angela. "You think Sheila left Garrett and Tony?"

Now she sounded airy and maybe impatient to end a conversation that refused to stay centered on herself. "Maybe. Or she could have been murdered."

Now Zoe flopped back in her chair in disbelief.

"Who would do that?"

A loud click of heels on tile made me think I'd made it to the end of our conversation and Angela was on the move. "Those clients of Garrett's? The people with so much power? They have resources. And if they let Garrett into the inner circle and he knew secrets, and then was ready to turn them down, it might put Sheila and Garrett, and maybe even that heartbreaker son of theirs in a tight spot. At that level, accidents happen." She clicked a few more paces and stopped. "What kind of accident did you say killed Garrett?"

15

I placed the phone on the desk and Zoe and I stared at it as if it might explode.

After a moment, she inhaled. "Did she just hint that Garrett and Sheila had been assassinated for knowing too much? That's not really what happened, is it? I mean, we're in the Nebraska Sandhills, not Sicily. Or, like New York. I really got into *The Sopranos* a while back and read all these books and articles about the Cosa Nostra and stuff. But that's not what's going on here, is it? I mean, it can't be."

I knew how she felt about the impossibility of those dramatic stories happening here, in Podunk, USA. Except, I'd experienced the big national breaking news story that you see on the *NBC Nightly News* and, in my case, gets coverage in a CNN special. As one does when you have a mother with a violent activist history. "Let's see if we can find out Garrett's clients and what they were into."

I found Dougherty, Fleishman, Haney and Associates' website again and looked through the pages. It didn't reveal any clients' names.

Zoe scooted her chair close and stared at the screen. "I should have brought my laptop. This antique is so slow. How can you stand it?"

"Since I don't have a reliable signal at home, this doesn't seem so bad." I clicked on group shots of well-dressed people at various charitable events.

The only people I recognized were Garrett and Sheila, him in a tuxedo and her in different evening gowns, all dazzling.

"Wow." Zoe breathed in. "First of all, those dresses are amazing, and it makes me wonder if I've made a tactical error by marrying Blaine and hoping to finance living on the ranch by being sheriff. I mean, I could go find some rich guy with potential and take him on as my career plan. And look like a million bucks in this off-the-shoulder number with sequins. And second, where does Angela Romero get off saying Sheila had a fat ass, because this woman here," she tapped the screen. "Is hot AF."

I clicked through more posed photos, the kind you see in prestigious university alumni magazines or in the theater programs they passed out at the Broadway musicals in Denver. Diane had season tickets and I'd been her guest occasionally. "Might be nice to dress up once or twice like that, but not if you had to put up with the rest of the BS like saying the right thing to the right people, or make sure the photographer gets your best side. Give me jeans and boots any day."

"I wasn't serious. It'd take more than money to pry me out of the Sandhills." She whipped out her phone. "I'll google Garrett Haney and see what I come up with."

We kept to our own searches for a moment, then Zoe said, "Whoa. Look at this."

I sat back and watched her face as she read, knowing her sheer cuteness would make people doubt her ability to be a sheriff. Would that be a good investigative tactic, like underestimating a bumbling Columbo? "Okay, there's a bunch of stuff about this guy, Coleson Crenshaw, and this energy corporation and some big mess with him breaking mining laws."

Coleson Crenshaw. It was one of those names you know you've heard but in relation to something you don't care much about so you can't really place it. Like you know Thomas Paine, but someone has to remind you he said, "Give me liberty or give me death." Or was that Patrick Henry?

"So, anyway, this guy's company got sued for environmental disasters about his mine close to the Mexico border. And basically, he got all these favors from the court and his lawyer was Garrett Haney."

"When was this?"

She scrolled up to check the byline. "Two years ago."

While she kept looking, I searched Coleson Crenshaw. And there he was. I pushed back a little from the desk so Zoe could read the screen along with me. "Coleson Crenshaw is very interesting."

Zoe started to read. "Holy crap. Who wrote this?"

The accusations were hair-raising. "It's a super-liberal online paper, so we need to keep that in mind. But maybe it's got some truth to it."

Before she'd finished the article, Zoe started punching into her phone. We were quiet for a few minutes, and she said, "Your paper isn't the only one. This is from the Wall Street Journal: 'There is widespread speculation that Crenshaw and his brother have funded numerous political campaigns around the country. It can't be proven, but our sources say it's likely the Crenshaws are responsible for placing more federal judges than most presidents.'"

I'd scanned my article and now started a new search. "Does it say anything about links to murders?"

"Is there some law enforcement search tool we can use?"

"Nothing that will help unless he's been arrested."

She mumbled as if reading quickly to herself. "Nothing mentioning arrests. They say he ruined careers, and one guy is quoted saying you don't want to make Coleson Crenshaw your enemy."

I raised my eyebrows at my search results. "I put in Coleson Crenshaw murder and look at this."

She whistled at the string of articles showing on my screen. She made the same search on her phone, and we spent the next half hour reading them. Each of us exclaiming and reading out snippets that sent chills up my spine. I didn't want Tony anywhere near Coleson Crenshaw.

When we took a break, I said, "The volume of speculation alone makes him a shady character."

She nodded. "But there's no convictions and not even any arrests. It could be that this Crenshaw guy and his brother are super-wealthy and way too involved in politics, and people hate them. So, their enemies manufacture lawsuits and accusations but there's never any proof."

I agreed. "Or it could be they're so rich and powerful they can make evidence and witnesses disappear." A thought struck me, and I whipped around to Zoe. "Tony said his parents fought about someone named Cole. Sounds like it was probably Coleson Crenshaw, doesn't it?"

That made my stomach flip. He'd been in the same house with Tony, Garrett, and Sheila. And now Garrett was dead and Sheila missing.

Zoe grew serious. "Oh. That's interesting. So, what now?"

I stood up and stretched. "I need some fresh air. Poupon could use a break from his hard work. I think we should take a drive."

Zoe jumped from her chair. "Sounds good. Where to?"

"Let's go out to the pivot where we found Garrett and see if we get any inspiration."

We filed out in time to see Ethel poke her head from her office on her way to get her afternoon coffee. She glared at me and let it wash onto Zoe. Guess she was still holding a torch for Ted.

Zoe fought a grin, but not valiantly.

Poupon fell out of line and if he didn't quite trot, he at least quickened his pace and gave two tail wags before slamming his butt down in front of Ethel and plying her with a pleading look.

Ethel gave him a smile so sweet I feared she'd go into insulin shock. "Here you go, handsome boy." She reached into her pocket and pulled out a plastic sandwich bag, the expensive zipper kind, and extracted what appeared to be half a hot dog.

Maybe times were getting tough at the Bender's place if she'd gone a step down from T-bones.

"You'll have to make do with this today, baby. I haven't had any time to cook with all the recall and new appointments going on."

I continued down the stairs.

Behind me, Zoe grumbled, "Good to know they invented passive-aggressive behavior in the stone age so Ethel could get in on it."

Having a partner was turning out to be fun.

When we reached the cruiser, I loaded Poupon in back and tossed Zoe the keys.

She caught them with one hand, her long arm shooting into the air with an athlete's grace. "You want me to drive?"

"Might as well get used to it. Besides, I'd like to know what Poupon finds so great about having a chauffeur."

It didn't take a lot of instruction for Zoe to learn the tricks of the patrol car. She worked the lights and siren. We called dispatch and I introduced her to Marybeth. We spent the remainder of the thirty-minute drive talking about the job. I passed on the line Milo Ferguson, Choker County Sheriff, had told me, "Sheriffing is ninety-nine percent ho hum and one percent oh shit."

I found it comforting that I didn't need to direct Zoe to the pivot. She'd grown up in the Sandhills with a family maybe not quite as extended as the Foxes, but big enough to spread through the whole county. Ted knew the county, too, of course, but I liked thinking of Zoe taking up the reins and making this job her own.

As we wound down the one-lane blacktop road, clouds bunched, heavy and gray against the blue. The smell of sweet clover whooshed through our open windows. Maybe we'd get some rain. With the pivot not functioning, the alfalfa could use a good soaking. Unless someone could get out here for the third cutting, which wasn't likely.

By now, word of Garrett's death and of Olivia's birth would be circulating. I'd had no doubt Louise had been out to Robert and Sarah's and filled their fridge with casseroles and at least a cake or two. The road to the Haney headquarters would be busy with pickups as people made condolence calls and dropped off more food than Ellie and Alden could eat in a year. The rituals of birth and death in the Sandhills gave comfort, maybe not for the family, but for the community.

The big heat of summer was over, leaving a sprinkling of a few perfect days in September. Days that glowed like rare amber and felt precious as any gem. Today, though, the wind was picking up and a crisp hint of damp spread over us as Zoe kept the cruiser in the two tracks through the alfalfa and parked it by the pump at the center and we got out.

A few more purple blooms spread across the field and Zoe paused to consider it. "If they don't get this cut in the next few days, they're going to lose a lot of the good from it."

I'd had the same thought. Michael and Jeremy would normally help, but the rift in our family made it hard for me to call them. Douglas was always busy at the University ranch. "Since you're here to take over the office, I'll help out. I think Robert and I can get this put up pretty quickly."

"Susan and Carly always say you're the one to call if you need help." She lowered her eyes to search the ground. "I'm sure Robert will be glad for another hand, but I'm not sworn in, yet. I know jack about the law, and I'm not allowed to do anything."

"That sounds like every sheriff I know. At least when they started. You can call Milo Ferguson whenever you want. He can get a little gruff, but he doesn't mean anything by it. And Kyle Red Owl is the best backup you'll ever find."

She bent over, taking deliberate steps to study the ground. "A lot of footprints out here. Mostly big ones."

"That's probably the state troopers who processed the scene."

She grunted. "But here are some small prints."

I slowly made my way to her and looked at the prints. Because the ground here was loose, not like someplace mud would create a mold, it would be impossible to glean any information we could use for proof. But maybe the footprints could give us a hint. I looked where she pointed. "They could be Tony's. He might have been out here with his dad."

We fanned out and she raised her voice above the wind rustling the alfalfa. "If Coleson Crenshaw is behind this, would he know Garrett was out here? I haven't heard anyone say anything about a stranger in town. And you said the woman at the law firm didn't even know Garrett was a rancher, so she wouldn't know where he went."

I inched out from the pump, keeping my eyes to the ground, not sure what I was looking for. "I don't suppose it'd be hard to find out Garrett's background if you had an investigator on it. We should look into a stranger coming to town." I told her about the guy at Fredrickson's with the Van Dyke beard. "They don't get a lot stranger, but he wasn't sticking around."

She didn't know what a Van Dyke beard was, so I explained. Then I said, "Twyla might know something." I thought about Newt and Earl. "Maybe it's time to introduce you to my confidential informers."

She jerked her head up. "What? Like moles?"

I laughed, thinking the brothers resembled literal, ground-digging moles and not the spying kind.

My phone rang and I pulled it out. "Hey, Sarah."

A newborn's weak complaints sounded, and Sarah grumped, "Enough farting around, you little bunny. I know you're hungry and it's time you eat."

Ah, babies. "I had a big lunch, but thanks for the offer."

"Very funny. She's fighting taking the...there." She let out a sigh. "Okay, score one for Mom." She shifted her attention to me. "We're on our way home and I need a favor."

"They let you out so soon?"

Robert must have heard me because he spoke loud enough for me to hear. "They didn't want to, and I don't think they should have."

She growled back at us both. "I'm perfectly fine. I promised I'd take it easy but laying around the hospital would not be a bonus."

I inched along, searching the ground for something out of the ordinary. "Taking it easy is the key."

"Roxy is going all Roxy on me. She can't bring Brie home because there's some drama or another going on. Like it always is. Can you swing by, get Brie and bring her home?"

The little grunting and squeaking of a baby nursing melted my heart. "I've got Zoe with me."

A tap on my back made me jump and squeal. Zoe had come up behind me and probably heard Sarah. She nodded and mouthed that she was okay taking the detour with me.

Since I'd need to drive Zoe the nearly twenty miles back to Hodgekiss to drop her off and double back almost another thirty miles on my way to Bryant and then take the fifteen miles out to Robert and Sarah's, this made my afternoon easier. "Okay. We're at the east pivot now and we'll head to Bryant."

She sounded annoyed. That didn't surprise me. Sarah hated big emotions. She liked her world to sail along on an even keel. Me being at the pivot would shove her dead brother to the front of her brain and that would be too heavy for her right now. "What are you doing out there? And what about Sheila?"

Zoe closed her hand around my arm and turned me back to where she'd been searching.

Without thought, I let her lead me. "I haven't found Sheila, yet. I talked to one of her clients who thinks maybe Sheila is with someone new."

Sarah huffed. "With someone? Are you talking about an affair? She left Garrett and is shacked up with another man and no one knows where she is?" I could almost hear her grinding her teeth. "No one knows because she's always been such a bitch she has no friends. If I had an affair and left town, you'd know."

Robert sounded shocked. "What?"

Zoe pulled me past the pump.

"You won't have an affair. It would be too messy," I said.

Sarah didn't answer immediately, and I was sure I heard a sweet kiss. When she spoke again, she sounded softer, so I assumed she spoke to little Olivia. "See? Isn't that better? You're going to have to learn that mother knows best."

"Unless that mother is Louise," I grumbled.

Sarah chuckled. "I don't want to ruffle your feathers, but you can't fault Louise's mothering skills."

I could, but I didn't want to go into that.

The silky tone left Sarah's voice and she was all business. "We're going to have to get Tony moved out here until you can find that slut."

In the background Robert spoke up. "Don't you think you should ask me first? I don't want that delinquent around my kids."

Sarah sounded like she'd made her decision. "He's a lot of things but he loves Brie and I'm sure he'll love Olivia. It's not permanent, and you know what, I wouldn't leave an alligator in Mom and Dad's care, let alone a ten-year-old boy."

Robert should give up right now. But he tried again. "Alden won't kill him in the next few days."

The phrase startled me.

Sarah bit back. "I'm not so worried about Dad as I am Mom. No kid is equipped for that kind of crazy."

They could go on like this for a while, so I broke in. "Tell Robert I'll help him get this pivot put up. It's more than ten percent bloomed, already."

Her voice caught, those pesky hormones playing fast and loose. "You're a good friend."

In the background Robert said, "I know it's ready, but I'll need to get parts for the mower...." The line went dead.

I stowed the phone in my pocket and addressed Zoe. "Did you find something?"

She pointed into a well-trod spot several feet from the pivot tower. At that moment, the gray clouds swept away from the sun, and it sent a brilliant flash across the field.

I looked to where Zoe pointed. Something caught the shaft of light and sparkled gold. Embedded in the soft, damp sand, Alden's pocket watch reflected the sun.

16

Zoe and I had taken a ton of pictures of Alden's watch, close ups with a quarter for perspective, incrementally farther away for distance measurements. After we sent them to Trey he'd called and had us bag Alden's watch for evidence.

"Glad to have you on the case," he said to me.

I grunted. "I'm not really investigating. I came here with Zoe to check it out. I'm trying to locate Sheila Haney in Scottsdale and ran into some interesting information concerning Garrett and a couple of his clients. Zoe can tell you about it."

She looked surprised when I handed her the phone. "Um. Hi. This is Zoe Cantrel."

I turned away as she and Trey made introductions and she caught him up on Coleson Crenshaw. They discussed the implications of Crenshaw and the likelihood of Sheila being a victim, and after a few minutes, Trey assured her he'd follow up on the information and they hung up. All in all, a good start to a working relationship she'd need as sheriff.

Now we both watched the prairie slide past the window as she drove us along the one-lane oil strip toward the highway. The hills spread along either side, edging up to the pavement and flowing away from us, the wind rippling the grasses creating the illusion of an endless golden ocean. Clouds flirted around the sun, making the sky almost like a disco ball of light.

Normally, the thought of being anywhere near Ted and Roxy would give me heartburn. But I liked the idea of taking Zoe with me. It would irk Ted to see us together. Imagine him having to be polite to two women the people of Grand County thought would be a better sheriff than him.

After a while, Zoe stirred, her face tight with thought. "Clearly, with the pivot running after the thunderstorm we're sure Garrett's death wasn't an accident."

"I can't feature anyone who'd worked on pivots at all not turning off the power. But it wouldn't be hard for someone to sneak in and turn it back on while Garrett climbed onto the pickup bed to work on it."

"Didn't Tony say Alden had sent him out to work on the pivot?" Zoe said.

"He did."

A line of Herford cows trailed along the fence. These would be Don Duran's herd. Good sized calves were interspersed among the big red and white mothers. They'd be plodding their way to a windmill for cocktail hour.

Zoe's keen eye surveyed the cattle. "Duran's got some nice-looking calves this year. Hope they bring in a lot."

I wasn't used to having someone inside my head making conversation while I traversed the vast county. Poupon wasn't much of a talker and totally uninterested in gossip. "They've had a tough year with Jen's cancer."

Zoe stopped at the turn to the highway. "Back to Garrett. You're sure that's Alden's pocket watch?"

I thought about the accident and how he'd jerked it from his pocket. "He had it the day before yesterday. The day of Garrett's accident. Garrett was killed that night and Alden hasn't been out to the pivot since then. That means Alden must have been at the pivot sometime between the accident and when I found Garrett."

She turned onto the highway, her eyes darting from the road to the pastures on either side, taking in everything. "It wasn't that hard to spot. I'd think the state patrol would have seen it if it had been there when they processed the scene."

Maybe. Or not. A scuff of sand or a broken stem could have hidden it. "Would we have seen it if the sun hadn't caught the reflection?"

She sucked her teeth. "I don't think Alden had anything to do with it. That kind of thing doesn't happen in real life, you know, a father killing a son. It's fine for TV but murdering someone is huge. Not just something you do if you're mad."

Zoe had a higher opinion of humanity than I did. "Not everyone is as rational as you are."

She tapped the wheel. "In novels and movies characters off other characters all the time with only the slimmest motive. I don't think killing someone is as easy as they make it seem. And for a father to kill a son, come on, it's not common."

"I always thought people, especially Sandhillers, are decent and caring and it's only the few who are bad. I'm not so sure anymore."

She glanced at me. "Is that what this job did to you? Am I going to be cynical and pessimistic? 'Cause I've got a baby to go home to every night and I don't want her to have to deal with a mom like that."

That startled me. Was I a gray cloud of doom? When was the last time I relaxed? Who had I shared a belly laugh with lately? Did I even remember feeling excited about something or someone?

Those questions tore down a flimsy barrier I'd patted into place around my heart. I couldn't stop the flood of memories. The phone call when Baxter told me about the documentary film director so intent on making contact he'd followed Baxter into the men's room at a gala. I'd laughed so hard I doubled over. Or Baxter threatening to take me to a Michelin-ranked restaurant in Chicago and me swearing I'd wear boots and Wranglers. And the worst memory of all. The night in the Wyoming cabin.

I held my breath against the torrent. If I didn't move, maybe I wouldn't crumble into a million pieces.

Zoe quickly added, "I didn't mean that you're hard to be around or anything like that. I know you've got a lot on your mind, with losing your job and wondering what to do next. You've always been the cool one of all your brothers and sisters."

I gave her a smile, but I was sure it was pretty anemic.

She wouldn't let up. "No, really. It's like of all the parents and adults, you were the only one fun to be around. When we'd come out to Frog Creek to hang out or watch movies or whatever, you were always dope."

As opposed to the me now, who stomped around expecting disaster to jump at me from every corner.

She could have stopped there, but she twisted the knife a bit more. "So, yeah, I'm worried this job might be kind of hard to not take home with me."

We were quiet for a while, and she studied the road with worried eyes. Then she said, "If Alden didn't kill Garrett, then maybe it was on Coleson Crenshaw's orders. And if that's what happened, do you think Sheila's disappearance ties into that?"

"Good question."

We picked apart the theories while we continued to Bryant. Ted and Roxy lived in a home built in the 1970s on the edge of town. It wasn't quite as old as the Sears prefab house out at Frog Creek. A strange salmon stucco color, it stayed cool in the summer, and with the heated water radiators along the floorboards, was like a cozy nest all winter. But it wasn't to Roxy's taste.

This one was newer and bigger, but it couldn't rival the two-story, spare-no-expense monstrosity at Carly's ranch. The house Baxter and Aria were enjoying this week.

That made me wonder how Baxter was getting along with his ankle and that cough. Then I tried to whip my mind away from that subject before it looped back to what was missing in my life.

Zoe pulled up along the curb, which was not so much a curb as a shallow lip marking the end of the yard and the beginning of the street. She sat back as if settling in to wait.

I grinned at her. "You should come on up to the house with me."

Zoe gave me an admonishing look, reminding me again that she was no one's fool. "If you've got something to prove to Ted, that's yours. I've got to work with him, so I don't need to rub my appointment in his face just yet."

I wrinkled my nose. "You're no fun."

There were no sidewalks or a front walk, just grass that needed mowing and watering so I crossed the lawn toward the cement stoop.

Roxy burst from the front door. She wore another pair of work jeans; these still had their bling on the pockets, but they were baggy. Her T-shirt was green instead of pink but still stretched and strained. In other words, Roxy was not being Roxy. What did I care? "Are you okay?" The concern slipped out before I'd slammed the gate on it.

She teared up and threw her arms around me. "I knew you'd understand."

Turtle fur and toenails. Things were bad enough I didn't need to struggle for air while being smooshed by Roxy's boobs. I understood she was a wreck. Even when she thought she'd lost Ted—well, any of those times including when he married me, and when he'd been shot, or when it looked like he might end up in jail, and when he'd nearly had an affair (well, he had slept with someone else, but Roxy didn't know that)—she'd always taken the time to curl, floof, and spray her hair into a fire hazard, and to wear something that accentuated her assets. There wasn't even any risk of asphyxiation from her perfume today.

I patted her lightly on the back. "Sarah sent me after Brie. Is she ready?"

Roxy straightened and pushed a strand of stringy hair behind her ear. She sniffed and dabbed at her eyes with the tips of her fingers, even though she wasn't wearing mascara, much to my shock. "I just got them down for a nap. They've been a handful. I'm...." She let out a sob.

I glanced at Zoe, and she held up her hands to indicate this show was on me. With nothing left to do, I lowered my voice in a calming way. "What's going on?"

She plopped on the cement step and, with no choice, I sat next to her. She blinked back tears and flapped her hands in front of her face to fan herself. "I don't know what to do. I was really looking forward to moving back to Grand County. I didn't expect to live at that old ranch house, of course. I have some money from when Bryan died, and I had plans for a new house drawn up."

Bryan was Carly's father. In a move of supremely poor judgement, he'd married Roxy. When he died two years after the wedding, she'd inherited a part of his estate. The 100,000-acre ranch had belonged to his father, and Carly had inherited that.

I consoled her. "You can still move to Grand County. Sid doesn't want to ranch and I'm certain if you and Ted tried, you could make Frog Creek a paying business." When I'd managed it, we turned a profit. Not a huge one, but I didn't need a lot to make me happy. That contented life seemed so far from me now.

She slapped her hands over her eyes and started another round of weeping while I waited. "I would be okay with that. I loved living in the country. And you know Dahlia, she wouldn't let Ted and his son live in poverty. She's so generous she'd make sure we had everything we needed."

Yeah, Dahlia was Lady Bountiful, giving to Ted, Roxy, and Beau. To me, she'd swipe the last bite right out of my mouth if I was starving.

Roxy drew in a shaky breath. "But Ted doesn't want to go. Honestly, I think he was relieved when they appointed Zoe sheriff. He says he loves it here." She let loose with what sounded like a chorus of strangled cats. "He feels too much pressure in Grand County, and he thinks Sid would want him to work on Frog Creek all the time and Dahlia would be demanding."

Ted had some good points. Since he was fairly lazy, being sheriff of a sparsely populated, sleepy Sandhills county would be ideal. He could cruise around in his patrol car or surf the net in the spacious office on the courthouse's second floor. When he was Grand County sheriff, I'd worked the ranch but if he moved back now, he didn't have that benefit. And he was right, Sid would expect Ted's help.

"So, we're going to stay here, in this dump." She cried some more, and I sat on the porch feeling slightly cheated that my recall and Zoe's appointment hadn't ruined Ted's life.

My brain scrambled for some way to escape this melodrama when the universe saved me with a phone call. I stood and edged away with a mumbled, "I've got to take this," hoping it wouldn't be Louise or someone I'd hate to talk to even more than I did Roxy. "Sheriff."

"Tim Morris." He started in right away. "We've got a Jane Doe that was found around the mid-May date you mentioned. Body mostly burned but they salvaged some DNA. She was driving a newer blue Lexus. Hold on and I'll get you the year and model."

I scrambled to the cruiser and startled Zoe. She sat up and stared at me as I grabbed a pen and small spiral notebook from the cubby. I copied down the details of the car when he came back on.

"Is it unusual to find bodies like this?" I pressed the speaker so Zoe could hear.

"Are you asking if this could be a coincidence with your Sheila Haney?"

Zoe nodded as if he was with them. I said, "I guess I am."

"Let's just say I'm interested enough to ask you to send some of your victim's DNA."

17

I sat in back of the cruiser with Poupon and Brie while Zoe drove us to Robert and Sarah's ranch, south of the highway and about ten miles north of the Blume, where Garrett and Tony lived. Brie tugged and patted Poupon's curls and he not only tolerated it, he leaned in for extras. I suppose familiarity bred contempt as far as he was concerned because he barely acknowledged me, and I was the one who'd taken him in when Diane and her family had enough of him.

"Day-um." Zoe said after several miles. "Sheila's dead in the desert. That pretty much points at Crenshaw."

Maybe. "Before we get ahead of ourselves, we need to send Sheila's DNA. I'll see if Tony has anything of hers. If not, we'll let Trey figure out how to legally obtain it from her house in Scottsdale."

She muttered, "Day-um," to the windshield again and waves of concentration lined her forehead as she seemed to mull it over the rest of the drive.

We pulled up in front of the ranch house, parking behind Alden and Ellie's shiny silver pickup. Sarah had several hanging pots of geraniums lining the wide front porch. Geraniums reminded me of old ladies because the Jumble Shop, run by the woman's auxiliary with most active members using walkers and canes, kept ancient terra cotta pots of them in their window on Main Street and they were always covered in dust (the flowers, not the auxiliary members). But these looked cheerful and vibrant, giving the house a welcoming feel.

The wide, green yard and two towering oaks made this place one of my favorites in the Sandhills. The breeze had slackened, and gray clouds clumped together like gossiping old men. The sun angled lower, threatening the end of the afternoon and promising a lingering evening, something that only seemed to happen in early fall.

Like the sky that couldn't decide to storm or shine, I wavered between joy at my new niece and grief for Sarah's loss of her brother. It would only be a more violent swing for all of the Haneys.

Zoe shut off the engine and climbed out. She was halfway up the walkway to the front porch when she must have realized I wasn't behind her.

Brie stood on the seat banging on the window. She'd been away from home and her parents longer than she'd ever been and she wanted out, now. "Daddy! Daaa-aaa-aaa-dy!"

Zoe's mouth opened when it dawned on her we were trapped in the back seat with no handles on the doors. She trotted back and released us.

I grabbed Brie under her arms and settled her tiny feet on the ground to barely keep her from spilling out. She took off full gallop as Robert shot from the house.

I swallowed down the lump in my throat as Robert bent to scoop Brie in his arms and hug her to him. A good soaking of love can turn the toughest biscuit into mush. Poupon took his turn jumping out before I got to exit. By then, Robert had joined us, Brie patting his whiskery cheeks.

He looked like he could use a shower, shave, and twenty-four hours in bed. "Thanks for bringing her. Sarah's folks were already here when we got home, and I couldn't leave for fear Alden and Sarah would bring out the heavy artillery before I got back."

Zoe gave him an amused look. Nice to know family drama didn't faze her.

His shoulders slumped. "I'm going to have to go to Grand Island tomorrow to get those darned parts. I can't find them anywhere closer."

I gave him a worried look. "Sarah's supposed to take it easy. I'll come out and hang with her."

The gleam in his eye was both frustrated and amused. "I suggested it. She won't hear of it. I'll let you guess what she said about needing a babysitter."

I started up the walk, Robert and Brie following, and Zoe bringing up the rear. "You'd think with everything going on, it would take the fight out of Alden and Sarah." I wanted to ask Alden a few questions about how his watch came to be at the east pivot. "Maybe I can distract them."

Sarah and Alden had a habit of butting heads. Over the last ten years Robert and Sarah had taken over much of the heavy lifting of the ranches and I'd watched Robert influence Sarah to use a little more sugar and a little less vinegar with her father. It didn't come naturally to her, but even she admitted it was more effective to wiggle in sideways with Alden than it was to hit him head on. I valued my life and friendship with Sarah too much to suggest that she and Alden might be a lot alike.

Growing up and in college, Sarah had avoided her parents as much as possible. She had nothing in common with Ellie, who seemed constantly in despair over Sarah's lack of gentility. And Alden was more interested in Garrett than a daughter. Then Garrett had rejected ranching and Sarah had embraced it and the whole dynamic needed to shift. I doubted they'd ever find a comfortable balance. Even though Sarah and Robert carried the future of the ranch on their shoulders, Alden hadn't taken the necessary steps to make succession legal.

Sarah and Robert hoped and trusted. I didn't have that kind of faith in Alden.

But today, when she was dealing with Garrett's death and the new baby, I'd bet Sarah didn't have the energy or interest in diplomacy.

If the Foxes had a conflict brewing, you'd hear yelling, slamming, a general ruckus. But Haneys had a different way of digging at each other. I entered the front door directly into the living room.

With her hair in a ponytail, wearing long basketball shorts and one of Robert's Western shirts with the sleeves ripped out, Sarah sat in an upholstered rocker that had been Grandma Ardith's before she went to the home. It was ugly as a newborn snake but was highly coveted in our family as the best nursing chair ever made. A flannel baby blanket draped over Sarah's shoulder with one tiny pink foot poking out as Olivia nestled underneath.

Sarah's face looked like it was carved from white marble and though her eyes weren't red, she wouldn't have looked fiercer if they were. Like Robert, a good sleep was in order. "You aren't listening to me. We need to hire someone for the Blume right away. None of us can take on any more. You're getting too old, and we've already got too much on our plate."

Ellie stood in the kitchen doorway, wringing her hands and keeping her focus on Alden. She looked confused and scared, as if Alden was the only thing keeping her tethered.

Alden sat on the couch opposite Sarah. He leaned forward with his forearms on his knees. "It's not up to you. This is my family and my ranch, and I'll make the decisions."

Sarah peeked under the blanket then back at her father. Her voice was low, but tension was strung on every syllable. I didn't like the pasty tint of her skin. "There you go with all that bullshit. You might not have noticed but Robert and I are perfectly capable of making decisions. And Tony will be staying with us, so that's even more for us to handle."

A deep crimson colored Alden's face. "I haven't decided about Tony."

Ellie's voice peeped from the doorway. "Tony can stay with us. Sarah is too busy with the new baby."

A cool breeze seemed to soothe Alden when he spoke to Ellie. "Now, Mother. Your nerves aren't up to chasing after another son. We've already raised our kids. It's someone else's turn now."

Funny how he ruffled all up when Sarah called him old, but he had no qualms putting Ellie out to pasture.

Sarah closed her eyes and sagged. "Tony should be around younger people."

The baby made those grunting, gurgling noises of someone enjoying a good meal. Sarah pulled the top of the blanket away a few inches and smiled down.

Alden slammed his open palm on the coffee table in front of him, making the baby startle and Ellie retreat into the kitchen. He rose, probably intending to shoot up but due to creaking and sluggish old bones, it took him a second. "Tony's staying with us and that's final. I don't know why you need to do that in public. It's obscene."

She whipped the blanket from her shoulder, exposing the little head of dark curly fuzz attached to her breast. "It's my home and I'll damn sure feed my baby where and when I want."

Robert brushed past me. "Hey, look who I brought home."

Brie squiggled to get free of Robert's grasp and he lowered her to stand in front of Sarah. Her eyes shone and she stared at the baby and Sarah, a look of wonder on her face.

Robert raised his arms to take in everyone in the living room. "How about you back off and let Brie get acquainted with her new little sister?"

Alden didn't move right away. "We came all the way out here to see the new baby and now you're telling me we can't?"

I reached out, not touching him, but herding him toward the door. "Let's give them a few minutes. By then, Sarah will be done feeding Olivia and we'll get a chance to meet her." For someone who hid from conflict under a bed when my siblings went at it, I had a bit of the diplomat in me when I needed it.

Ellie had disappeared, probably as good at avoiding conflict as I used to be.

Alden pointed a finger at Sarah. "When you start paying rent you can tell me who can live in my house. Tony is coming with us."

Robert's jaw tightened with an effort to keep from coming back at Alden. For ten years they'd lived in that house, supposedly part of their wages working for Haney Ranch. Robert and Sarah worked harder and smarter than Alden ever had, I'd wager. He lived the life of the semi-retired. And to have him still acting like king made my temper boil. I could only imagine what it did to Robert.

Zoe, Alden, and I shuffled out the front door to the porch, where Zoe settled herself in the swing and I perched on the railing. Alden folded his arms and stared across the front yard to the alfalfa field on the other side of the dirt driveway. The field had been mowed, raked, and stacked, the golden round bales dotting the pivot. Normally, seeing the hay put up and ready for winter would be a comfort. I'd imagine knowing your only son had died a day ago in an alfalfa field, didn't make this view easy.

But here we were with a perfect opportunity. Zoe and I exchanged a look that held a question of who should open with Alden, and the answer was that it would be me. "Where's Tony?"

Alden generally had the demeanor of a salesman, always talkative and friendly, even if you felt that one layer down he was impatient and irritable. Today, all of that pretense had evaporated. He scowled. "Tony's the one that had to get here right now. And the minute she gets ready to feed the baby, he takes off for parts unknown. I don't blame him. It used to be that mothers did that in private. If they did it at all. Ellie fed with a bottle. Sarah had a heart attack when I even suggested it." He hmphed. "Sarah insists she's doing the work of a hired man around here. I know I pay her for it, so how is she going to keep that up if she's got to play chuckwagon all day long?"

Behind his back, Zoe gave him a dirty look and flipped him off.

I'd have liked to slap him upside the head, since I knew the salaries the ranch paid for both Sarah and Robert together were slightly more than I earned as sheriff. But calling him a cheapskate and a misogynist wasn't going to get us anywhere. "She kept up okay after Brie was born. I'm sure she'll be fine now."

He tightened his arms and muttered, "We'll see. I'm down a man now as it is."

Zoe's expression said she'd rather shoot than listen.

I tried to sound gentle. "It'll be hard to process Garrett's death."

His nostrils flared. "That damned pivot will need a fortune in repairs. And I don't know how we're going to put up the hay. Most kids Tony's age could at least run the side delivery rakes. But that kid is about as worthless as his father."

Zoe opened her mouth to ask something, then closed it and nodded for me to go.

Not sure what we needed to know, I went fishing. "Garrett seemed to get along pretty well out here. And from what I know, he was a really successful lawyer."

Alden swung his head, drilling me with his gaze. "Garrett was a disappointment. I was my father's only son, and I knew from the beginning what was expected of me. And I lived up to that. Garrett had been raised to do the same, but the world got soft and young men don't understand duty. Garrett allowed as how there were easier ways to make a better living than ranching. As if what I did wasn't good enough for him."

Zoe studied Alden's back, taking in every word, her face hard.

I wanted to encourage Alden to keep going. "Garrett had to have been smart to do as well as he did."

Alden turned and directed his words away from the porch. "Smarts wasn't Garrett's problem. He was lazy."

Maybe. It's what Angela Romero thought, too, but I thought Garrett had plenty of ambition. "I don't think a lazy man could have been partner at a law firm like his."

Sarcasm tinged Alden's words. "Oh, I'm sure. But if he was doing so great, why would he run home with his tail between his legs?"

Zoe lifted an eyebrow my way to say it looks like we might be getting somewhere. I prodded. "He had some problems at the firm?" I didn't bring up the botched case Becca had mentioned.

Alden sniffed. "He messed up somewhere. I didn't know the details, but he was on that damned phone all the time trying to make things right. He was like that. He'd create some havoc and then apologize and try to get everyone to love him again. It worked for Ellie, but I saw through that game."

To me, Garrett always seemed like he'd rather be respected than liked. I'd imagine he felt more angst at losing a case than in disappointing the political ambitions of someone like Coleson Crenshaw. After learning how hard Alden had been on him growing up, I figured Garrett was out to prove something. But, like Sarah, I had the impression he was spooked about something. Coleson Crenshaw insisting on the political track? "It seems strange Garrett would have been working on the pivot without shutting off the power."

Alden lifted the side of his mouth in a sneer. "He was always cutting corners. Trying to find the easy way out. I turned the Blume operation over to him and I haven't been out there for over a week. I should have known it would end up something like this. Ellie never took her eye off him. Even when he went to school she fixed every problem he ever had."

Zoe's distaste for Alden was clear in her tight face and stiff neck.

Alden sighed. "I blame myself, though. Ellie is like a kitten. She's soft and sweet and never had the heart to discipline Garrett. It was up to me to teach him how to be a man. But he refused to learn. And now he's gone, and we've got this kid who's already been ruined."

Zoe probably didn't give Alden the benefit of the doubt, but I figured all this hateful talk was the only way he could deal with the pain of losing a son he loved but never understood.

Maybe Ellie had coddled Garrett, Sarah shared Alden's opinion on that. But Newt Johnson had hinted Alden used a heavy hand with Garrett and I'd witnessed Alden do violence against Garrett. Well, Alden had given Garrett a welt near his eye by snapping him with a towel. Maybe not a lethal weapon, but violent just the same. "We're searching for Sheila so Tony may not have to stay in the Sandhills for long."

Alden spun around to me. "The hell you say. This is where Tony belongs. That featherbrained wife of Garrett's won't get her hands on Tony if I have anything to say about it."

I couldn't stop myself. "She's Tony's mother and legal next of kin. Of course, he should be with her. Besides, you said it yourself, you and Ellie have already raised your kids. And Sarah and Robert have two of their own."

His face pinched like he'd bitten a jalapeno. "I never said Sarah can't raise him. And as Garrett's sister, and living here at the ranch, she should. Tony is my heir. He needs to be here to learn about the ranch and be able to take his rightful place now that Garrett can't."

Zoe didn't try to hide her shock. She shifted forward, a storm building on her face.

I struggled to keep a passive face. I probably didn't succeed. "So, Sarah and Robert are supposed to be hired help forever? They aren't going to own any part of it?"

Alden looked annoyed. "My granddad and dad and then me have put together fifteen thousand acres of some of the finest land in the Sandhills, not to mention three alfalfa pivots. You think I ought to divvy up the ranch that it's taken three generations to build? Have you seen what happens when you do that? What's left is too small to support a family and one or the other of them sells out and pretty soon, your name is erased from the country."

This wasn't my fight, except I loved Sarah and Robert too much to keep quiet. "You incorporate. It would stay the Haney Ranch, but your officers would be Sarah and Robert. They're already doing most of the work."

He let out a pfft of scorn. "Her name is Fox. The day she married she became your brother's responsibility. My responsibility is to my wife. I will always take care of Ellie. And then to my heirs. Of which, I have one left. And I'll be damned if I'm going to let a woman, especially one who lives in a city, raise him."

"But Robert and Sarah have run this ranch for ten years. Don't you think that as your blood, your daughter and granddaughters would be valid heirs?"

Alden exhaled and looked at me as if I were a remedial student. "I see what you're doing. You're trying to weasel an inheritance for your brother. I didn't make him stay here. He's been getting a salary and free housing all these years. His obligation is to take care of his wife and his daughters until they're married. That's what a man does."

Welcome to the eighteenth century. I'd never exchanged this many words with Alden and, for that, I thanked the good green grass. Zoe had lost all of her earlier amusement at the family dysfunction. It looked like her jets were firing and she'd fly off the porch swing directly at Alden's head.

I changed the subject as quickly as possible to avoid a justifiable homicide. "Sarah said you spent a lot of time with Garrett before he left for college."

Alden grunted. "I did everything I could think of to make a man out of him. But none of it worked. So off he goes to college and law school and sets up shop in Arizona, about as far from the Sandhills as you can get."

Not far enough, considering the opinions this jerk held.

Zoe's tolerance had apparently run to ground. She hopped off the porch swing and stalked Alden. "You know that the state patrol is saying Garrett's death wasn't an accident."

At several inches taller than me, Zoe stood a hand's width taller than Alden. He met her gaze but still looked at her as if she were a child interrupting an adult conversation. "And you know that because they've suddenly taken you into their confidence?"

I jumped in. "Zoe is the new Grand County Sheriff. Commissioners appointed her yesterday."

Alden looked away and hmphed again. "You were bad enough, but this is ridiculous. Have you even graduated from high school?"

As fake as his smarmy veneer had been, I preferred it to this swamp-breathing mud-brain.

Zoe drew herself up. "Salutatorian. And have a bachelor's degree from the university with honors. So, let's get to your son's murder."

The screen door opened, and Ellie slipped out. "Alden?"

He swung around to her. In a normal voice devoid of the sneers and superior tone he'd used with us, he said, "Go on back in the house."

She hesitated. Her glistening eyes, full of confusion, went from me to Zoe and back to Alden. "Did she say Garrett was murdered?"

He took two strides to the door and gave her a gentle nudge inside. "They don't know what they're talking about. I'll collect Tony in a minute, and we'll go home. Why don't we go into town to the Long Branch, so you don't have to fix supper?"

"But we've got a houseful of food from condolences."

As if we needed proof Alden was a jerk, he confirmed it. "I sent Hal and Bertie over to collect all that trash and get rid of it. Put a note on the door that we didn't want any callers."

Ellie put a hand to her mouth and blinked rapidly. "Do you think you should have done that? People will want to stop by."

He injected some sweet into his voice. "You don't need the hustle of people around. I'll make sure you're okay."

As long as I could remember, everyone in the Haney household worked to keep Ellie's life as unruffled as possible. Even though Ellie's delicate nerves irritated Sarah, she'd gone along with protecting Ellie. I could hardly believe it, but Sarah said if Ellie got too upset, she'd become irrational.

Ellie gave us all another round of frightened glances, then retreated into the house.

Zoe planted her hands on her hips and gave Alden a challenging stare. "You know, Kate and I were just out to the pivot, having a look around."

Alden growled back at her. "If you have all that extra time, why don't you get the mower and help us out."

I could volunteer that I'd offered to do that, but I wasn't doing it to help Alden.

"We made an interesting discovery." She baited him. Not the way I would handle it, but she had her own style.

Alden bristled up. "I don't give a good goddamn what you're playing at while you're taking our tax dollars."

Zoe didn't seem at all put off being cursed at by someone older than her father. "We found your pocket watch. The one you had hours before your son was murdered. It was in a place you said you hadn't been for at least a week."

Alden's face changed like a kaleidoscope when you twist the end. He started out turning red, as if he'd explode in a fiery mess. Then something like an ice floe stopped him, flames doused, and color drained away. "I must have...." He trailed off and we could almost see cogs slipping in his brain. "It couldn't...." He dropped his gaze to the planks on the porch. Then his head snapped up and it appeared that his thoughts had gained traction.

He glared at Zoe. "I always had respect for your dad. I thought he'd raised you girls up right. But now I see you got the same disease everyone else has. You think you got the right to go around being all bossy and right-eous. You don't know a damned thing about life, girlie. And I take exception to you accusing me of going after my own son."

Zoe held her ground. "How do you think the watch got out there, Alden?" I supposed she used his given name to show she was his equal.

He bared his teeth as if he might bite. "You get off my porch. Off my land. I got nothing to say to you."

He swung open the screen door and only kept from slamming it because it had a pneumatic arm.

Zoe flipped her braid behind her shoulder and spun toward the steps. She skipped down the stairs. "You know all that stuff I said about a father not capable of murdering a son? I take it back."

18

It was hard to talk Zoe down from arresting Alden on the spot, but I managed to explain we needed more evidence and we should discuss it with Trey. If we arrested Alden too soon and couldn't keep him, it wouldn't help us out.

We hadn't waited around to talk to Tony, so I hadn't had a chance to ask him about collecting his mother's DNA. I would have to catch up with him tomorrow.

Zoe pulled into the parking spot behind the courthouse. "We've got a pocket watch and Alden saying he thought Garrett was a failure."

Poupon stood up and shook, hair flying in the backseat, proof that even a poodle can shed a little.

I flicked my hand in dismissal. "I've heard parents say a lot worse about their kids. What he said doesn't mean much and isn't evidence of murder."

Her eyes flashed in exasperation.

"This investigation isn't my responsibility. I'm going to try to find Sheila because Sarah's my friend and she asked me to. But I'm no longer sheriff." I opened my door and stepped out.

"You are until I'm sworn in," Zoe reminded me. She let Poupon out of the back.

I took the keys she offered. "Still, the state patrol is lead on this, so I'm not going to spend any more time on figuring out who killed Garrett. And, in fact, I'm going to get a nice steak and some fries and a cold beer at the Long Branch." And try to convince myself I didn't care about justice.

Zoe raised her eyebrows. "Eating there twice in one day can't be good for your arteries."

Poupon followed me as I walked toward the alley leading to Main Street. "I'm young and strong, my arteries aren't my main concern." My livelihood, my loneliness, Robert and Sarah's precarious future, even Baxter's cough weighed heavier on my mind than my cholesterol levels.

Poupon and I stepped into a lively bar. Some ruckus was happening in the corner, and it took a couple of seconds for my eyes to adjust to the gloom before I was smacked with the reality that the one causing the scuffle was Dad.

Twyla had hold of Dad's arm and was tugging him away from Coop Ambler, a man about ten years younger and twenty pounds of muscle heavier than Dad. She glanced over her shoulder at me. "If you can't get that damned hound of yours to attack, maybe you could lend a hand here?"

For his part, Coop was standing back, his arms to his sides. But he kept hollering at Dad. Who knows what they fought about.

Dad wrangled with Twyla, struggling to get free so he could launch himself at Coop. He let out a string of cuss words that would impress Sarah. Not only had I never seen Dad lose his temper, but he hated cursing, and it might have been the only rule he insisted on in our home. The fact that he was obviously itching to throw punches shifted the whole scene into an alternative universe. I felt paralyzed.

Twyla started to lose her grip. "Would you quit your gawking and get over here?"

That did it. I sprang toward the melee and pushed between the two men. With my hands on Dad's chest, I walked him and Twyla backward. "Come on, Dad. Knock it off."

His eyes looked glassy, and I got a full-on mist of Jack Daniels when he opened his mouth. "Goddamnit, Katie. Let me go. That son of a bitch needs taught a lesson."

It's some kind of miracle I didn't keel over in shock. But Twyla and I succeeded in shoving him to the door. Contentious woman that she was, my scrawny aunt didn't let loose of Dad's arm when she swung open the door and finally stepped out of the way while I gathered enough momentum to bulldoze us out the door and onto the sidewalk.

I pushed him back several feet and let him go. He tried to get through me to the door. "I mean it, Katie. Coop needs some sense knocked into him."

I held my ground and managed to back him off another few feet as his fight tapered off a bit. "What's your beef with Coop?"

Dad's mouth curled into a snarl. "He's an ignorant piece of shit and I've had enough of his big mouth."

Coop Ambler liked to talk politics and argue. From what I'd experienced by hearing him with others, he'd take the opposite position from anyone he engaged and often had only half his information correct. He was as irritating as a mosquito on a perfect summer evening, but aside from an annoying itch, fairly harmless.

I continued to walk Dad backward away from the door. "He hasn't changed in twenty years so what's the sense of going after him now?"

The door to the Long Branch opened and Twyla shooed Poupon out. He sauntered out with the attitude of a royal who'd chosen to leave.

Dad spun away from me and stomped around the corner to head up Main Street. He'd let his hair grow longer than normal. Where he'd had a salty buzz cut for years, it now tickled the top of his ears, brown streaked with gray. He needed a shave and he'd taken to wearing faded Levi's instead of the canvas Dickies he'd favored since before I'd grown old enough to take notice. The jeans hung from his hips. He was beginning to look more and more like his sister, Twyla, a woman who lived on Jack Daniels and spite.

Dusk colored the sky with the slightest pink that rapidly morphed to periwinkle, deep violet and black. Cool air heavy with rain pushed against my bare arms. Storms seemed to be seeping in all over my life.

Poupon and I followed Dad up the street, his pounding footsteps getting lighter and slower as the fight drained from him. When we made it to the Legion Hall at the top of the hill, he plopped on the retaining wall and stared down the street, his back bent and shoulders slumped.

The house he'd lived in for forty years winked back at us.

After a few minutes, while the last of the sun slunk away, he said, "I shouldn't have been in the bar. I know better." I hated the regret in his voice.

"What's going on?"

He straightened up. "Oh, nothing, really. I'm retiring. Forty-five years on the railroad is enough for anyone. So, I thought I'd celebrate."

"And you wanted to share the moment with Coop Ambler. Good call."

"Like I said, I shouldn't have been in there."

With how much I hated other people interfering with my love life, I still waded into the water. "Why not celebrate with Deenie Hayward? She'd love to know you're retiring."

He puffed up his cheeks and let air escape. "She's got better things to do than hang around an old dog like me."

I moaned. "You poor thing. Come on, Dad. I don't know what's gotten into you, but I think it's time you straighten up, don't you?"

He kept his eyes on the house across the tracks. "I think this is the real me. Your grandma, she had her hands full with me growing up. I'm sure you heard all the stories. I raised a lot of hell. And finally, when I'd broke about as much of her heart as I could, I enlisted, and they sent me to Vietnam. Might have been the kindest thing I ever did for a person."

I settled in. "Twyla said you were a wild kid. And I ran into Titus Simonson a while back and he allowed as how you used to carry on back in the day."

Dad hooted. "Old Titus. He was a crazy man. The scrapes we got into. It's a wonder we survived it all."

Weird to be talking to your father like this. "But then you got married, worked a steady job for forty-five years and raised nine kids. I'd say that's really who you are."

His sigh sounded heavy enough to sink a flotilla. "Was. Your mother was the plumb line. She needed me and she loved me, like I'd never known before. It was like I'd been looking my whole life and I finally found where I belonged."

Sharp and jagged, his words sliced into my lungs and I couldn't breathe. I'd thought I belonged at Frog Creek. Then I thought I might belong as sheriff. I'd belonged as a Fox until Louise had taken that from me. It killed me that Dad felt that same abandonment.

Dad smacked his lips. "But it's over. She's gone and from what we know now, the real Marguerite was never really here. And I guess I can't go back to before then. For one thing, hangovers are worse than I remember. And truth be told, if Twyla hadn't got in the middle of me and Coop, he'd have decked me."

I couldn't fix our past, no matter how much I wanted to. "So, call Deenie. You two are good together." Was I really advising my nearly-seventy-year-old father to date a woman the same age as his daughter?

He thrust himself off the wall. "I like her too much to inflict myself on her. My heart is tied to your mother."

I stood, too, done for the moment. Poupon rousted himself and pointed his nose down the hill, ready to go somewhere the napping was more comfortable. This subject wasn't exhausted, but I figured I'd go at him in small doses so I didn't poison him on the idea of Deenie. "You need something to eat, and I doubt Twyla's going to welcome you back to the Long Branch. Come home with me and I'll grill some burgers." It wouldn't be the steak I was anticipating, but a second hamburger in a day wasn't the worst thing that could happen to me.

We loaded into the cruiser, and I was sorry I'd need to relinquish the patrol car to Zoe soon. I liked my Ranchero Elvis better anyway, but Poupon didn't fit as well in the bucket seat as he did stretched out in the back of the cruiser.

Dad and I drank iced tea while he started the charcoal, and I patted out burgers. I managed to find a few tomatoes and peppers not decimated by the hail and tossed them into a salad, a luxury with numbered days before the impending frost would wipe them out completely. We chatted about insignificant topics, avoiding the painful potholes of Mom, Louise, my job, and love life.

We filled our plates and settled on the front porch to listen to the frogs croaking on Stryker Lake. Poupon had given up staring at me with plaintive eyes—as if I'd ever fed him from my plate—and plopped down on the porch, chin on paws, eyes closed, when the roar of an engine came over the hill and headlights popped into view. Whoever it was would probably mean trouble, so I took a giant bite of my burger, trying to enjoy it before the next catastrophe wreaked havoc.

Dad stood and set his plate on his chair, watching the approaching vehicle.

Poupon noted the unattended plate and glanced at me to see if he might sneak the burger. I lifted my lips in a snarl and growled. He huffed and lowered his head back to his paws.

When the vehicle pulled up, I recognized Louise's old Suburban. I quickly shoved the burger between my lips and filled my mouth with warm, juicy comfort. Whatever she was doing at my house wouldn't be good.

Dad opened the porch's screen door and descended the steps to meet her as she crossed to the cracked sidewalk. "Hey, Sugar, what are you doing out here?" He had nicknames for most of us. Sugar seemed fitting for Louise, who showed affection by leaving baked goods in her wake. Glenda had been Goldie; I don't know why. Susan was Cutie. I didn't have a nickname. Maybe I was too plain.

Louise pounded toward him like a tank in Tiananmen Square. "What in the world has gotten into you? Jan Riek called me and said you were raising cane in the Long Branch. And then your pickup is parked on Main Street. I was worried sick that you'd gotten into an accident or wandered off somewhere. If Olin Reick hadn't seen you get into Kate's car, I wouldn't have any idea where you'd gone. And do you think I could have called 9-1-1 about it? No, because the law enforcement community around here is scandalized by Kate and the mess she's created."

That put a blade of fight into my chest. What mess had I created? The recall was on Louise.

Even Dad didn't know how to react to that tirade. I took another bite of my burger, although now it tasted more like the charcoal I'd cooked it on.

She stopped short in front of him, but most of her took another moment to settle. With her hands on her hips, she said, "Why are you here? And what are you going to do about your behavior?"

He made a half turn to me. "Katie made me supper. I can share my hamburger with you if you want."

She opened her mouth in an offended expression that settled her chins to her neck. "I would love to cook for you. You don't even have to let me know, just stop by. You don't have to bother Kate; she doesn't like to cook."

Actually, I didn't *not* like to cook. For me, it was more a matter of having the time. I tended to be busy until I got so hungry I needed to eat immediately. That didn't leave a lot of opportunity for slow cooking.

Dad glanced at me. "We ran into each other, and she invited me out."

Louise swallowed and clamped her mouth shut for a moment. It would have been great if she'd have accepted that Dad was safe and fed and turned around for home. I assumed I'd get over resenting her meddling in my life. Eventually. But my charity bone felt a little fragile and I wanted her out of my sight. Sharing with her felt sour. No burger, no conversation, no family camaraderie.

Her voice cracked but she stitched it back together. "You never come over anymore. No one does. I thought when I moved into the house people would drop by. I always have food and my door is open. Remember how our home was always filled with everyone's friends?"

Sure, Glenda had a coterie of pals, Diane had one or two, the boys seemed to have a whole posse that stampeded in and out. I don't recall Louise having many friends, except Norman, who she married right after graduating high school. And me, if I wasn't hanging out with Sarah, I liked my alone time, something rare in our home bursting with Foxes and their friends.

I kept gnawing through my burger and salad, even if it tasted like dried leaves and twigs.

She stomped her foot, sending a tremor through her. "Why not? I've done everything I can to bring this family back together."

Dad walked across the yard, probably intending to give her a hug. Good for him. He was her father as well as mine, so it seemed like his duty to comfort her. He'd tell her what a great mom she was, how much everyone appreciated that she tried so hard to keep us together. He'd probably go on about what a loyal and loving wife she was and how she held up the Fox responsibility in the community. That's Dad, always ready with a fuzzy blanket of love and acceptance to drape around our shoulders when we felt vulnerable.

I resisted the compassion that knocked at me. This was the woman who had decided she didn't like how I chose to live my life. She'd ripped away my career and left me dangling at the end of a pole like a worm about to be eaten by the big bad trout of the world.

Okay, maybe that was hyperbole, but, dang, it's scary being out of a job, all alone, and living in an area with job opportunities as abundant as water in the desert.

Irritated that Louise had turned my thoughts into bad similes and metaphors, I stood up with my plate, heading for the kitchen. I stopped when I heard something that shocked me like chomping on aluminum foil with a tooth filling.

Dad's voice carried a stern admonishment, maybe the first I'd ever heard from him. "You can push too hard, Sugar. And this time, you've gone way beyond your place. I can't say I blame Kate for being furious."

She must have been as stunned as I was. She made a gurgling noise. "But I know how broken you are because Mom left. If we get the family back together, we can take care of you."

I stood in the doorway to the house, plate in hand, wondering what was happening.

Dad must have heard himself and decided on a course correction. The Dad who wanted to bust Coop Amber's face seemed to step back and the guy I'd known all my life pushed through. He spoke quietly, with a voice full of understanding. "I don't need fixing, Sugar. I need the time and space to figure out how I'm going to keep going when it feels like the lights have gone out in my world."

Tears glistened in her eyes, visible from my porch light. "But people are talking. First it was Kate making us look bad. And now." She stopped and sucked in a breath. "You're too old to have bar fights and go around with women like Deenie Hayward."

I opened my mouth to defend Deenie, but Dad spoke first. "And you're too old to be so judgmental. Deenie is a fine woman. She's kind and generous and always gives people the benefit of the doubt."

Louise shifted her weight, and probably her perspective. Like me, she was used to Dad being a soft touch. He and Mom weren't big on discipline. If the school called with a complaint or some neighbor let it slip we'd caused trouble of some kind or another, they'd react with disappointed stares and questions about why we did it and what we'd gained, and how we'd do better next time. For the most part, guilt shaped our characters. I don't know if my folks got lucky or if it was a smart way to raise kids, but most of us had turned out okay.

Louise gave Dad a disbelieving glare. "Deenie's a fine woman? I don't even know how many times she's been married. And she works as a waitress. My goodness, Mom was a world-renowned sculpture artist. How can they even compare?"

Mom had some success, sure. And even more now that Marguerite Myers was revealed as Miriam Fine. That notoriety had skyrocketed the price of her work. But I was more irritated with Louise dissing Deenie than with her exaggerating Mom's qualities.

A little of that barroom swagger seeped into Dad's posture. Apparently, he wasn't having Louise's remarks any more than I was. He upped his volume enough that Poupon raised his ears and opened his eyes. "That's enough of that kind of talk. Deenie hasn't always had an easy road, but she's been honest and true. Doesn't owe anyone anything. She laughs easy and generally has a good word to say to anyone. Can you say the same?"

Tears seeped down Louise's round cheeks. Deserved or not, he'd buried the spear deep. "I've always tried to do right and not shame the Fox name."

Dad backed off from his criticisms but didn't seem contrite. "I can see that. But going after Deenie like this and filing a recall against your own sister isn't reflecting well on the Fox name."

She gulped with a strangled sound. "But Kate chased Mom away. It's her fault our family is divided. How can you defend her?"

He looked over his shoulder at me and smiled before turning back to Louise. "I asked Katie to find your mother. She didn't know—none of us did —who Marguerite was. We're all trying to come to terms with that. But none of that can be laid at Katie's feet."

Louise was sobbing now. "But if she hadn't—"

Dad's voice rang out in a shockingly firm way. "Enough. The reason people don't come to your house is because you're no fun to be around. You demand everyone live their lives by your rules."

Louise sucked in a sob and pointed at me. "What about Kate? She doesn't even have rules."

He wagged his head slowly. "Of all you kids, Goldie and Katie are more like the woman I knew your mother to be. They look at the world with clear vision and try to do their best to help others and be kind."

Louise's lips opened and closed as if she wanted to argue.

Dad kept on, his voice taking on an edge. "It's you who has driven a wedge through us. Jeremy always worshipped Kate, but out of all of you, he depended on Marguerite like a duckling follows his mother. Thanks to you, he doesn't believe he can count on Katie when he needs her the most. And I never thought I'd see a rift between the twins, but you managed to make that happen."

Louise shook her head, sobs cascading from her.

I set my near empty plate next to Dad's and started down the porch steps to stop Dad from total annihilation. Louise might be a lot of things, but I couldn't let her stand in this barrage, even if she deserved it.

Louise's mouth was distorted with her wet sobs. "But you don't understand. We were special. Everyone admired our family. People wanted to be at our house because there was always something going on."

The way she cared so much what others thought of us seemed sad. I was proud of being a Fox but there was a core of myself inside. Probably what the world called self-esteem. And honestly, sometimes I struggled with my own worth. But it occurred to me Louise's inner core depended on being a part of the family. No wonder Mom leaving and the Fox name being disgraced crushed her. She didn't believe in herself, she believed in Us. She must be terrified now.

Dad looked at her in confusion, like she spoke a foreign language. "Our family limped along like any. We struggled to make ends meet. You kids fought and made up, like every other family. The only difference is that there were more of you."

She wiped her flowing nose with the back of her hand and swiped it on her jeans. "No. Mom was a mysterious artist. And Glenda was so special. Then, when she died, there was this tragic aura around us. And of course, everyone wanted to be with the twins because they were so fun. And Jeremy and Susan were adorable. We were like a Partridge Family."

Except no tour bus, no goofy songs, and no album sales.

A few years ago, I'd stumbled upon the knowledge that Louise had a breakdown when her kids were young. She'd taken off one night and ended up in a bar in Broken Butte, determined to go home with one or more men. One of Dad's work buddies had gotten her out of the bar. Dad had to remember how fragile she'd been then and maybe still was.

Whatever she'd done to me, she was hurting now, and I needed to help her. I hit the bottom stair and started across the yard.

Dad stepped closer to Louise and put an arm around her shoulder. "It's okay, Sugar. We're still a family, even if your mother left us. For all her faults, she was the love of my life. She lied to us and that cuts mighty deep. But she taught us kindness and compassion."

She leaned her head into his shoulder. "We learned from you, too. How to be accountable to each other. How to be proud of the Fox name and make it mean something in our community."

He scoffed. "I'm probably too proud of the Fox name. I love and think the world of all my kids. You've been a good mom, though I think you'd do well to ease up on the reins a bit. I don't mind telling you, though, I admire Katie a great deal. She's worked hard and given her all to whatever she sets her mind to. She kept with Ted longer than most would have. She's been a darned good sheriff. She's picked herself up more times than I can name and through it all, she's been there for every one of you. I'd like to think that's what being a Fox means."

Louise flinched against him as if he'd slapped her. She lifted her head from his shoulder and, dry-eyed, stared at him. "You are most proud of Kate? And Glenda is so special? What irony. I suppose you think Jeremy is better than the rest of us, too."

My stomach did a flip and crashed. How had Louise found out? She'd known about Glenda, but not me and Jeremy. Dad had riddled her with the bullets of recrimination, and she was about to return fire. If she did, our family might truly disintegrate. I hurried to close the gap and stop her. "Louise, wait."

She glanced at me, a hard gleam in her eye. "It's not like I didn't know you have your favorites. I think it's ironic. Glenda was—"

Dad interrupted. "I know I wasn't her biological father. Your mother was pregnant when I met her. Back then, I didn't know Marguerite's past so

I could accept the baby. I'm not sure how I would deal with it now, knowing her father was a murderer."

Louise let out a mean chuckle. "That's the least of it. Your precious Kate is—"

"Louise!" I tried to stop her.

Poupon barked and scrambled off the front porch, whether to join me in battle or to roughhouse in fun, I didn't know. I would have loved it if he'd go for Louise's jugular.

Her words slapped the air with a savage vengeance. "And Jeremy. Both of them. All three of them. They aren't yours."

I grabbed her shoulders and shoved her away from Dad, as if she were actually hitting him.

She turned on me, her eyes glittering. "You thought I didn't know. You and Diane always keeping secrets from me. And now you've got Carly on your side. Everyone laughs at fat old Louise. But I heard Diane talking to Carly when they thought I was in the kitchen. Because everyone always assumes I'm in the kitchen."

Dad hadn't moved. He stared at me his mouth open, and I couldn't read his expression.

I understood Louise's pain at being left out. But she'd lashed out at the wrong person. "What is wrong with you?"

She stepped back from me. "I'm tired of everyone always saying Glenda was the best of us. She wasn't perfect, you know. She left me in Broken Butte one time. You can ask Norm. And she was always pawning Carly off on anyone who would babysit. You should know, even before Glenda died you were practically Carly's mother."

Dad still didn't move.

I yelled back at Louise, thinking maybe cursing might pull Dad out of his shock. "You're full of shit."

She didn't back down. "And you. Sheriff. Respected. You couldn't keep your marriage together. You have to act like you're Carly's mom because you can't have kids of your own. You're probably going to manage her ranch, so don't give me any sob story about not having a job."

Growing up, I'd been on defense in any Fox skirmishes. I never threw punches, just learned to duck and weave and slip out of most situations. I was intimately familiar with the underside of my bed. But now, it took all my restraint not to fly into Louise and punch her mouth shut.

I swallowed bile and acid churned in my gut. While the frogs croaked, and a cricket chirped into the darkness, I fought to feel the ground under my boots. The night sounds usually soothed me, but there wasn't much going to save me now. I hissed through clenched teeth. "Get the hell out of my yard."

Maybe the sounds triggered something in Louise, though. She seemed to suddenly come back to her senses. She looked at me, then at Dad. With a hitch in a breath, she covered her mouth with a doughy hand. In a second, she pulled it away and whispered, "I'm sorry."

I inched toward her, my fists clenched, her apology like rain in the ocean. Poupon stayed at my side and nosed my hand.

Louise squeaked out, "I didn't mean that about Glenda. I was her little sister always tagging along, no wonder she got irritated." It appeared as though she played back the tape of her tirade in her head. "I know you love Carly like your own daughter."

Even though she had several inches and the weight advantage over me, I felt menacing as I scowled at her and slid closer. She'd had a breakdown once before and maybe that's what had happened here, but that didn't excuse this carnage.

She took a step backward. "Okay. I'm going. But think about it, Kate. Isn't it better to get the truth out there? We can deal with this in the open. You're mad now, I get it. But we can talk tomorrow or the next day."

I wouldn't be calling her tomorrow, the next day, or any other day. "You don't want me to be part of your family. I agree to that. Bye, Louise."

She hesitated and started to say something else, but I turned my back and clicked for Poupon to keep up with me. I stomped across the grass, thinking Dad and I would talk this through after she left.

It wouldn't change the way we felt about each other. He'd raised me thinking I was his and DNA wasn't going to alter our bond. But him coming to grips with Mom's betrayal during their marriage would take some healing time.

I heard Louise open the door to her Suburban as I neared Dad.

He blinked as if emerging from a dark cave. "Hold up," he called out to Louise. "I need a ride back to town."

He didn't acknowledge me as he trotted past on his way to Louise's rig. I hadn't considered there was a choice to be made, but he'd clearly decided to go with his real daughter.

That's when my heart tumbled through my ribs and bounced onto the dark grass. I couldn't even turn around to watch as they drove over the hill.

19

If I'd slept at all, I'd be able to say my phone ringing at five o'clock woke me. As it was, I'd have to settle for saying Zoe called me as the first pink slashes lit the clouds, still heavy with unshed rain. My head felt as stuffed with emotions as the clouds looked burdened with moisture.

After Louise had driven Dad away, I wanted to jump in Elvis and chase them down. I needed to hear Dad say that finding out I didn't carry his genes wouldn't change the way he felt about me.

Then I figured he'd need time to process Mom's affair. It was bad enough his wife of over forty years had left him for a long-lost love, but knowing she'd cheated throughout their marriage was a volcano on top of a hurricane in the middle of a blizzard. I couldn't pressure him when the foundations of his world kept crumbling under his feet.

Maybe I could talk to Diane. But it had been late, and it was never a good idea to interrupt Diane's sleep.

I wanted to know when she'd told Carly and why. But really, I wanted a sister's support. Maybe Diane felt that since Glenda was Carly's mother, Carly ought to know her blood line. Who knows what went on between Carly and Diane. They shared so many secrets that had nothing to do with the Fox clan in Nebraska, I tried to keep my curiosity to a minimum.

Since I wasn't ready to break the news to the rest of my brothers and sisters that Glenda, Jeremy and I had been the result of Mom's ongoing affair with the man she called the love of her life, that left me to mutter to Poupon and pace from the kitchen to the front porch when I wasn't doing battle with my bed sheets.

So, when Zoe called, I'd eaten breakfast, was already on my third cup of coffee, and was wired and cranky. "What's up?"

Road noise sounded from her end. "I'm about to hit town. Can you meet me at the courthouse?"

"I guess so." What else did I have to do today besides worry that not only had I lost my mother, but my father might have abandoned me, too.

She spoke with a steely edge, as if threatening me against arguing. "I think it will look more official if we use the cruiser. And since I'm not sworn in, you need to actually do the arresting."

I assumed dispatch had called Zoe with some disturbance. Could be Newt and Earl were caught rummaging where they ought not rummage. Maybe Leonard Bingham drank into the wee hours and took exception to something his wife said this morning. Leonard was a mean drunk and, because of his history of punching first and apologizing later, his wife dialed for help at the first inkling the situation trended south. I'd be glad to go along with Zoe to help her out.

I dumped kibble into Poupon's dish. He sniffed, gave me a look that clearly showed his disappointment, and planted his butt next to me in protest. I held the phone away. "You'd better eat now or forever hold your peace." To Zoe I said, "Who are we going to arrest?"

"Alden Haney."

Whoa. I choked on my next breath. "Are you sure this is how you want to play it?"

"I didn't get much sleep last night thinking about this. I know you said we ought to wait until we had more to go on, but a man who would kill his own son is dangerous. Maybe you and Trey think he's okay, but there's an old lady and a kid out there. If he comes unhinged and hurts either of them, I won't be able to live with myself."

Sarah and I had been best friends since kindergarten. I'd spent a lot of time at their place, helping out with cattle work and roundups and chores around the ranch. But their home had also been the site of slumber parties, hours and hours of gossip, makeup experimenting, coloring hair, movies, and laughter. Sarah's parents were mostly background characters in our growing-up years. Alden would flash that fake everybody-loves-me smile, then he'd disappear into his office or off somewhere on the ranch. Ellie took care of meals without much creativity and the house seemed tidy, but she seemed to spend most of her time reading paperback romances.

While I enjoyed the quiet, orderly Haney home, Sarah seemed to revel in the chaos of Fox Central. Some in-laws seemed to barely tolerate our over-involved family, but Sarah always felt like one of us.

Sarah butted heads with her dad from time to time, but she didn't complain about him any more than most kids moaned about their parents.

Poupon must have given up hope of a better meal option and began to crunch through his breakfast.

A few months ago, I'd witnessed Alden losing his temper with Garrett when they didn't know I was in the shop with them. But he'd recovered quickly and pulled his smile from his pocket. Yesterday he'd been different than I'd seen him. He didn't try to cover up his foul temper. He'd been downright combative.

Maybe Zoe was right. I'd been relying on my impression of Alden through the years but how much attention does a kid really pay to someone else's parents? Trey wasn't on hand to witness him firsthand. But Zoe was experiencing Alden unfiltered by history. And he seemed to be a talking electric wire. "Okay. We can hold him for 48 hours. Hopefully, we can find something on him in that time."

It took a few minutes to get changed into my uniform. Why not? If we wanted to look official, that would help. With Poupon enjoying his post-breakfast nap in the back seat, we caught up to Zoe at the courthouse. She stood by the back door and jumped into the passenger seat.

I studied the sky as we sped along, calculating how long until the clouds couldn't hold back and we got nailed. "You need to call Trey and let him know your plans."

Zoe sighed. "I can already tell this phone thing is going to be the hardest part of the job for me. I hate making calls."

The first fat drop smacked the windshield. I'm sure Zoe thought the same thing I did—and probably what most Sandhillers thought—a well of gratitude for the moisture that would grow the grass that would feed the cattle that would keep us all in groceries for another season. Even if it meant sloppy roads and chilly air.

While she argued with Trey, I watched the long, yellow grass bend under the wind, acre after acre of undulating waves. I'd hate to leave the Sandhills. If Dad would no longer call me his daughter, would I end up ostracized from my family as well as unemployed? If Dad denied me, maybe his sister Twyla would, too, and I'd lose my last resort—bartending at the Long Branch.

That left me shacking up with Diane or going into debt to get my master's degree from the University of Nebraska (Go Big Red). Or maybe loading up Poupon and going to work on a dude ranch in Montana.

Zoe hung up. "He wasn't thrilled, but he ended up giving in."

"I'll bet you don't get many people holding out long against you." She was going to make a great sheriff.

"Helps when I'm usually right."

Ah, the confidence of youth. Or maybe just of someone like Zoe. I admired that.

We pulled up to the ranch with the wind and rain battering the cruiser. The storm roared like a rhino in rut. Well, I suppose an aroused rhino would roar, what did I know?

Zoe leaned forward and squinted up through the windshield. "We could sit it out. There's blue sky coming."

I followed her gaze. Yep, to the west the deep violet of the clouds gave way to a winking blue. "As Grandma Ardith used to say, 'I'm not made of sugar.'" I opened my door and sprinted toward the porch. The drops drilled into me, cold and almost violent. Just another bit of punishment on this dreadful day.

Zoe's door slammed behind me, and we hit the first step at the same time.

She leapt the next two stairs onto the dry porch. I'd swear she was barely damp when I felt drenched. Bless her heart and those long legs. Her fist pounded on the door.

No one answered. "The storm is making so much noise I'll bet they can't hear us." And Tony would have earbuds in, or his game turned up loud.

Zoe creaked open the front door. "Alden? Ellie? It's Zoe Cantrel." One pause, then as if trying it out, "Sheriff."

Something crashed toward the kitchen in the back of the house. "Ellie?" I shouted.

There was a shuffling of feet and then pounding and she appeared in the hallway at the kitchen. "Here. Oh, here. Thank God. Hurry."

I lurched forward, my feet moving before I could think what had caused her panic. Zoe followed. I rounded the doorway and tried to take in the whole gloomy room. In the house built in the early 1900s, the kitchen took up a fair amount of space. Alden and Ellie had renovated it about twenty years ago, making the one small window into a gaping picture window with a seat. In this morning's storm, though, the light was muted.

Ellie stopped by the stove, her hands over her mouth, eyes glistening with tears, staring at the area with an eight-seat pine dining table. At first, I noticed the overturned coffee mug and brown liquid puddling in a plate with a half-eaten sweet roll.

Zoe brushed past me to the lump on the floor. She was on her knees rolling Alden to his back when I joined her. "Alden. Alden, can you hear me? It's Zoe Cantrel. Hang on, we're going to help you."

She spoke with such calm authority I was both relieved and jealous. Over my shoulder I hollered at Ellie. "Have you called the ambulance?"

She went through a series of peeps and squeaks like a baby rabbit in the jaws of a coyote.

I took that to mean she hadn't. Forgetting there was no cell service at the Haney place, I stuffed my phone back into my pocket and used the landline. Instead of calling dispatch in Ogallala, I dialed Eunice Fleenor directly. She picked up on the first ring as if she'd been waiting for my call.

"On our way," she said when I gave her the few details.

Zoe had loosened Alden's shirt. She glanced up to Ellie. "Does he have a heart condition?"

This time, Ellie was able to nod.

"Glycerin tablets?" Zoe started patting Alden's breast pockets, then his jeans. She worked her fingers into his left front pocket and extracted a pill bottle.

Without asking Ellie again, Zoe read the label, then flicked open the lid and dumped a tiny pill into her palm. She raised her voice as if speaking to someone hard of hearing. "Alden, I'm going to put this under your tongue."

Since Zoe seemed to be doing all we could for Alden, I stood up and put my arm around Ellie. "Why don't you sit here. Eunice Fleenor will be here any minute."

Still making mewling noises, she allowed me to settle her in a kitchen chair at the other end of the table from where Zoe stayed with Alden. I got her a glass of water.

She lifted it with shaking hands and took a sip. "Is Alden going to be okay?"

From the look of his gray-blue skin and his labored breathing, I wouldn't give him great odds. "Zoe knew exactly what to do. She's got it under control. When the EMTs get here they'll give him oxygen and whatever he needs and get him to the hospital."

Wind rattled the window and rain pelted it making everything that much more frantic.

She clasped her hands on the table as if holding onto herself for strength. She would only be able to see his feet from where she sat but she stared at them and nodded.

"What happened?" I asked.

Her lips trembled. "He came in because it looked like the storm was going to hit. I heated him up one of those rolls and coffee. Sometimes he likes a snack this time of morning. Back when the kids were younger, he'd never take the time to come in the house during the day, except for dinner. But now that he's slowed down, seems like he's in here a lot."

Nervous chatter, I guessed. But it distracted her.

"So, I warmed up the roll and then I went to start the laundry. I didn't know anything happened until I heard you knocking. I came in here to see if he wanted me to get the door and that's when I saw him."

I glanced around, seeing only Alden's plate and cup, no other dishes. "Where's Tony?"

Ellie sniffed and looked at Alden's feet. "He's at Sarah's."

At least he didn't need this trauma on top of his father's death. "That's good."

Zoe twisted her neck to look at Ellie. "I thought he was going to stay with you and Alden."

Ellie's fingers twined and pulled against each other. "Alden decided it was too much work for me, so he took Tony back to Sarah's last night."

"That's probably for the best." I didn't really feel this way. Sarah had enough to worry about with a newborn, a toddler, and recovering from prolonged labor. I was sure friends had offered to bring food or babysit, but like Alden, Sarah wouldn't accept it. Difference was, she'd be nicer about saying no.

Zoe pulled a placemat from the table and fanned Alden's face.

Ellie focused on me. "You really think it's a good idea?"

"You don't?"

She pursed her lips, all the wrinkles coming to a point. "I think Tony would be better off with me. I have the time for him. He's never had much attention or direction. It's time someone gives him the care he deserves." Ellie lowered her voice as if imparting a secret. "That Sheila was never much of a mother. She had that poor boy in so many classes and programs he doesn't know how to entertain himself."

Zoe kept fanning Alden, but I got the impression from the way she held her head that she was listening.

I hadn't noticed the storm let up, but when I heard the rumble of the ambulance out front, I realized the rain had run its course. I glanced outside as the first ray of sunshine fought through the clouds and struck the kitchen table, giving the plate with Alden's coffee-soaked roll a slightly green gleam.

I dashed to the front door in time to open it for Eunice and Harold and one other EMT. I was glad to see Tyrell Ostrander, a man in his early thirties. We needed new volunteers since Harold and Eunice wouldn't be around forever.

They clattered into the kitchen. Zoe stood and backed up, giving Eunice space. She explained what we'd experienced and the dose she'd given him.

Eunice sent Harold and Tyrell back to the ambulance for the gurney. She set to work strapping oxygen on Alden and speaking to him in that same loud, calm voice Zoe had used. She paused and glanced up at Zoe. "Good work, kid. You learned something in those classes."

I raised an eyebrow at Zoe in question.

She shrugged. "I took an emergency medical course in North Platte last summer. Ten hours. I thought it might help if something happened on the ranch. This is the first time I've had to use it."

Another reason to admire this young woman. Grand County could be in a lot worse shape than to have her as a sheriff.

It didn't take long for them to load Alden into the ambulance. Ellie, Zoe, and I stood outside in the damp grass as Harold hopped in back and Tyrell closed the doors and took off for the passenger side.

Long, lean Eunice bent over slightly to speak to Ellie, probably thinking she sounded caring and sweet, but sounding more like a teacher demanding homework. "We've got an extra responder today so no room in the back of the ambulance for you."

I stepped in. "That's okay. We'll follow you to Broken Butte."

Eunice hadn't waited for my response. She lunged for the driver's door and swung herself inside before I'd finished my sentence.

We stepped back to let the ambulance speed away.

During the whole event, Ellie's spine had straightened a bit. She'd quit wringing her hands and now stood in the yard, the smell of clean air and damp sand around her. She spoke up with no quaver in her voice, "You don't need to take me to Broken Butte."

I shook my head. "I don't think it's a good idea for you to drive right now. You're too upset."

Ellie rested her hands on her hips and watched the road where the ambulance had retreated. "I won't be driving on the highway. Just country roads."

Zoe's head snapped toward her. "You don't want to go to the hospital?"

Ellie started for the house. "There's nothing I can do for Alden, but Tony needs me." She had a jaunt to her stride. "The rain has made it so fresh out here. It's lovely, but I'll need my sweater."

She didn't seem upset the way she had when we arrived. It was that strange calm she had after Garrett's death. Weird enough it worried me.

"Let us help you. I'll drive you in your pickup and Zoe can follow in the cruiser. That way you'll have your rig when you're ready to come home."

Ellie stopped before she reached the porch and turned to us. "You don't understand why I'm not falling apart that Alden is gone. Is that it?"

Zoe answered for us. "Well, yeah."

Ellie drew in a long breath, her chest rising, then she let it out in one puff, looking from me to Zoe. "I'm relieved. That's the truth. I might even feel better if he died on the way to the hospital."

20

Zoe and I both stared at Ellie. A robin let out a string of happy notes, discordant with Alden's emergency and Ellie's response.

Ellie studied the upper branches of a nearby blue spruce. "Don't you love that sound? It reminds me of home."

Zoe sounded cautious. "Where is home?"

Ellie brought her attention back to us. She chuckled. "I haven't always been here, you know. I lived in Maryland. The springs, there, oh my, they were glorious. The daffodils and dogwoods. The hyacinths and tulips. It was a wonderland of color. Not like here. You can't safely plant until Mother's Day and even then you're stuck with marigolds or petunias."

I still didn't know what to say. Ellie had lost her son two days ago and her husband was suffering a heart attack, and she was nostalgic for the home of her youth. Strange. Maybe her inability to process trauma was why Sarah and Alden worked to insulate her.

Ellie waited for a second before she went on. "And the autumn. Such color. The smells of wood fires and the cozy lights in the evening in all the neighbor's homes. Here, one day you're listening to the robins sing and the next there's snow blowing horizontally and your whole livelihood is threatening to freeze to death. The leaves skip right from green to brown. And there are no neighbors, so of course, no cozy homes."

Zoe glanced at me, then back to Ellie. "You've been in the Sandhills for a long time. You've never liked it here?"

Ellie waved her hand. "At first I thought it would be an adventure. Alden was handsome and charming. He had a ranch and I thought he was rich. I had some romantic notion of being like the Ewings on *Dallas*. But then I got out here and it was nothing like that. Alden didn't have a lot of money. He worked all the time. And there was that temper I never knew about."

We'd got a glimpse of that yesterday.

Zoe took charge. "It can be hard to live with someone who's volatile."

Ellie climbed up the porch steps and lowered herself to a wicker chair. She engaged Zoe as if having coffee with a friend. Her skin took on some healthy color and it seemed to smooth her wrinkles. She smiled in a relaxed way that wasn't what I'd expect. "I was going to be a concert pianist. That was my plan when I met Alden. I was studying and already had some success. But he swept me off my feet. Before I knew what was happening, he'd whisked me out here, promising me my own home and saying I'd never have to get a job. And a few months later, here I was, twenty-five years old and pregnant. No friends."

Zoe had followed her up to the porch and sat in the chair next to her. I leaned on the railing.

The twenty-four-year-old Zoe, with a baby, didn't show offense at Ellie sounding despondent at the same situation. "I've been told it's hard for someone who didn't grow up around here to make friends."

I didn't think that was true. There weren't enough people in Grand County to get too picky about letting someone join in the fun. New people were folded into the community if they wanted to be.

Ellie's mouth pulled into that pursed expression again. "Well, I *am* more educated than most. I've seen some of the world, lived in a big city. People around here were intimidated by me. I never tried to be superior, but...." She paused and tilted her head. "As my mother used to say, 'The genes tell.'"

How Zoe kept an even face, I'd never know. She didn't comment on Ellie's snobbery and changed the subject. "So, Alden had a temper?"

Ellie nodded for emphasis. "A terrible temper. Not in the beginning. But once he let it out, it was a beast that was harder and harder to contain. I should have left the first time he hit me. It was such a shock, I didn't really know what to think."

All my nerves jangled as if I'd been the one decked. This isn't what I'd expected, and it left me sideswiped. Who could hit this timid little lady?

"It happened often?" Zoe's eyes filled with compassion.

Ellie looked out to the yard, maybe waiting to hear the robin again. "Not really. I learned how to smooth things out for him. After I knew getting dinner on the table too late, or not having meat at every meal upset him, I made sure I never let that happen. The same thing with a messy house or spending too much on groceries."

I felt sick for the terror this woman had lived through. Sarah had never hinted at this kind of abuse. Had Ellie kept it hidden all these years?

Ellie looked Zoe in the eyes. "Back then, women were just beginning to be independent. Most of us had been raised to be good wives and mothers, to respect a man's authority. I never considered leaving him. He was a good provider, and I didn't think I could make it on my own. After I'd abandoned my career, what did I have? I was too mortified to tell my parents. And I'm sure they wouldn't have believed me anyway."

Zoe laid a hand on Ellie's resting on the chair arm. "I'm so sorry."

Ellie patted Zoe's hand. "I got pregnant with Garrett right away. So, I had to make the best of it. Mostly, Alden was good, and I knew he would never let me take Garrett from him." She choked up and her eyes misted. "I tried to protect little Garrett. Alden thought I spoiled him, but I wanted to keep Alden from hurting him."

Tears collected in Zoe's eyes. "But that didn't work?"

Ellie gave herself a moment to control her emotions, cleared her throat and began again. "No. I don't know that Alden hit Garrett. But he was abusive to him. Yelling and slamming things. Alden wanted Garrett to take over the ranch, but I encouraged Garrett to get away. And I'm glad he did."

"But he came back," Zoe said.

Ellie's wrinkled hands shook, and she raised them to her face to cover her eyes. "I was so happy. I thought everything would be wonderful, just like I'd dreamed as a young bride. It all seemed perfect because Sheila was gone, and it was only Tony and Garrett. It was like the family I'd dreamed about."

Zoe leaned in closer. "But it wasn't?"

Ellie focused on the blue spruce where the robin had been, her color fading again and the deep worry lines reemerging. "Alden's temper had faded in the last ten years. He still became angry at small things, but he'd mellowed and stopped hitting me. I thought maybe he understood that it was wrong, you know, with all the movies and TV shows and news." She addressed Zoe. "Like the Me Too movement has made older men understand that the way they used to act was wrong."

It didn't surprise me that Zoe couldn't let that one go. "They always knew it was wrong."

Ellie didn't seem to hear her. "But everything Garrett did upset Alden. He constantly compared him to Robert and threatened to leave the ranch to Sarah. He started throwing things again."

I had no business butting in, but that didn't stop me. "He should at least leave part of the ranch to Sarah."

Ellie gave me a puzzled look. "You know, Alden favored Sarah. He'd never lift a finger to her. That's good, of course. She's had all the advantages I never had. She has a husband who is respectful and loves her. She thinks she's entitled to what should rightfully be passed on to the son, the one who carries the Haney name."

Steam started to rise in me. "Sarah has given time and sweat, her whole life and heart into this ranch. That's not entitlement. Garrett left. You can't compare them."

Ellie explained to me as if it was a standard rule. "Sarah spends more time outside than I do. But we all know a woman can't run a ranch like a man can. They don't have the muscles or the aptitude for it. Sarah and Robert are welcome to stay here, and Robert will always have a job. He's a very good manager. But Sarah knows how it is, or she should because she was raised that way. She'll understand when her daughters marry and take someone else's name." She made a sympathetic smacking noise. "I'm sorry she doesn't have a son."

Zoe cocked her head. "Sorry that she has daughters?"

Ellie chuckled again. "Daughters are fine. I know some mothers and daughters are very close. Sarah always wanted to be a son and go with Alden." She glanced at me and Zoe. "Oh, I know that's not popular thinking. With Ruth Bader Ginsberg and all. Despite the way Alden treated me, I do believe in men being the authority. Our job, as women, is to raise our sons to be respectful and protect their families. And if we do a good job, they'll take care of us. A daughter's job is to take care of her husband and children."

Zoe and I shared a mutual look of disbelief at this distorted worldview. Zoe said, "You think sons are worth more than daughters?"

Ellie nodded. "In a way, yes. Look at the world and all the troubles we're having now. Violence and no one wanting to get along. For heaven's sake, our government only fights. They don't care about the people. And I think that's because we've lost our way. If women took the time to care for our children instead of thinking they need to do everything a man does, then I don't think we'd be in the fix we're in."

Did Ellie realize she was talking to female sheriffs? Ellie's daughter, Sarah, was the strongest woman I knew, comfortable with herself as a rancher, business partner, and mother. How could this woman have raised someone like that when she thought women were inferior to men?

Ellie stood up. "This has been nice, but I need to take care of Tony."

I pushed off from the railing. "I insist on driving you." I wasn't sure what I'd do with her once I got her to Sarah's. I'd rather take her to a hospital for a psych evaluation, but I didn't know how to carry that off. Sarah might be able to help out.

Ellie rubbed her arms. "I never did get that sweater, did I?" She did a little old-lady grunt when she stood and started for the house. She passed me and said, "You can drive your cop car. I'd rather have this young girl drive me."

Zoe's eyes twinkled as Ellie slipped into the house. "The old folks love me."

"Ellie isn't older than sixty-five."

"Like I said, old folks."

For a moment we both stared at the door, then at each other. I had no words and I supposed Zoe was at a loss, too. She rolled her eyes and flapped her hands in dismissal and stomped down the porch into the sunshine and cool breeze. Probably the best way to deal with this.

Ellie returned from the house with her sweater and purse, and she climbed into their shiny pickup with Zoe at the wheel. I urged Poupon from his nap in my back seat to the front yard for some forced relief. He complied but didn't seem grateful.

It took fifteen minutes to drive from Alden and Ellie's place to Sarah and Robert's. The Haney enterprise was a thriving business with more than enough land to go around. If Alden didn't recover and Ellie was in charge, she'd have to rely on Robert and Sarah. Maybe she'd change her tune about sons and daughters.

The clouds continued their march to the east, leaving the sky a brilliant, cloudless blue. It seemed the definition of infinite and it sparked some optimism in me. I'd find something new and start over again. I'd done it before, and I could do it again.

But I'd done it as a Fox, with the whole clan on my side.

I gave up solving my own problems and called Sarah. The baby sounded mildly fussy, and Brie chattered nonstop. Over the small-scale chaos, she said, "Between Garrett and the baby and Dad's stupid behavior yesterday, we haven't even talked about the recall. After I get Olivia down for a nap and Tony takes Brie to feed the chickens—" A wild shriek from Brie told me she was ready to escape the house. "I'll grab the shotgun and take care of Louise for you."

She didn't know the half of my feud with Louise and how I almost wished she wasn't joking. "I'm not going to be your favorite person when I tell you why you can't go on a traitor hunt with me today."

She spoke away from the phone. "Tony, can you get Brie some juice before she crawls into the fridge herself?" She spoke to me. "What's the next disaster?"

I hoped she was sitting down nursing the baby and not pacing with her. Either way, it couldn't be helped. "Alden's had a heart attack. But he's—"

She interrupted before I had a chance to assure her. "Fuck!"

Tony's "Whoa," came through my end.

I jumped in quickly to head her off. "He's on his way to Broken Butte right now. Zoe gave him glycerin and Eunice got him stable. I think he's going to be okay."

"You've got to be kidding me. First Garrett and now Dad? What's going on here?" The baby started to wail. "It'll take me a few minutes to get hold of Robert and get him home. I'll take Olivia with me to the hospital."

"Hold on," I said. "You don't need to go to Broken Butte now."

"The hell I don't. Mom will be a mess, and someone needs to take care of her so the professionals can help Dad. Robert's on his way to Grand Island for parts but he can turn around."

Ellie didn't give Sarah any credit for being a great rancher, a wonderful mother, an amazing best friend, and, now, it was clear she sold Sarah short in the daughter department.

"Don't call Robert. You aren't going to Broken Butte because—and I know this isn't going to be the best news—Ellie is coming to your house."

She was louder than the baby. "What the hell are you talking about?"

I tried to impart calm to her. "She doesn't want to go to the hospital with your dad. She thinks Tony needs her."

I knew Sarah tugged in her control because she stopped cursing. "Dang, dang, dang. This is the last thing I need." She drew in a breath. "And here she comes now. I'm going to kill you for letting this happen."

She didn't mean it, so I didn't take it personally. "Backup is on the way. I'll be there in less than five minutes."

She hung up to the sound of the baby crying, Tony talking, and Brie yelling. More like a protest rally than a circus.

I stopped behind Ellie's pickup in time to see Zoe stepping into the house. I didn't wait for Poupon to stretch and step out, just left the back door open for him and trotted to the house. When I swung the screen open and walked in, Sarah and Ellie stood in the middle of the room with Brie clinging to Sarah's leg.

Sarah cupped Brie's head of soft brown curls and spoke to Ellie in a firm but kind voice. "That's not a good idea, Mom. Tony is fine here and he's actually good help."

Ellie clutched her purse to her chest. "This house is too confusing and loud. He's just lost his daddy. He needs peace and comfort. I'll cook his favorite foods. Make him feel loved."

Zoe leaned against the wall by the door, looking as uncomfortable as if she wore a suit of red ants. I knew how she felt.

Ellie tried to get around Sarah, but Sarah shifted to block her, dragging Brie along. "Why aren't you at the hospital with Dad?"

Ellie sidestepped, straining her neck to see around Sarah. "Is Tony back there?"

"He's rocking Olivia," Sarah said. "Don't you think someone should be with Dad?"

Ellie frowned toward the hallway to the bedrooms. "You shouldn't make Tony do that. He needs to be looked after, not doing the babysitting."

Sarah huffed with impatience. "He likes it. She likes it. And I like it. I don't see the problem. Now, tell me about Dad."

Ellie stepped back, showing the first anger I'd seen from her. "For heaven's sake, Sarah. Your father is with trained doctors. They can do more for him than you or I can. He won't even be aware of visitors for some time. Tony needs me more than your father does right now."

Sarah scooped Brie into her arms and stepped back, letting Ellie through. "If you won't be with Dad, I'll have to. And they aren't going to be happy about a newborn in the waiting room."

Ellie didn't stop but disappeared into the bedroom.

Sarah bounced Brie on her hip and the two of them shared a short conversation about bunnies. I figured Sarah wanted the toddler to know she wasn't forgotten.

I waited for them to finish their moment and for Sarah to plop into the rocker with Brie on her lap. She looked exhausted. "I don't know what's going on. I really can't go to Broken Butte and leave Mom here."

I ventured, "She doesn't seem all there, you know?"

Zoe gave Sarah a confirming tilt of her head. "She was with your dad when he had the heart attack. I think it's traumatizing for her. Maybe she needs to rest."

Sarah sighed and dropped her head back. "When Mom gets upset she gets confused. Sometimes she comes up with things that don't make any sense. Dad can keep her even most of the time."

"Has she seen a doctor?" Zoe asked.

"Believe me, I've tried to make that happen. I don't know why they're so resistant. This has gone on since I was in high school, so I guess they're used to it." She sat up and looked at me. "What's the deal with Dad?"

I told Sarah all the details as we knew it. "Eunice seemed to think Alden would be okay. But I'm sure it rattled Ellie."

Sarah patted Brie, who had cuddled into her mother's lap. "Mom's never been able to handle much stress. Dad always protects her. I suppose she's lost without him telling her what to do."

"She said she was a concert pianist," Zoe said.

Sarah laughed. "Says Mom. Her sister told me Mom was a marginal player at best."

That reminded me of Sarah's family. "Isn't your aunt an attorney?"

Sarah kept rocking and grinned. "Sure, like Meryl Streep is an actor. She's lead corporate attorney for a national insurance company."

Zoe raised her eyebrows. "Your mom has some notions about women in power."

Sarah set her face. "Mom thinks she's so much better than Aunt Marie because she has a husband and kids. Marie never married. She's got a whole big life Mom is too repressed to admit she's jealous of."

I lowered my voice and glanced at the hallway to make sure Ellie and Tony weren't in earshot. "She says your father hit her and was abusive to Garrett."

The rocking stopped, and Sarah's jaw dropped. Then she started laughing. "Oh my God. Mom is so full of crap. Dad worships her. So much it'll make you sick. He brings her coffee in bed every morning, carries anything heavy for her. Asks 'how high' when she says 'jump.' I mean, he dotes on her. I can't believe she'd say that. And that you'd believe her."

Zoe looked uncertain.

Sarah shook her head. "Do you know one time Mom told me this story about her father promising he'd take her to Europe after she graduated from high school, but she got mono and the trip was cancelled. I asked Marie about it, and she reminded me their father had died when Mom was a sophomore." She rocked a few times. "She loses track of reality sometimes but she's harmless. Unless you believe her."

I didn't want to bring it up but thought it might be important. "I witnessed Alden attacking Garrett."

She drew her head back. "When was this? Attacking? Like with his fists?"

I explained the shop, the snap, the welt by Garrett's eye.

"I'll be the first to admit Dad was hard on Garrett. But what you've said doesn't mean Dad attacked him. Garrett could have hurt himself working on the tractor."

Zoe took a step forward. "We suspect Alden killed Garrett."

Sarah's disbelief and anger spit out at me. "You're kidding."

I frowned at Zoe for jumping into this now. "We're looking into other suspects." I hurried on, while she stayed speechless. "Which is why we need Sheila's DNA. Do you have something that would work? Maybe she used a toothbrush or brush here?"

Sarah looked at me like I was nuts. "She wouldn't touch anything of mine, and she hasn't been here for years. Not even at Mom's. Why don't you ask Tony?"

Zoe shifted impatiently.

"Because we need it to ID a body found burned on the desert. Dates and car line up with Sheila's disappearance."

A thud behind me made us all turn. Tony slumped against the wall where he'd come from the bedroom. His mouth dropped open, and he stared at me with eyes full of anguish. "Mom? You're saying Mom is dead?"

I hurried to him, talking quickly and knowing nothing I said would do any good. "No. This is only to rule it out. We shouldn't worry until we know for sure."

He pounded a fist into the wall at his hip. "Great. Now I'm a fucking orphan." He ran toward the front door.

Sarah held out her arm but missed him when he flew past. "Tony. Wait."

I started to follow him, but Sarah stopped me. "Give him a minute. If you go out now, he'll try to be all tough, so let him cry alone." She ran her palm along Brie's head. "You're thinking if that's Sheila, the same person killed her and Garrett?" She threw her head back and sucked in a breath. "I can't believe I said that. And that we're talking about someone killing my brother and that you think it might be Dad."

I rushed in. "Or someone else. There's another possibility."

"But your father was in Scottsdale about the time of this murder. Who is likely Sheila," Zoe said. "And from things your father said yesterday and evidence we found, it looks pretty convincing he killed Garrett."

Sarah's face glowed with outrage, but she kept her voice level, either to keep Brie from getting alarmed or to keep Ellie from hearing. "Remember I told you Garrett was scared? And he was on his phone all the time. I think someone from work was threatening him. Maybe his family, too."

"We were on our way to arrest Alden," Zoe said. "I was worried about the safety of your mother and nephew. What Ellie said about him only confirms what I suspected."

"Did you tell Mom you thought Dad killed Garrett?" She let out a breath. "Even saying that sounds crazy."

"We—" I started, but Sarah held her hand up.

"You know, just go. I don't know what's going on. But I don't believe Dad is a murderer. Mom might be bonkers, well, I'm sure she is. But let me sort this out. Do me a favor, though, don't arrest Dad. He's in the hospital and not going anywhere, so give me a minute here."

Zoe looked doubtful. She might have expected Sarah to get hysterical or boil over somehow. I knew that all the swirling, confusion, and uncertainty simmered well below the calm face. I believed Sarah when she said she'd take care of this.

Sarah looked me directly in the eyes. There was over thirty years of friendship, all the pain of growing up, the joys of marriages, the agony of divorce, an infinite number of moments where our bonds were strengthened into an irrevocable trust.

It wasn't even a conscious decision for me. She asked. "Of course."

21

Zoe didn't say anything while I loaded up Poupon. Before we could leave, Tony walked from the barn. Tears hung in his eyes and his cheeks looked raw as though he'd repeatedly swiped them dry. He swayed slightly as if he'd been hollowed out and moving took effort.

Zoe cocked her head. "Dude. How're you holding up?"

He looked at his shoes. "Do you think that's my mom?"

Zoe landed a soft hand on his shoulder and squeezed. "We're going to find out as soon as we can."

He gazed at Zoe with adoration, despite the bad news he was absorbing. I guess not only old people loved her. "You think someone killed my dad, don't you?"

My heart shattered into a million Tony-sized pieces. "It looks like it."

He took that in. "I'm kind of glad because that means Dad wasn't stupid about turning off the pivot."

I swallowed the ache in my throat. "He was a brilliant man. He loved you a lot."

Tony's brown eyes glittered with purpose, the same way Sarah's could when she was determined. "I know who did it."

Zoe focused like a bird dog on a duck. "Who?"

Tony's gaze was serious as he looked from me to Zoe. "I don't know his name but that day we had the accident on the highway. Right before we left, some guy came out to the ranch."

Zoe leaned into him. "Did you know him?"

Tony locked eyes with Zoe. "I saw him before at home. And Dad knew him. I thought he was a friend of Dad's, but they were fighting and the guy left." He slammed his fist into his thigh. "I didn't ask Dad about him because I was pissed Dad was making me start school here. I should have said something. Maybe it would have made a difference."

Zoe squeezed his shoulder again. "Dude, you couldn't have stopped this. Can you tell us what this guy looked like?"

Tony huffed in disdain. "He had this lame beard. This triangle thing. Looked stupid."

Oh. The guy from Fredrickson's. Zoe and I exchanged a surprised look. Tony had seen him in Arizona. The Van Dyke guy came from Arizona. Did that connect him to the law firm and Garrett's mistake, or was he maybe an enforcer of Coleson Crenshaw's?

Tony scrubbed at his face again, even though there were no tears. "Do I have to go back in there? Grandma is killing me."

That phrase startled me, then I realized he didn't mean it literally. Giving up the sheriff gig might help me regain my equilibrium and quit overreacting. I tried to sound understanding. "She's going through a hard time."

Such a cute kid. He looked so much like his father and aunt, even down to that commanding attitude. "Like I'm not? My dad is dead, and I don't know what happened. And my mom might be a goner too. And now Grandma's strangling me. Talking about taking me to Maryland where we're going to eat crabs and see the fall foliage. Give me a break."

Zoe leaned on the cruiser and concentrated on Tony. "Yeah. That sounds pretty whack. All of this pretty much sucks. You know she's an old woman who's suffered a big blow. I don't think your Aunt Sarah will let her whisk you off to Maryland. Just be nice to her and try not to worry."

I assumed Zoe hoped if Tony could concentrate on someone or something else for a moment, he might ease into his grief.

I didn't have long to contemplate the unfairness of the situation because my phone rang. Carly's face with her grin and freckles met me when I pulled my phone out. She sounded rushed, and after a quick hello got to it. "Rope had some kind of incident. He passed out. Baxter called and told me, or I wouldn't have known. Rope says he's fine, but the last load of cattle is going out this afternoon and I don't want him out there. Baxter said he and Aria will take care of it, but...."

I slapped at her with my words. "You set me up, sending me out there yesterday to run into Baxter."

Carly had learned to lie so effectively I didn't know if she was sincere. "Set you up? Aren't you and Baxter friends? Anyway, I didn't know what time they were getting there. So, will you help me out again?"

Zoe hugged Tony and he leaned into her, then she said something to him, and he nodded. With a hanging head, he started back toward the house.

I normally wouldn't hesitate. I'd already be on my way to the Bar J, both because I would help Carly in any way and because I love cattle work. But being anywhere near Baxter was like throwing my emotions into a blender for a heartbreak margarita. Seeing him yesterday hit me like a hammer, pounding out the truth that we'd never be together. I should stay as far away as possible. But having a chance to see him, no matter how painful, was also a drug I couldn't resist.

"Sure. I'm on my way back to town now so I can be out there in about an hour."

Zoe watched me. "Is that Carly?"

I nodded.

"Tell her I tried that kombucha and it really sucks but she should get the grapefruit rosemary stuff because...." She trailed off when she saw the look on my face. "Tell her I'll call her later."

Carly must have heard. "Training day? Cool. Tell Zoe hi."

If Zoe and Carly were half as good friends as Sarah and me—and I was sure they were—they wouldn't need me passing messages. We signed off and loaded into the cruiser.

Tony stood on the porch with his shoulders hunched, looking as gray as the sky and as heavy as any rain cloud. He watched us drive away with a look of sheer abandonment. I wished there was something we could do for him, but maybe he'd find some comfort in his tiny nieces.

Zoe had only driven about a mile down the road when my stomach flipped and I thought I might throw up. What the ever-loving f-f-f-football was I thinking skipping on out to the Bar J? Baxter. And Aria. Together. I had no business torturing myself. Losing Dad after being kicked out of my job ought to be enough for anyone to absorb.

This wouldn't end well.

For anyone.

22

Zoe switched to her pickup at the courthouse, and I took over the cruiser and made a quick stop at Fredrickson's on my way out of town. There was one last slice of pizza in the warmer and that would do me. Poupon would be glad for his Slim Jim.

When Norm rang up my gourmet lunch, I asked, "You know that guy from Evergreen Enterprises?"

Norm looked puzzled and shook his head.

"The one with the Van Dyke beard."

He still looked baffed.

"The black Cadillac who had Newt and Earl spooked?"

He got it and chuckled. "Sure, him."

"Has he been back?"

"Nope." So much for that.

I thanked him and took off, scarfing down my lunch on the drive to the Bar J.

As Carly predicted, Rope hadn't been persuaded to go to Broken Butte to get checked out. But somehow, Baxter and Aria had convinced him to sit in a pickup and direct the operations from where he parked near the loading chutes.

The stock truck driver was already there and backed up to the chute.

Aria was on the ground along with the driver, urging cattle up the chute and into the truck.

The most amazing part of the whole operation wasn't that they had it running smoothly and didn't need me, it was seeing Baxter sitting on the back of a horse at the corral gate. I pulled up and, again, rolled down the windows for Poupon, telling him to stay put. Not that he'd ever roused himself to chase a cow, but if he took the notion, he'd scatter them from here to eternity.

I stepped out of the car and leaned against the back panel, arms crossed, doing everything I could to keep from howling with laughter at the sight of one of the most powerful cable news moguls hunched in the saddle. He wore jeans, but they weren't long enough for stirrups, so the gap between the hem and his tennis shoes showed skin on one ankle and a wrap on his injured one. He wore a ball cap, something I'd never seen him do, and it looked good on him. To be honest, I still wanted to throw myself into his arms. But resisting was easier when he looked so comical. Between Aria and Rope, they'd chosen an old mare for Baxter who wouldn't be tempted to stampede across the prairie.

Aria waved and grinned. She shouted, "We told Carly we'd handle this."

I didn't want to get the animals stirred up, so I didn't holler back but gave a thumbs up. The sand was damp from a meandering shower, but not enough to make puddles. Cows huffed but only gave an occasional moo, clearly a relaxed operation.

Aria must have rounded up the herd alone. It wasn't a great feat for an experienced hand, but I hadn't expected a city girl to accomplish it.

Baxter sat on the horse, hands wrapped around the saddle horn, scowling at the world, and looking tense enough a good whack with a bat would shatter him.

Hooves clattered up the ramp and the side panels clanked as the load shifted and the cattle stirred inside. As the driver and Aria followed the last of the cows up the chute and he closed the door and slid a bolt in place, I couldn't resist any longer and walked back to where Baxter hunkered on the dozing horse. "Howdy, cowboy." I didn't try to hide my amusement.

He glared at me. "Shut up. I'm only doing this to help out Carly."

"You can get down now. The work's all done."

He looked to the left, maybe hoping if he didn't see me, I'd magically vanish, a trick Poupon could have told him wouldn't work. When I didn't, he said, "I sprained my ankle. It's why I'm on the damned horse and not on foot. Aria decided I'd be more help back here in the saddle than hanging in the pickup with Rope."

If he'd been any help at all I'd be surprised. Aria must have positioned Baxter back here mainly so he'd feel like he was helping. Resourceful and kind. A lot to like there. "So, you're stranded until someone helps you down?"

The truck door slammed, and the engine started up and Aria joined us. "He looks good up there, doesn't he?"

We looked at each other, both suppressing laughter, and then, as if on cue, it burst like a flood.

"Very funny," Baxter said. With one rein in each hand, he tried to tug to the right and make the sleepy horse go to the barn. Of course, the horse didn't make any move.

That made us laugh even harder.

In frustration, Baxter kicked, startling the horse not from pain, but probably because Baxter let out a yell when he jarred his ankle. The horse meandered toward the barn and we followed, not bothering to resist our guffaws.

When we'd had our fill of laughing at Baxter, Aria sobered. "Sorry you had to make the trip but I'm glad you came out here anyway. I wanted to get your advice."

What could I possibly know that she didn't? Medical knowledge, cow sense, financial acumen, cultural icon, she had it all. "Sure."

Though the grass in the pasture was fading to golds and some reds, it still had enough nutrition to graze. Carly had sold off the bulk of the herd, keeping only her best breeding cows that could be cared for by one person. She planned to restock when she could be here full time. With few cattle on the place and only a couple of horses, the forage would be plenty to take care of Bar J's needs for the next year. The sun felt warm, but the breeze kept everything fresh. September days could be like this, golden and perfect.

"The real reason we're in the Sandhills is not so Glenn can advise Carly. I pushed him to bring me out here because I've got a plan."

It sparked my curiosity—what plan could involve the Sandhills? A few years ago, preppers came out here to live off-grid. Maybe Aria was turning one hundred percent granola.

"I want to raise Scottish Highlands cattle."

Huh. She wanted to breed cattle? Not what I expected.

Her excitement fizzed. "They are the red ones, with horns and all the hair, not really tall."

"Yeah, I know what Highlands are. Why would you want to do that?"

How could you not fall for her enthusiasm and bubbly laughter. I didn't blame Baxter one bit. "Aside from the fact they are adorable, there's a big market for them. It's not uncommon for one heifer alone to bring seven thousand dollars."

As if she needed more money, but holy cow. Or heifer. Literally.

"I've looked all over for a bit of land. I only need maybe five hundred acres or so. Just enough for forty head. As you probably know, small parcels are hard to come by. But I love it here. And if Glenn is helping Carly, he'll have a reason to be here."

What would it be like to blithely say she wanted to buy five hundred acres? That could run her upwards of half a million dollars. A ranch that size wouldn't support a family, unless you had the means to supply it with high priced livestock breeds. Most regular people around here didn't have that kind of money sitting around. And purebreds like that need more tending than a herd of black baldy beef cattle.

She'd brought up Baxter being out here and that made me think. "I don't know how much he'll be here. One person could manage what's here now. And if Carly puts the land in the environmental easement, the organization will manage what little needs to be done. Which won't be much since there won't be any cattle out here."

She eyed Baxter, who barely managed to keep his horse plodding toward the barn. "I probably shouldn't tell you this, but it's Glenn."

"What's Baxter?"

"The nonprofit who's leasing the Bar J. See, he knows Carly wants to come back in two years and that you aren't interested in managing it until then. So, he told her he found an organization to lease the ranch, but it's actually him. He made it up and gave it a bland name and is paying Carly. All legit. But he doesn't want Carly to know." She grinned at me. "He said she's stubborn like you, and if she finds out, she'll call it charity and won't do it, and then he's afraid she'll quit school early."

He'd go to that great length to help Carly? It melted my heart and I struggled to not admire him even more. "That's, uh. It's a lot."

She looked at me from the corner of her eye. "He promised Carly's father he'd look after her. Some pact from when they were at the military boarding school." She paused. "He's got a loyalty streak that runs deep as the Mariana Trench, and he never forgets anything. Probably one reason he's so successful."

We walked in silence for a second. Then she stopped and turned to me, making me stop, too. "All that loyalty and integrity causes him stress. And it's not good for him."

My heart jumped. I'd known it the minute I'd seen him yesterday. He'd looked peaked, as Grandma Ardith would say. Kind of the gray pallor he'd had the first time we met. And that cough. But he'd started an experimental treatment for his rare lung disease and had been better these last two years. I wanted Aria to tell me all the details, every single breath he took or didn't take. But he wasn't mine. I had no right to be anything but polite. "I'm sorry to hear that. Is he okay?"

She watched me but answered almost casually. "He's got the best doctors. He's in a cutting-edge study for lung ailments and, of course, I've got some connections as well. What he really needs is to relax more. I'm trying to convince him to step away from the network, but he's fighting me. If I could get him out here more—and take away his phone and computer —I'm sure it would help."

We started walking again and I kept my focus on the grass and sand under my feet. The doughy lump of worry forming in my own lungs wasn't mine to feel. Baxter had Aria to take care of him.

"Which brings me to what I want to ask you. Do you know of anyone who might be willing to part with a few acres?"

I exhaled deeply, at a loss.

She sounded excited. "I've been looking for someplace I belong for a long time. You know?"

Yeah, I knew.

"I've started and stopped a half dozen careers. Maybe it's because I never had a family like yours to anchor me."

Anchor or drown?

"From the moment we landed that silly 'copter on the meadow here I've felt such peace, and I think maybe this is where I really belong."

I didn't know which sentence she uttered ground at me most.

"So, I need to have one foot out here. Not a whole ranch with beef cattle. Something one person could handle."

It takes a lot of acres to make a living out here and people didn't often give up bits and pieces. "Troy Stryker owns a couple of sections close to town. He's fourth generation and lives in Denver. Never comes out here. But so far, he says he's not interested in selling."

She clapped her hands. "Perfect."

"I wouldn't hold out much hope. I suppose a hundred people have asked to buy that land and he's never budged."

The confident way she shrugged reminded me of Zoe. Again, I wished for that kind of swagger. "He hasn't been asked by me."

We made it to the barn to see Baxter had the horse in a stall and was dragging the saddle off her back.

Aria gasped. "Glenn! You shouldn't be on that ankle. It won't heal if you don't take care of it."

Baxter hugged the saddle to him when she reached for it. "You wrapped it tighter than a tourniquet. I'm fine." He must have heard the curt way he'd addressed her because he softened his face. "Didn't mean to snap at you."

She dropped a light kiss on his cheek and turned to the horse.

Baxter hobbled to the tack room. "Sorry you came all the way out here," he said when he walked by me.

I waved it away. "No problem."

Aria picked up a brush and gave the old horse a vigorous going over.

I watched Baxter struggle with the saddle but assumed he wouldn't want my help.

He grunted, clearly not used to lugging the awkward thing around. "Carly told me you got recalled. What are your plans now?"

Ouch. It felt like I wore "loser" embroidered across my chest. "Not sure. Maybe go back to school. Diane wants me to move to Denver and help her with her kids."

He chuckled. "Sounds like Diane. She knows how to spin someone's disaster to her best interests."

The last encounter he'd had with Diane hadn't been anyone's finest hour. Except maybe Roxy. "She thinks she can get me into a good job with her firm."

He slid the saddle on the bar, brushed his hands together, and snickered. "I can't picture you at a corporate job, locked inside all day."

Me, either. "I never thought I'd see you on a horse, so I guess we all might have hidden talents."

Aria laughed, "I'd hardly call it a talent. But your help was invaluable."

He scoffed and hobbled out to where Aria was finishing up with the horse.

My mind circled what I'd learned yesterday. Knowing the super-rich were a small club, I asked, "Have you guys ever had anything to do with Coleson Crenshaw?"

Aria burst out. "Ugh. He's an arrogant blowhard. Your typical old white guy who thinks the world is made for him." She glanced at Baxter. "Not like you, Glenn. You're not old, and you're kind and considerate and spend a great deal on saving the environment."

He grimaced. "White and male is enough of a bad label these days."

She placed her palms on his cheeks. "You poor, rich, baby."

Rich now, sure. But he hadn't started out that way.

Baxter considered. "Cole has been linked to all kinds of nefarious dealings. Especially with his energy company and mining."

"Yeah," I said. "I heard he wanted to open a pit mine in Arizona and got shut down."

Baxter gave me a questioning look. "You follow environmental issues now?"

I quirked my eyebrows at him. "I keep tabs on everything, as you know."

Aria threw an arm around my shoulder. "Don't underestimate this badass."

Baxter opened up with the first genuine smile I'd seen since he arrived. "Oh, I know better than that."

I gave them an "oh-please" look. "Actually, the attorney who lost that case was Sarah's brother. The rumor I heard is that Crenshaw wanted to groom him to eventually run for governor, but Garrett backed out and came home. And died two days ago in suspicious circumstances on their ranch."

Aria sucked in a breath. "Oh my god. I don't know who Sarah is, but—"

Baxter interjected. "Kate's sister-in-law and best friend. Married to Kate's favorite brother, Robert."

Aria froze and stared at him.

He shrugged. "It's a complicated web of relationships. Everyone is related to everyone in some way."

She nodded slowly. "Are you saying this brother of your sister-in-law was murdered? And he was working for Coleson Crenshaw and maybe botched a case? Or Crenshaw wanted him to be his political lackey and he bugged out?"

I heard how crazy it sounded but agreed. "Yep. The bad part is that Garrett has a ten-year-old son, and it looks like his mother might also have died recently."

Baxter said, "You don't know?"

I explained about the body found in Scottsdale, and all the while Aria wore a horrified expression. When I finished, she and Baxter exchanged a worried look.

I looked from one of them to the other. "What?"

Baxter gave Aria a dip of his head to go on. She did. "Two years ago, maybe more, I don't remember all the details. Cole supposedly was having an affair with a married woman. They said the husband found out and threatened to go public. Cole is married and didn't want to upset that arrangement—my guess is because of money since his wife is super-wealthy."

"Wait, isn't he rich, too?" I asked.

She acknowledged that with a tilt of her head. "Sure, but rich people are greedy. Anyway, bottom line is, the husband was murdered, and they questioned Cole, but he had great lawyers, and it went nowhere. What was really appalling was the woman had a kid. And she and the kid died in some freaky accident. I don't remember what. But the suspicion was that Cole had them all taken out."

I snorted in disbelief. "Why would he kill a child?"

Aria said, "I've heard people say that her son knew all about the affair and Cole wanted to shut him up. We'll never know because it looked like an accident. I think one of those true crime shows did a series about it, but they couldn't really accuse him because of libel laws."

Baxter chimed in. "It sounds outlandish. But I know Cole. We've been on some environmental boards and done the gala junk, and he's got one creepy vibe. I'd believe he could be a kid-killer."

Garrett was dead. Sheila might be dead. Tony told me he'd seen Gregory Fisher at their house arguing with his dad. "You said you've dealt with Crenshaw in your environmental work. Is his company Evergreen Enterprises?"

Aria nodded. "Yes. Why?"

I was already racing toward my car.

Behind me, Baxter shouted my name. "He's dangerous. Be careful."

23

As soon as I got onto the highway heading south, I called Sarah. It took several rings, an answer and hang up, and a few more rings after I called again. "Sorry." She sounded worn out. "Brie brought me my phone and we had a few missteps. I called Dad. He didn't sound so bad. I guess it wasn't a full-fledged heart attack. Or it could have been, but Zoe stopped it."

I raced down the highway. "Did you talk to him about your mother's accusations?"

She spoke slowly, as if she pushed the words out. "I started to but all he wanted to know was if Mom was okay and why she wasn't there. I told him she was with me and that seemed to really upset him. The way he was so worried about her, I didn't have the heart to ask if he'd been using her for a punching bag all these years. It makes me more worried about Mom. I think she's losing it. I mean, she seems way worse than I've ever seen her. As soon as Robert gets home, I'm going to take her to a doctor."

"Did she say anything else about Alden?"

She lowered her voice. "Yeah. She said she really hoped he didn't get out of the hospital because she thinks he's dangerous. But she's been rattling on about what a great pianist she is and doing concerts in Baltimore when she and Tony are there. She's not taking that boy anywhere.

She's batshit crazy. I have no problem thinking she made up stuff about Dad. Not that she doesn't believe it."

I thought about Alden and the rage we'd seen boiling under the surface. "When I saw him yesterday, I got the feeling he was losing control of his temper. Zoe's convinced he killed Garrett." Sarah sounded so weary, I hated throwing this at her.

"He processes all emotions by getting mad."

Who did that remind me of? Only, Sarah wasn't violent.

"Since he just lost his only son, I'm not surprised he's full of rage," Sarah continued. "But he'd never hurt his family. I mean, he threatened to kick us off the ranch because apparently all I do is bring more mouths to feed onto the place and Robert can't stick around long enough to get the east pivot put up."

"That sounds nuts. Especially since Robert's off getting parts so he can mow the alfalfa."

"That's my point. He spouts off. He's mad. He's not going to do anything about it. How often have you heard Diane say she's going to kill someone because they didn't do what she wanted?"

She was right. But my heart still raced. Not because I thought Alden was a threat, but because Gregory Fisher, Mr. Van Dyke and probably Crenshaw's man, could be out there anywhere. "You said Ellie is still there? And Tony?"

"Yeah. Tony is keeping Brie occupied but she's due for a nap. Mom is outside watering the mums. I'm about ready to pass out. And I think this baby is ready to sleep finally. I'm going to leave Mom and Tony on their own and the girls and I are going down."

"When will Robert be home?"

"Not until late. The dealer is waiting on a UPS delivery, so it's going to be a long night for him."

"For you, too, with a newborn." I didn't want to worry Sarah more, and the idea that Tony was in danger seemed pretty remote. I'd stop by her place on my way home and hang out until Robert got there. "I'm heading out to the Blume. Want to look around and see if I can find out who Garrett was afraid of."

"Keep me posted. I'd love to help but I can't keep my eyes open."

I called Zoe as soon as I hung up to fill her in before I lost service. I let her know what Aria and Baxter said and that I wanted to take another look around Garrett's house to see if I could find some threat from Evergreen Enterprises.

I heard a grin in her voice. "That's fine. But, you know, thinking that Gregory Fisher murdered Garrett and his wife, and maybe wants to take out Tony is even crazier than Alden killing Garrett."

I thought about what Sarah said. "Someone had to think through killing Garrett. Electrocution isn't a crime of passion. I'm not saying Alden couldn't have flown into a rage and murdered his son, but I can't picture him planning it out. That's psychotic and Alden is frustrated, not crazy."

She didn't sound convinced. "You go after your theory, and I'll go after mine. I think I'll drive to Broken Butte and talk to Alden."

Seemed like as good a plan as any. We agreed to meet up later and compare notes.

I drove the rest of the way in silence, kind of missing Zoe's conversation. I didn't try to start anything with Poupon. He wouldn't answer the way Zoe did.

I rolled down the windows to let in the last of the afternoon. Even though the day had been full of sunshine and golden fall glow, the approaching evening carried a tinge of chill, and more clouds clustered like witches calling a coven. I may not be as worn thin as Sarah, but fatigue drummed in my temples and the dreary weather wasn't giving me a boost.

I couldn't help craning my neck to look at the pivot when we passed. The sight settled a heavy weight in my chest. The field was pocked with more purple blooms. Ideally, a field should be cut at just 10% flowered. Robert and I needed to get out there right away. Maybe tomorrow.

The house hadn't changed any from the night I'd spent there with Tony, but it looked abandoned somehow. I parked and let Poupon out. He stepped lively to the porch, probably thinking he'd see Tony.

I didn't bother to knock, just turned the knob. I hadn't locked it when we left, but most people never locked their homes out here. I pushed open the door and froze at the threshold.

"Stop," I commanded Poupon.

Maybe he read the shock and urgency in my voice because he halted and swung his head around to me.

I gave his collar a gentle tug back to the porch. "You wait here." And much to my surprise, he sat his butt down.

It took me a second to let the shock work through and get my breath. I didn't want him disturbing the scene inside. When Tony and I left, the place had been tidy. We'd even done the breakfast dishes. Now it looked like a category four tornado had ripped through it. Couch cushions and pillows strewn all over. Drawers pulled out and upended, scattered paper and debris everywhere.

I took tentative steps toward the kitchen and discovered all the cabinets had been emptied, glass and silverware littered the floor.

The place had been tossed. Whoever had done it had searched thoroughly. I minced my way toward the bedrooms, knowing I'd find them in the same state.

I assumed Gregory Fisher had paid a visit. And he hadn't been nearly as thoughtful a guest as I'd been. I didn't touch anything for fear of contaminating any prints, and I pulled my phone out to call Trey. Remembered there was no signal and used the landline, needing to look up his number. How did we used to live this way?

While I talked, I scanned the room. The silverware was tossed with old *Esquire* magazines, sofa pillows and those silly three-legged chairs looked as if they'd slid across the wood floor like the intruder had played shuffleboard. Thank God Tony hadn't been here.

After I told Trey what I'd found, he said, "I'll send a crime scene team up there. They won't make it for another hour or two, though."

"I don't know what he was looking for or if he found it. But I'm not going to stick around. I want to check on Tony, make sure he's okay."

"Why wouldn't he be?"

"I don't know." And that was the truth.

I gave him the information about Gregory Fisher and Evergreen Enterprises, and updated him on Alden. "This Gregory Fisher gave me the heebie jeebies. And seeing this...I think he could be dangerous."

"Noted," Trey said. "We'll get on it immediately. In the meantime, you and Zoe keep your eyes open."

I rubbed my forehead against the worry. "All of this seems like bits and pieces that don't fit together. And if you add Sheila's possible death in with it, we've got a bowl of spaghetti and no way to straighten the noodles."

He sighed. "It's complicated. I'll put someone on Evergreen Enterprises and Gregory Fisher, though I'd be surprised if that's a real name."

"I doubt you'll find any connection with Crenshaw. He's too smart and slippery."

"Probably, but I'll call a friend in the FBI and see if he can help."

I couldn't think of anything else, but the fear was a hard pit in my gut.

Trey seemed ready to get to work. "Okay, then. You know, I think Zoe Cantrel is going to work out well, but she's young and pretty headstrong."

I laughed. "I've heard that said about another sheriff."

He probably grinned back. "That sheriff worked out pretty well. Taught me to give a newbie some slack."

We hung up and I collected Poupon from where he'd been napping on the porch. It appeared that Garrett had reason to be frightened of Coleson Crenshaw and his henchmen. But if Fisher had killed Garrett and come here looking for whatever evidence Garrett might have against Crenshaw, what could that have been?

Garrett was always on his phone whenever he was away from the house and gained a signal. If he and Tony were reduced to old technology, maybe they had an answering machine. It might hold some clue.

I went back inside and picked my way through the living room until I found the machine. No blinking light, so no unheard messages. Just to be sure, I hit the play button and listened.

There were messages from Alden, sounding exasperated and complaining about Garrett being late on mowing the alfalfa. I couldn't argue about that; I'd be cranky if it'd been my field losing its best harvest. Not a hanging offense, though. One from Sarah for Tony. "If you're bored, get your dad to let you ride the quad to our place, I'll let you play Minecraft. Tell him Aunt Sarah said it's safe and only ten miles on country roads." That was nice of Sarah.

The last message was from Ellie offering to make runzas if her boys wanted to come for dinner.

No clues there. I closed the door behind me and was halfway to the car when a freight train slammed into my chest. "Oh, no. Damn it!"

I ran back inside and dialed Sarah. No answer. I hung up and dialed again, hoping she was sending Brie to get it, or maybe waking from a nap and groggy. Or maybe she'd turned the ringer off so they could sleep. "Come on, Sarah. Pick up. Pick up."

When it slid to voicemail, my heart nearly exploded with fear. If Gregory Fisher had the same idea I did about outdated technology, and he'd punched the answering machine, he'd know Tony had an aunt who lived close. It wouldn't be too tough to find a Sarah living within a ten-mile radius. Especially for a professional fixer.

I jumped in the cruiser and buried the gas pedal.

24

Obviously, I breathed on the endless dash to Sarah's, but I wouldn't be able to prove it. Damn that Robert was in Omaha. Curses that I hadn't taken the Gregory Fisher threat seriously enough. I prayed I'd find Sarah napping and mad as a hornet I'd woken them up. That Tony would be playing Minecraft on Sarah's couch while Ellie nattered about whether they should have macaroni and cheese or beanie weenies for supper. But I couldn't do anything except raise dust on the country road and slide around every curve.

After what seemed like three moon cycles, the house came into view. Ellie's pickup was no longer out front. I couldn't spare a thought for her right now. Not until I knew Sarah, Tony, and my little nieces were safe. My tires slid as I braked in front of the house. Again, I threw Poupon's door open and left him to fend for himself as I ran for the porch, hopped the steps, and burst into the house.

Oh God!

The smell of propane nearly choked me. It hung thick in the air. "Sarah!" I screamed her name and bounded through the living room on the way to her bedroom. I needed to hurdle a Little People house of Brie's and watch my step to miss a sippy cup.

I probably screeched her name in an endless wail until I saw her closed door. I wrenched it open to find Sarah sitting up on the bed, a quilt drooping from her shoulders. She blinked and frowned and immediately reached for Olivia, who was cuddled by her side and had started to kick. Brie lay on Sarah's other side with her thumb resting between her lips. She opened her eyes and gazed at me in bewilderment.

"What the hell, Kate?" Sarah had confused eyes and furrowed brow, struggling to clear fog while she fumbled one-handed with the clasp on her nursing bra. I didn't think she registered the gas smell, though the bedroom door had been closed and the window open.

"Out." I ran to the other window and struggled with the sticky frame. Dratted old houses with their wood windows. "Gas. Out, now." I whisked Brie from the bed and lunged for the door.

Brie let out a shriek of fear and cried out for her mama. That stabbed my heart for the poor, brave little tiger.

Sarah stumbled after me, baby clutched to her. She must have got her first whiff of the gas. "Shit. What's going on?"

I took the porch steps in one leap, nearly colliding with Poupon. He barked and hopped to the side like we were playing tag, then followed me as I jetted to the other side of the drive and deposited Brie next to him.

Sarah was on my heels.

"Tony?" I asked.

Sarah glanced around for Ellie's pickup. "Damnit, Mom must have taken him home with her."

At least that was something. A bumbling Ellie couldn't be as dangerous as Gregory Fisher. But if he found out Tony wasn't here, he might figure out about Ellie and Alden's connection to Tony and be on his way there soon. I ran back toward the house.

Sarah tried to grab my arm but missed. "Don't. It's bad in there."

Before I ducked in the door, I gulped twice and sucked in a long breath. The most logical place to look was the kitchen and I bee-lined through the living and dining room. The gas stove stood along the far wall. One glance told me all the burners were cranked on and the oven door wide open, no flames, just gas spewing. Maybe there was a candle lit somewhere. Maybe Gregory Fisher meant to gas them and not burn them.

I held my breath long enough to turn the gas off but ended up having to inhale before I got the danged old wooden kitchen windows open. I gagged and it felt like my nose hairs shriveled. With one gasp of fresh air from the opened window, I rushed back outside to Sarah sitting in the road nursing Olivia, and Brie patting Poupon's curls.

"We need to get you out of here," I said.

Sarah's brown eyes held a combination of confusion, worry, anger, and mostly exhaustion. "You didn't find the leak? We can't just leave the house to blow up."

"Someone set the stove to gas you. I think it might be someone working for the man who killed Garrett. Coleson Crenshaw."

Her brows shot up. "THE Coleson Crenshaw? Why would Garrett be involved with someone like that? We saw this true crime show about him."

I glanced at Brie and decided even if she was listening, she wouldn't understand. "It's possible Sheila has been murdered."

Sarah gasped. "What? By Coleson Crenshaw?"

I waved that away. "Not conclusive. But Garrett's place was tossed, and I'm worried whoever killed Garrett and maybe Sheila is coming after Tony."

She shook her head. "But he's a little boy. That doesn't make sense."

Where would Sarah and the kids be safe? I could take them to my place, but I wouldn't be there to protect them because I needed to find Gregory Fisher. Unless you were hungry, Louise couldn't help. Douglas lived too far away. I landed on an idea. "Whether it makes sense or not, I don't want to take the chance any of you are in danger. We'll swing by and get Tony and Ellie and I'll take you to Carly's." No one would figure out that connection and if they did, Aria and Baxter were there.

A sputtering motor sounded from down the road, and we turned to see a quad buzzing toward us. As it neared, we identified Tony.

Brie jumped up and down, making Poupon dance, too. "Tony. Tony. Tony."

In the past few months, I'd wondered if Tony had any redeeming qualities, but if he'd charmed his little niece, who could be as discerning as her mother, he couldn't be all bad.

Tony pulled up and shut off the engine, covering us in a plume of dust. Boys, even those beloved by toddlers, were generally oblivious about dirt.

Sarah popped a bright-eyed baby from her breast and lowered her shirt. "Did you go with Mom? Is she okay? What are you doing back here?"

He straddled the seat and hoisted Brie to sit in front of him. She grabbed the handles and pretended to drive. "She's fine." He pleaded with Sarah. "I'm sorry, okay. I tried to tell you I don't want to go back there. Grandma is smothering me, man. And she's, like, so weird. Calling me her little man and saying how I'm going to save the day. It's creepy."

I frowned at him. "You ran away?"

He tilted his head sideways as if challenging me. "It's not running away if you're going back to where you're supposed to be. Gramps told her to leave me here. He'd be mad if we disobeyed him." He made meaningful eye contact with Sarah. "And we know we don't want to make Gramps mad."

Sarah stood and the baby's head dropped on her shoulder. "Does Mom know where you are?"

He rested his chin on Brie's head and let her wag it back and forth. "Maybe."

Sarah drilled him with a look.

"Probably not. She said she was going to lie down and so I kind of went for a ride."

I threw in, "I wonder she didn't hear the motor."

The side of his mouth tipped up in a sly look. "Could be because I pushed it until I got away from the house."

"Tony," Sarah warned. "We need to call her and tell her you're okay."

He gave her a whine, like any ten-year-old would. "Come on, Sarah. She'll only come get me again and take me prisoner and it's getting gross the way she keeps telling me about how much fun we're going to have together when we get to Maryland."

This time I agreed with Tony. "You can call her later. I think the gas has probably dissipated enough you can grab a few things you need, and then let's go. Tony is safer with you."

25

While Sarah filled the diaper bag, I grabbed a few things for Brie. Tony ran out to the shop to get Sarah's pickup and drove it to the house. Despite Alden saying Tony was worthless, he was catching on to some of the fun of being a country kid.

Brie insisted on riding with Sarah, and Tony wanted to be with Brie, so Sarah ended up with all the kids. We didn't cave when Brie begged to load Poupon with them, so the two of us followed in my cruiser.

After calling Baxter to alert him and Aria that we were on the way and why, I called Trey and Zoe. Zoe's phone flipped to voicemail, so I assumed she was with Alden. Trey said he'd send the crime scene team to Sarah's after they finished at the Blume. Maybe they could find fingerprints, but I doubted it.

The sun sank while we drove, taking the day with it, leaving behind cold clouds that clung to their rain, only giving off enough moisture to make everything feel damp and ominous.

Aria and Baxter met us at the old ranch house that had been built by Carly's great- grandparents. They'd opened the windows to let fresh air in, which Sarah was grateful for.

"I made spaghetti," Aria announced.

Baxter beamed at her. "And bread. She baked a couple of loaves this afternoon so I'm glad you're here to share it. A person should only eat so much bread, but when it's fresh, I can't resist."

It's too bad I couldn't hate Aria, but her perfection could be annoying.

I surprised Sarah—and me—when I gave her a hug. "Sorry I made you come all the way out here. Until I figure out what's going on and who's behind all of this, I want you safe. Try to get some rest."

She turned her head from me, and when she spoke with a cracked voice, I figured it was to hide tears. "You old worry wart. But look, someone cooked me dinner and all I have to do is take care of the kids. This is practically a vacation."

I pointed my finger at Tony. "You help your old auntie and keep an eye on Brie. Or I'll hog tie you and take you back to Ellie's."

He gave me a serious nod that convinced me he'd do his best.

Aria and Baxter walked me to the porch. "We'll take care of them," Aria said.

I watched Sarah plop down on the old couch, looking like she'd crossed the Mohave on foot. "Someone tried to hurt them. I doubt anyone could figure out where they are now, but I feel better with you here."

Baxter and I made eye contact and a spark flashed before he looked away almost immediately. "Of course."

I hesitated and addressed them both, though I meant it more toward Aria. "Do you have a gun?"

Her look was grave. "No. But I know how to shoot."

I'd hoped as much. I pulled my gun from my holster and handed it to her. "I pray you don't need it."

They stood on the porch and watched me drive away.

I hated not being here to keep an eye on them, but I needed to find Gregory Fisher or get Trey to somehow stop Coleson Crenshaw from targeting Sarah's family.

Night officially started its shift. With the clouds so full and heavy, a dirty gray covered the sky, the clouds themselves illuminating the sky to keep the night from a blackout.

I called Trey on my way to town, but he didn't have anything to add. "Sheesh, Kate. We only started looking into it this afternoon. The crime scene guys picked up prints and they'll need to eliminate you and Haney to see if anything else shows up. Same with Sarah's house. Crenshaw is out of the country, so that's a dead end, not that he'd be doing anything himself. And no Gregory Fisher in the right age."

That wasn't any comfort. I thanked him and dialed again. Still no answer from Zoe. I needed to gas up the cruiser and maybe grab some of Fredrickson's finest pizza again—if it hadn't been in the warmer for longer than an hour.

Ten minutes later I stood under the bright lights pumping gas and drumming my fingers on the roof as the first giant drops of rain exploded against the canopy. A gust of cold wind ruffled my hair and tugged a few strands loose from my ponytail.

Tuff Hendricks pulled up in his Ford F250 on the opposite side and jumped out to fuel up. In his mid-twenties, he was broad-shouldered and had the hard muscles of someone who worked outside all day. He gave me the same pained look he'd offered when he was in grade school, and I'd tripped over a hurdle at a track meet. He'd always rooted for me. "Sorry about the recall. You were a great sheriff."

I clicked my tongue. "Nice of you to say even after the two speeding tickets I gave you."

He winked at me. "It's all the others you didn't give me that matter more."

I watched the dollars adding up on the pump, thinking that I'd miss driving around on county gas. But I wouldn't be doing that much driving if I wasn't protecting and serving the citizens of Grand County. "You'd best watch your heavy foot from now on. The new sheriff is a tough one."

He laughed. "I went to high school with Zoe Cook. She's not a problem."

My pump clacked off. "She's Zoe Cantrel now, and I don't think she's going to take guff off anybody."

Headlights swept across us as a car whipped into the station and braked in front of the store. I nearly lost my breath when I realized it was a black Cadillac with Arizona plates. Gregory Fisher opened his car door and set a loafer-clad foot onto the concrete. The patron goddess of investigation—whoever that was—smiled on me.

I slammed the handle back into the pump, leaving my gas cap

dangling and the car where it was. While the rain wetted the pavement and blew across the parking lot, I watched Gregory Fisher push out of the Cadilac and tuck the back of his golf shirt into his khakis. He frowned at the sky as if insulted by the rain. That silly beard called attention to itself.

I dashed across the lot while he turned and headed for the door. He had barely gone two steps when I barreled into him. My 5'3" and a hundred-twenty pounds shoved him several feet to slam into the windows with a mighty crash.

His eyes flew wide before squinting into fight mode and he grimaced, yellowed teeth amid the dark whiskers. "What the hell?" He jerked back but not with any real purpose.

Before he could corner his shock at being attacked by a petite woman, I leaned on him, my hand grasping one of his wrists, the other reaching for my cuffs. With the skill and timing I'd learned goat tying at rodeos as a kid, and the muscle memory of playing Cuff 'Em with my nieces and nephews, I smacked the cuffs on his wrist and yanked his other down and clipped it, too. Because I'm smaller than most, including bulls and horses, I've learned to use surprise to my advantage.

Too bad for Gregory Fisher, he hadn't developed quicker reactions. He still looked like he was gathering for a fight when I'd already corralled him. "You can't—"

Tuff said, "Whoa," with unmasked admiration.

With one hand on the collar of his polo shirt and one on his cuffed hands, I jerked Fisher around and shoved him against the building. "Why are you here?"

Gregroy Fisher was over two hundred pounds of pure muscle. Even with his hands cuffed behind his back, he was a handful. He struggled against me, and it took all my strength to keep my feet planted. Fisher's lips curled back, little porcine eyes sparked with malice. "I stopped for a pop and snack. What is your problem?"

Tuff sprang to my side. "You need some help?"

I didn't look at him. "Thanks. Stay back. For now." Then I spoke to Fisher. "I want to know who you work for and what you're doing in Grand County."

That stupid triangle of a black beard didn't hide his thin lips curled in a snarl. "That's my business."

I grabbed hold of his shirt, yanked him toward me, and slammed him into the store again. Good thing he kept underestimating me. If he'd been expecting it, I'd never have been able to manhandle him. "I've got no problem tossing you into a cell and keeping you there."

"You can't do that."

Tuff hadn't moved behind me, but I could sense he was ready to spring into action. "If she has any trouble, I'm right here to help her out. Trust me, you don't want to get on her bad side. She's got the whole county backing her up."

Shut up, Tuff. I kept my focus on Fisher. "Never mind talking to me. You can save it for when your lawyer gets here. But understand, the nearest airport is hours away from here."

He jerked from side to side. It wasn't easy hanging on to a guy nearly twice my size without clenching my teeth and grunting, but I'd had a lifetime of not letting my brothers and sisters know they bugged me. Whatever else I got from my family, I'd learned to keep a poker face. "I don't know what you think you've got on me, honey, but this is harassment."

It didn't make his situation any worse, but calling me honey didn't help it any. "I'm arresting you for the murder of Garrett Haney."

He let out a disbelieving ha. "That's rich. He was alive and kicking last time I saw him. You can't get me for that."

I jerked him away from the building, startling Tuff. With me shoving Fisher every step, I walked us to my cruiser. "I can. I have a witness you were at his house before he was murdered. And I have evidence you tossed his house." I didn't, but he didn't know that.

He pulled back. "A witness? No one even lives around here. Witness. A horse? Wait, a cow?"

"You can figure out your excuses in jail while you wait for your lawyer."

He resisted my bulldozing, causing the cold rain to drizzle on my neck and making me even madder. I'd had about all I was going to take from this sleaze bag. When he balked one too many times, I bumped my knee into his rear end. Not enough to bruise, but enough for him to feel it.

Tuff let slip a soft snort from where he followed on my heels.

Fisher smelled none-too-fresh, like a guy who'd been too long without a shower, with a garlicky kind of undertone. When he twisted his pointy chin over his shoulder, his breath was even worse. "If I killed Haney, why would I be hanging around? Honey, I'd have been long gone by now."

I opened the back door to Poupon, who'd been slobbering and dancing in the back seat waiting impatiently for his Slim Jim. If he'd had the usual poodle grooming with manicured face and clipped ears, he might not have been imposing. But I preferred the natural look, so he appeared to be any old big, hairy dog. And he'd been anticipating his treat. A gaping, slathering mouth greeted me, and he looked ready to take a bite out of the nearest hand.

Fisher pulled back and shouted in alarm. "Jesus H. Christ."

Maybe the raindrops were laced with luck. Poupon didn't usually scare anyone except Newt Johnson. "He's trained to attack on command."

Tuff let out a strangled noise that might have been shock, but was more likely a stunted laugh.

Fisher's head whipped left and right, and his pig eyes glistened in fear. He jerked me back to avoid the vicious beast. "Okay. Okay. Yeah. I was out there."

For the first time in the three years I'd been calling him my deputy, Poupon had finally earned the title. I swung the door closed and pushed Fisher against the car. "Why were you there?"

He sucked his thin lips between his teeth and his gaze traveled to Tuff, who seemed poised to put a fist in Fisher's face. If the ridiculous fluff Poupon inspired fear in Fisher, maybe Tuff would keep him on edge, too.

I raised my eyebrows to urge Fisher to talk.

"I work for Evergreen Enterprises. You could call me a kind of a fixer."

I folded my arms and glared at him. "And you *fixed* Garrett Haney."

"Haney really screwed over the company. He didn't file paperwork with the court and screwed up the whole thing. They hired a new lawyer to take over. But Haney, he takes off without handing over the proprietary information and all the trial docs. I got sent to find them."

"And to kill Garrett," I said.

"Whoa." More from Tuff.

Fisher threw his chin back. "I already told you I didn't kill Garrett. I don't do that kind of work."

It felt like he almost added *anymore*.

He bit his lower lip, drawing that stupid beard toward his mouth. "Evergreen wanted the papers."

"You work for Coleson Crenshaw. He's not known for gentle ways."

He looked puzzled. "I guess I work for Crenshaw in the way a Walmart greeter worked for Sam Walton. Crenshaw doesn't give two goddamns about what I do."

"But Crenshaw had his eyes on Garrett and Garrett let him down."

Fisher shrugged, trying to regain some of his tough-guy persona. "If Crenshaw offed everyone who turned him down, he'd be swimming in corpses."

Had I been chasing zebras when the hoofbeats had been horses, as Trey accused?

His eyes flicked to the closed door and Poupon slobbering in the backseat.

"What about turning on the gas at the other ranch house?"

If he was lying, the guy was better than either Diane or Carly could hope to be. Real confusion shone in his eyes.

I circled my finger to tell him to keep talking. "You went out to the ranch and had words...."

Fisher seemed like he wanted credit for his work. "It wasn't easy to find that place. Figuring out that Haney was out in this wasteland wasn't hard once I tracked down his family. Haney isn't an uncommon name, and I located his parents. But you got all these ranches out here and no street names, just dirt roads going no place. And maps don't show what I needed."

Which is why having a sheriff who's lived here forever is helpful.

The more he talked, the more he sounded like a mobster. "But, yeah, I found the place and then Haney says he doesn't have the docs. But I know he's lying. I'm gonna go back the next day and offer him the payout I was authorized for. I mean, they gave me five grand to entice Haney to turn over the docs, but if I can get it for less, then, that is a bonus for me, right? So, I let them stew about it for a day. But then the dipshit gets himself killed. So now, what am I gonna do, right? I go back to my boss and say I didn't get the docs, then I lose my job."

Sure, I knew how devastating unemployment could be.

"So, yeah, I searched the house. Didn't find anything. And now I got to drive all the way back to Scottsdale and that ain't gonna be fun."

A rattle and squeal of tires made us all spin around.

Zoe sped under the canopy, leaving wet tire tracks behind her. Window down, she hollered at me. "He's gone."

Her intensity set my nerves jangling. "What? Who?"

She waved her arm. "Come on. Alden Haney left the hospital, probably two hours ago. I tried to call but you didn't pick up."

"My phone is—" I'd called Trey and heard another call come in but had forgotten about it.

If Fisher was telling the truth about not killing Garrett, and Alden was at large, then....

I grabbed Fisher by the shoulders and shoved him toward Tuff. Reaching into my pocket for the key to the cuffs, I handed it to Tuff. "Take him to the courthouse and put him in the cell. The key is in the lower drawer of the file cabinet. Stay with him until someone official shows up."

"Hey," Fisher said. "You can't do that."

Tuff looked proud and scared. "Whoa."

I ran to the passenger side of Zoe's pickup and shouted at Tuff. "Use the cruiser. Take care of my dog."

26

While we drove, I called Sarah. She didn't answer her phone. Of course, bad weather would disrupt cell service. The landline at the old house had been disconnected. I called the new house where Baxter and Aria were staying, but they didn't answer either. I assumed they were at the old house with Sarah and the kids.

Knowing Gregory Fisher wasn't after them gave me some relief.

But someone had killed Garrett. And if that hadn't been Fisher, then that left Alden. I tried to call Ellie, but no one picked up that phone, either.

Another call to Trey to tell him about Alden's escape and catch him up on Gregory Fisher. He said he'd send a trooper to the courthouse to retrieve Fisher and question him. I left it up to them to charge him with breaking and entering or let him go.

I stared down the road, as if I could help Zoe maneuver in the barrage of rain. "If Alden killed Garrett, what about Sheila?"

She frowned at the windshield. "You said Alden went to Scottsdale about the time Sheila disappeared. And isn't that when Sarah said Ellie started slipping?"

"I can't see Alden as a serial killer. He'd have no reason to kill Sheila."

Zoe mulled that over. "Alden told us Garrett's place was on the ranch, but Sheila hated it here. Maybe he got rid of Sheila to clear the way for Garrett to come back. But then, Garrett was a disappointment, as Alden said, so he got rid of him, too. Hoping Tony would fulfill all their dreams of a male ranching legacy."

Rain sheeted the windshield and I struggled to see the road even though I wasn't driving. The whoosh of the tires on the road added a sense of urgency. "That's crazy."

The back tires slid to the right and I sucked in a breath, instantly seeing the heifers in bloody bits on the highway two days ago.

Zoe's teeth clenched as she counter steered one way and then the next until we righted. Our breath came heavy in the damp cab.

I wanted to tell her to slow down, that saving a few minutes wasn't worth us skidding off the road, but I was in too big a hurry to get there to worry about our safety.

After the sluice of wipers on the windshield and the rush of water under our wheels and a few more tense seconds of hydroplaning on the highway, we sailed up the dirt road to Haneys' house. Lights shone from the windows but there was no vehicle parked out front.

Zoe shut off her engine.

The rain would have masked our approach, so we didn't bother with much stealth as we ran to the front door. The cold drops smacked my face and one plopped into my eye. I hesitated a moment trying to decide whether to burst in with the element of surprise, knock and see if everything was okay, or ease the door open and sneak inside.

Zoe didn't wait for me to figure it out. She chose option number three, gently turned the knob and pushed across the threshold. We stopped inside and listened.

A moan of pain came from the kitchen at the back of the house. No longer sneaking, we clattered down the hall.

Nothing prepared me for what we found. Zoe must have felt the same way because we both stopped and stared.

The woman sprawled on a kitchen chair brushed blonde hair from her forehead and turned a mascara-streaked face our way. She panted and gasped. "Thank God. At least they sent someone to help me."

It had been a few years, and last time I'd seen her she'd had auburn hair, so I wasn't sure. "Sheila?"

Zoe stirred and approached her and that's when I saw the blood soaking the calf of her jeans. They were threadbare in places and rolled up past the ankles, probably an intentional and stylish worn look, but blood wasn't part of the chic. "Are you okay?" Zoe asked.

Sheila dropped her head back and moaned before whipping her focus back to Zoe. "Of course, I'm not okay. The bastard shot me. I may never walk again."

Stupid question but I was processing. "Alden shot you?"

Zoe knelt down and gingerly tugged at the denim on the side of Sheila's calf where it looked like a bullet might have torn it.

Sheila screamed. "Ow! Do you know what you're doing? Who are you, even?"

I pointed to Zoe. "She's the new sheriff and has had emergency medical training, so yes, she knows what she's doing." At least Zoe had the confidence of someone with expertise. "We've met before. I'm a friend of Sarah's, Kate Fox. The former sheriff."

None of that seemed to give her comfort. "I hate this nowhere, hillbilly, Godforsaken place. Where they can shoot you and leave you helpless and there's not one qualified professional to help."

I could see why Sarah didn't care much for her sister-in-law. "Did Alden take Ellie? Do you know where they were going?"

Sheila closed her eyes and winced. "I don't know. When I got here Ellie was sitting in a chair bawling and Alden was yelling at her. They didn't hear me drive up, I guess. I surprised them and Ellie jumped up and ran out. I didn't know she could move that fast. Alden went after her."

We got here too late. Alden was abusing Ellie and Sheila interrupted. Ellie ran and Alden was after her. I had to find them before he hurt her.

Zoe pulled out a multi-tool from her pocket, making me like her even more. She opened the blade and started to cut away the denim.

Sheila gasped. "Do you have to do that? These are bespoke."

Zoe ignored her and sliced the fabric.

I raised my voice. "Focus. This is important."

Sheila snapped back. "You don't have to tell me, I'm the one who's shot."

I glared at her.

She huffed. "I don't know what happened from there. All I wanted to know was where Tony and Garrett are. But those old coots are running around and yelling and the next thing I know Alden shoots me when my back is turned. I heard him yank the phone cord from the wall and doors slamming and they're gone and I'm lying in a pool of blood."

"How long ago?" I insisted. I'd be interested to know why she'd come for her family, but it was far less important than saving Ellie.

She threw up her hands. "I don't know. I'm suffering here. Doesn't anyone care I've been shot?"

Zoe gave her a deadpan comment. "We thought you were dead."

Sheila moaned again. "I might have been. I could bleed out if I don't get help."

Zoe allowed a small grin. "You're not going to bleed out. The bullet blew right on through. I imagine this hurts but you can brag about the scar." Zoe caught my eye. "Can you find a first aid kit?"

Sheila squeaked in distress. "A scar?"

I'd spent plenty of time at Sarah's when we were kids, which meant lots of bandages and disinfectant on skinned knees. I hurried to the bathroom and returned with the kit.

Sheila looked like a drowned raccoon with all her make-up and tears smearing her face.

Zoe took the kit and started cleaning the wound accompanied by Sheila's cries and moans. Sheila handled the situation exactly opposite of how Sarah would have. Put a bullet in Sarah and you might get a grunt or a wince. Scratch her child, and you'd better be able to run fast.

I shoved my face toward Sheila, and she blinked in alarm. "Think. Did Alden say where they were going?"

She bit her lips. "Wherever Ellie was going, I guess. Since I heard two cars drive off, I assume he's chasing her. In my own car. A Lexus isn't built for roads like these."

Zoe glanced up at me. "Do you think Sarah called Ellie and told her they'd gone to the Bar J?"

And Ellie was leading Alden there.

Zoe tilted her head to me. "Go. I'll take care of Sheila. Hurry."

I started down the hall, then whipped back to Zoe. "Tell her." I hated leaving Zoe with the awful task of informing someone their husband was dead. And probably murdered by his own father. "Just, fill her in."

Trial by fire, Zoe.

But I was already on the run.

27

The rain couldn't decide if it wanted to withhold its favors or give generously. I constantly adjusted the wipers on Zoe's old pickup as I raced through the night to the Bar J. I didn't take the route going south to the highway, through Hodgekiss, then up the highway on the west side. That's probably the way Ellie would go since she didn't get out much and didn't know the county as well as I did.

By going north on the gravel road, I could cut across Shorty Cally's winter range and come to the Bar J from the east. The rain made the road slick in spots, but Zoe's pickup had good tires that kept me on the road. Zoe would contact Trey. Sarah was out of reach. I called Milo Ferguson, the closest sheriff to the Bar J, but it would take him at least an hour to get there.

I loved the Sandhills mostly because of the open range. The endless hills with no signs of civilization. The quiet isolation. Tonight, I hated that vast prairie with its lack of roads and so many places hidden from human eyes. I needed to reach the Bar J, and time was running out.

I threw open every gate and left them that way. When this was all over, I only hoped various herds wouldn't be mixed and needing days to sort them all out.

In the darkness and rain, with the wipers beating a frantic rhythm, I followed a two-track trail across a pasture. Somehow, I lost it for several miles and had to drive along a fence line to find the gate from the western-most Cally pasture into the eastern edge of the Bar J. Three-quarters of an hour had already ticked by on the clock since I left the Haneys. I bumped cross-country, hoping I was moving in the right direction to intersect with ranch headquarters. I'd been out here enough times helping round up and work cattle, I had a feel for where the house should be. But it was taking too long. I could only hope Ellie kept her vehicle on the road and that Alden hadn't caught up to her.

It felt like crawling through loose sand leaving plenty of time for a crazed man to take out a whole town and escape. My logical mind told me that Ellie and Alden might be moving faster on paved roads, but they needed to travel twice the miles to reach the ranch, so chances were I'd get there sooner or at least not long after them. Probably. Maybe. But every inch felt like miles. I rounded the last hill and nearly shouted with relief to see lights spilling across the yard from the new house.

In a matter of minutes, I pulled in front of the house. Through the sweeping front windows of the great room I watched Aria crossing from the kitchen toward the fireplace. She paused at a sofa and leaned over, draping her arms around what I realized was Baxter's head. She planted a kiss on him, and it felt like a fist into my bruised heart.

They were supposed to be staying at the old house, not having a romantic getaway up here. Carly's house was fifty yards away, past the barn and corrals and a few other outbuildings. I squinted through the mist. Lights from the downstairs window of the old house broke against the gloom and sparked on the wet grass. My stomach dropped when I realized all my calculating about the route had been wrong. Ellie must have chan-neled a NASCAR driver to get here so fast. Where there should only have been Sarah's pickup, Haney's silver Ford and Sheila's Lexus were parked out front.

I slammed on the brakes and tore from Zoe's rig, racing through the sudden downpour and up the porch steps to the new house. When I barged into the foyer, Aria spun around and Baxter sprang to his feet and twisted toward me, a wince of pain sliding across his face.

He took in my dripping frenzy. "What's happened?"

"When did you leave Sarah?" I nearly shouted in my urgency.

Aria answered, her posture poised as if ready to jump into action. "About an hour ago. Tony and Brie went to bed upstairs, and she and the baby were dozing on the couch. It felt like we were disturbing them by being there. Why?"

I pushed my wet hair from my face and tried to think. "Alden and Ellie are parked out front. Alden chased Ellie out here and he's got a gun."

Baxter limped around the sofa to me. "Sarah's parents? He's got a gun? Are they here to protect Sarah?"

I couldn't take the time to explain so I blurted, "Alden's the murderer and I think he might be after Ellie and Sarah."

Aria's look of confusion shot between the two of us. I loved that she didn't ask for details but went to the important point. "A man with a gun is threatening them."

I nodded, my mind churning to make a plan. Tony and Brie were upstairs. Maybe Alden would leave them alone and deal with Ellie and Sarah first. Baxter's ankle was wrapped so he wouldn't be great on the fly. I spun around to the big window and stared at Carly's house, noting the windows. With the storm raging, it would be hard for anyone inside to hear or see me peeking in the porch window. "I need to see what's happening."

Aria seemed ready to join me. "If Alden's got a gun, don't you need one, too?"

Sure, that would be the easy way to do it. Like they do it in the movies, burst through the door, shout *Police, drop it.* "I gave it to you."

She and Baxter stared at each other as growing dismay colored their faces. Baxter said, "We left it with Sarah."

That could be good. Sarah would defend her children no matter what cost. "Alden won't expect me. And Sarah is smart and tough. Between the two of us, I think we can figure out how to disarm Alden." Sarah and I had wrangled cows and boyfriends. Worked our way through high school, college, marriages, childbirth, blizzards, and everything else. We could use every bit of our intuition and knowledge of each other to tag team taking down her father.

By the calculating look on his face, it appeared Baxter had been making his own plans. "The kids are upstairs. I know where there's an extension ladder in the barn. Aria and I'll get them out the window at the back of the house and bring them here." I loved his total faith in me.

Aria bolted for the row of hooks by the front door where their rain jackets were hanging. Baxter limped behind her. She didn't count him out because of his injury and neither did I. Of course, he'd do what he could to help the children without concern for himself.

I beat them out the front door. Tired of playing patty-cake, the rain bulleted down so hard it almost felt like hail. Cold and aggressive, it attacked, running down my neck and into my eyes as I raced toward the old house.

I passed between the pickup and Lexus. Something caught my eye and made me jerk against the pickup and peer into the Lexus window. Something—someone—smashed a hand against the window, leaving a smear of blood as it slid down.

Terrified I'd find Ellie in a pool of blood, I yanked open the passenger door, trying to shield the body from rain. The overhead light shed a yellowish glow on the blood-smeared steering wheel and dash and at the body in the front seat.

Alden slumped across the front seat, wheezing and groaning. His eyes squeezed closed. One hand clamped on his chest and a crimson blossom covered his shirt, with blood pooling on the leather seat under him. He blinked with effort and focused on me.

I lifted his hand and the blood gushed before I slammed it back down and cast about for anything to staunch the flow.

He panted. "Ellie."

Aria appeared behind me. She took a second to assess the situation. "Gun shot?"

Alden was barely able to give one weak nod.

She opened the back door and grabbed a white sweatshirt, something Sheila probably paid more for than I'd spend for a new TV. She shoved beside me and replaced Alden's hand with the sweatshirt, pressing down.

I shouted at Alden, "Where is Ellie?"

He sucked air in with difficulty. "Stop. Her."

A horrible thought started to form. "Ellie? She did this?"

His skin took on a chalky hue and he started to go limp.

Aria pressed on his wound and shouted. "Alden. Help us. Where is Ellie? Who is she with?"

With agonizing effort, he opened his eyes and looked at me. "I couldn't protect her. Failed."

I grabbed Alden's bloody hand. "What does she want?"

Raw pain filled his eyes, along with that hint of fight I recognized from Sarah. He'd lost everything, maybe even his life. But he struggled not to quit. "Tony. For." He winced and panted. "Herself."

Aria twisted her face to mine. "Glenn is getting the kids. I'll stay here. You go."

28

Ellie. The quiet woman who hardly left the house. The almost ghostly presence in the background of our lives, providing lunches and rides to town before we got our driver's licenses. The woman Sarah said was an object lesson for how she didn't want to be.

Ellie never seemed to have an opinion or a backbone. Helpless with ranch work, and not interested in even keeping the books for the business side. If Sarah and I thought of her at all, it was to wonder how she filled her life. Cooking and cleaning were only necessary chores for us as we plunged into ranching or, recently for me, being sheriff. We thought all Ellie did was read romance novels. And her life had moved on, leaving her looking at old age with nothing to show for it.

How could someone so ineffectual plan and carry out the electrocution of her own son? It seemed impossible this meek woman could point a gun at her husband of four decades and pull the trigger.

But she had. And now she threatened my best friend.

The battering rain covered my footsteps as I thundered toward the house and onto the porch. The picture window started about three feet from the porch floor and extended up four feet from there. Light from the living room spilled out, casting shadows from the well-used wicker chairs. Carly's great grandmother had covered the window with lace curtains and

Carly planned to take them down. She hadn't gotten around to that, thank goodness. I squatted next to the window and inched my face over so no quick movements would catch Ellie's eye.

The couch, with a slipcover Carly bought to not only hide the stains but contain the stuffing leaking from holes, was placed in front of the window, the back rising a few inches above the sill. Despite amassing a pile of money, Carly's granddad hadn't squandered much, if any, of it on his home.

Olivia was in her car seat on the floor in the middle of the living room on the threadbare and dingy carpet. She kicked her feet and waved her tiny fists, her face a mottled raspberry of wrath as her screams were masked by the thundering rain.

Sarah stood by a recliner that was covered in an old quilt. She looked pale and unsteady, supporting herself on a shaking arm propped on the chair. Her face was streaked with tears.

My first impulse was to storm through the front door. But with Ellie armed and me with only my good looks, it wouldn't be a contest.

I skittered down the porch and blinked the rain from my eyes as I ran to the kitchen door in back. A light shone from the barn and Baxter limped from the gaping door, dragging a ladder.

Hoping Ellie wouldn't hear, I eased open the door, an old wooden one that looked like it hadn't been replaced since they'd built the house. My muddy feet slipped on the old linoleum, and I gently pushed the door closed. With light breaths, I snuck through the dark kitchen, hoping to surprise Ellie and tackle her before she could react.

Dim light from the living room came through the opening from the kitchen. I approached the door and crouched down, ready to spring. In slow motion I inched my head by the doorway to locate Ellie and time my leap.

"Come on in, Kate. Glad you could join us." Ellie's gun pointed at me, though her hand shook slightly. Still, this close, she wouldn't need great aim.

Sarah's face melted and her shoulders sagged further. "Oh, Kate." It held her loss of hope I'd ride in and save them. And probably her sorrow we'd all been dragged into this.

"It's okay," I said, knowing it wasn't but not knowing what else to say.

Sarah's voice lost its normal steel but she tried, "Listen to me, Mom."

Where was the gun that I had given Aria? I scanned the room and finally located a glimpse of the handle on the top of a bookshelf toward the dining room. Of course, Sarah, feeling no threat, would stash it out of the kids' reach.

Ellie's thin gray hair was plastered to her head by the rain and her voice was shrill and grating. "No. I'm tired of listening to everyone else. First it was my parents. They didn't believe in my talent, so I had to marry Alden."

Even in the late seventies Ellie would have other choices than to marry the first yahoo that came along.

She addressed us like a prosecutor convincing a jury. "Then it was Alden. My whole life he told me what to cook for dinner, what we could buy for the house, how to dress, when we'd go to town and what we'd do. Never a vacation. Not like my sorority sisters and their husbands. No new house and furniture."

And yet, Sarah said Alden doted on Ellie. The woman had her own reality.

In her two days outside the womb, Olivia had developed some lungs. She let loose with wailing that ended in a silent moment before she built steam again.

It wrenched my gut to see the newborn in such distress.

Ellie flipped her head in Sarah's direction. "And then you came along."

Sarah turned the color of plaster and I prayed she hadn't started bleeding again. She pleaded with Ellie. "Let me pick her up, Mom. She needs me."

Ellie raised her gun in Sarah's general direction, an aging woman with a heavy tool. But a gun had the power. Until now, I'd have questioned Ellie's ability to shoot. The gaping hole in Alden's chest proved her prowess.

When Sarah flinched, Ellie held the gun on her a second longer, then lowered it. She gave Olivia a cold stare. "As Alden always said, it won't hurt her to cry. I never let Garrett cry. See how that turned out for me?"

A dull thud sounded, and I hoped it was Baxter propping the ladder against the house. To keep Ellie from noticing, I accused her. "You turned the gas on in Sarah's house. Why would you do that?"

Olivia hitched and sputtered, working herself into a froth of rage. Bless her little heart for helping mask Baxter's noise.

Ellie looked confused then her face cleared. "Oh, that. Sarah wanted to take Tony away from me. I couldn't let that happen." She made it sound like the most natural explanation in the world.

Sarah's mouth dropped open in shock. She turned to me in help-lessness.

A scrape sounded on the ceiling, and I kept on. "Sarah loves you. She's always taken care of you." I used the phrase that seemed to be important to Ellie, to be cared for.

Ellie frowned. "She's a girl. Men carry on the legacy. They protect the family."

The birth and losing all that blood was catching up to Sarah. I'd been optimistic to think she could help me in some kind of action-movie take-down of the bad guy. I realized how bad it was when her legs buckled, and she collapsed.

I lunged forward to help her and Ellie shrieked, "Stay away from her!" She jerked her arm up and swung the gun in a wild arc. I froze.

Olivia kicked and kept crying, getting weaker.

Sarah dropped her head for a second, then lifted her chin and pushed herself to her knees. Her hand shook as she brushed tears and hair from her face. "What are you going to do?"

Ellie glanced above her, as if seeing upstairs. "Tony and I are going back to the east coast and away from this hell hole."

Sarah shook her head. "You killed Tony's father. He'll hate you forever."

Ellie didn't like that. She scowled at Sarah, and I braced to jump in front of a bullet. But Ellie pursed her lips. "Garrett left me no choice."

I couldn't help my incredulousness. "He was your son."

Sarah inched toward the crying baby.

Ellie didn't seem to notice. "When Garrett told me he still loved Sheila and they were talking, I knew she'd dig her claws back into him and he'd leave. And when he did, he'd take Tony. They were going to leave me. I couldn't let that happen."

Sarah gained another millimeter toward Olivia, who had started to wear down, her cries becoming weak hiccups.

Ellie whirled around to Sarah, and I spoke with urgency. "How did you know what to do at the pivot?"

"You all think I'm stupid. And weak. Not worth paying attention to. I know how electricity works. I read the literature on the pivots when everyone else thought they knew so much."

She seemed proud of her plan. "I told Garrett his father needed him out there. No one suspects little old Eleanore of anything."

Ellie straightened her shoulders in a self-righteous stance. "And then you started nosing around and I had to leave Alden's watch where you could find it."

If I attacked her, Ellie's finger could twitch on the trigger. She may not be aiming, but a bullet flying in the living room could hit anyone. If she held the gun up, it might go through the ceiling to the kids. To Baxter.

Another thump sounded and this time, Ellie frowned and stared at the ceiling. "Those kids should be asleep by now."

Sarah zeroed in on Olivia, so it was up to me to take care of Ellie. "Setting up Alden didn't work, though."

"Alden figured out about the pivot." Her lips rose in a cagey grin. "So, I crushed his Viagra in his coffee. I'd read about it in a novel. It would have worked if you hadn't showed up."

Sarah was only a few inches away from Olivia. The baby wasn't moving any more. She might have worn herself out.

A louder noise and vibration shook the light fixture. Ellie jumped and started toward the stairs. "What the heavens, Tony? Tony!"

Sarah lunged for Olivia as I jumped for Ellie.

Ellie shouted and a gunshot exploded.

Sarah screamed.

29

Sarah curled around Olivia on the floor. Ellie stood on the second step. She stared at the pistol in her hands as if the shot surprised her. Then she saw me coming for her and swung the gun in my direction. I dove to the floor as the second shot shattered the front window and glass rained down.

Sarah stayed curled around the baby, not moving. Had she been shot? No blood seeped into the carpet but that didn't mean anything.

"Ellie," I shouted. "Put down the gun."

She must not have liked me telling her what to do because she shot again, hitting the sofa about three feet from my head. Stuffing flew to join the rain and glass. "I'm taking Tony. He's mine. The rest of you can rot here." Was it possible she believed she could kill her whole family and ride off into the sunset? I never pegged Ellie as a Lady Macbeth type, but she'd mastered the deadly lunatic.

I jumped to my feet and ran toward the stairs. She probably wasn't a marksman, but in this small space, at such close range, even a trained monkey could hit his mark or at least do real damage.

She squeezed off one more wild shot, spitting out a chunk of carpet and wood on the floor close to Sarah and the baby. Sarah screamed again and rose up like a fierce grizzly. She had to be operating on pure adrenaline and mother-bear fury—emotions Ellie wouldn't understand. She roared and raced across the living room.

Ellie must have goosed herself with adrenaline, too, because she bounded up the stairs like an antelope and not a feeble senior citizen. In her state of mind, she'd shoot Baxter on sight, and I couldn't be sure she wouldn't take aim at Brie and Tony, too.

Light from the living room faded as I sprang up the stairs ahead of Sarah, hoping I could contain Ellie before Sarah got to her. Ellie had threatened Sarah's children, and it didn't matter who she was, Sarah would tear her apart. Not that I cared for Ellie's safety, I wanted to protect Sarah from a murder charge.

Ellie hit the top of the stairs and barreled into the first bedroom on the left. I heard a loud thud and then Ellie shrieked. Noises of a scuffle sounded as I raced into the dark room.

The drapes billowed from the far wall. There was only light enough to make out two people struggling in the cold, with rain spitting through the open window.

Sarah tried to push behind me. She bellowed, ready to do what it took to protect her children. "Brie!"

The gun went off, a flash and deafening blast. It was impossible to tell who yelled or screamed or what was happening. The figures in front of the window, obviously Ellie and Baxter, continued to wrestle.

Ellie had a gun and some kind of demonic power fueling her. Baxter was unarmed with a bum ankle.

The hall light flicked on, and Sarah yelled again for Brie. She spun around and disappeared. I prayed the kids had escaped, maybe from a small pass-through in the closet between the bedrooms Carly used to hide in when she was small.

I think I must have shouted Baxter's name.

If he lost his grip or made a wrong move, Ellie could maneuver her gun into his belly and pull the trigger. He was a TV mogul, not a Ninja fighter. And even if Ellie was an old woman, tonight she fought like a creature released from Hell.

"Ellie!" I bellowed, hoping to distract her for even a millisecond.

Enough time for me to jump between them or for Baxter to get the upper hand.

The gun discharged again. A spark lit up in the corner by the brass bed, and then Baxter let out an anguished cry. The taller figure, Baxter, fell back and slumped against the wall under the flowing drapes.

No! She'd hit him. Baxter, the most irritating, arrogant, stubborn, wonderful man I'd ever known. Shot down because I'd dragged danger into his world.

Without thought I charged into Ellie. She was nothing more than fragile bones surrounded by wrinkled skin, and she wasn't expecting the speeding rocket of fury that hit her. The gun flew from her hand and clattered on the floor, sliding toward the open door and the scant light from the hallway.

Her body, slight and frail, crumpled under me. I heard a crack and felt bone give way. She let out a squawk of agonizing pain and when I rolled off, she curled into a ball, clutching herself and making more noise than a raging banshee.

Leaving her to writhe in misery, I scuttled across the floor through the icy rain. "Baxter. Are you okay? Oh, please. Be okay."

At the same time, he scooted toward me. "Kate. Are you hurt?"

We reached for each other, grasping hands.

The overhead light snapped on. Aria scanned the room in an instant, her gaze skimming over us quickly and resting on Ellie, who thrashed on the floor, her cries now little more than whimpers.

I backed away from Baxter and pushed myself to my feet. "I think her hip broke."

"Glenn!" Aria ran across the room and knelt down in front of Baxter. She grabbed his arms and studied him. "What happened? There's blood."

His voice was strong and as full of life as I'd prayed for. "The bullet must have ricocheted off the bed and nicked my arm. But I think I reinjured my ankle."

He was alive. His warm hands had gripped mine and our eyes had held each other for one short second before we'd pulled apart. I felt as if I'd been sucked into a whirlpool and drowned, only to be spit out to gasp at the pain of losing him again.

Baxter was with Aria. They were together. She'd take care of him. I forced myself not to rush to his side. He wasn't mine. I'd repeat that until it sunk in.

Sarah staggered past in the hallway. She paused to cast an emotionless gaze on Ellie writhing on the floor.

Ellie stopped and turned her head toward Sarah, giving her a look so full of hatred it curdled my blood.

Sarah turned away, gripped a silent Brie to her chest as if they were one and thudded down the stairs.

Pale and shaking, Tony slid into the doorway. He seemed to melt and dropped to the floor when he saw Ellie. The devastation on his face looked like a city after a bombing. Gray, lost, destroyed.

I hurried over, knelt, and pulled him into an embrace. His flat voice vibrated against my chest. "That man came in through the window. We were going to climb down but there were gunshots and Grandma started up the stairs. He told us to hide in the closet. I told Brie we were playing hide and seek but I think she was too scared to talk. Then I found the door into the other closet."

I hugged him, wanting to stop his trembling. "You saved Brie. I'm so proud of you."

He shook hard and leaned into me.

Splinters sliced into my heart for this sad little boy and the long road to healing ahead of him. But I had some good news. "Your mother is alive. She's in the Sandhills."

He pulled his head away and searched my face as if verifying my words. "Mom? Is here?"

"She came to get you."

He lowered his head into my chest, pulled in one long breath and started to bawl.

30

Three days later I walked down Main Street on my way from the courthouse to the Long Branch. The afternoon had turned blustery, and more rain threatened from the west. That might mean a soggy football game for Homecoming. Since Zoe had just been sworn in and I was no longer sheriff as of ten minutes ago, I wouldn't be standing on the sidelines as a law presence. I planned on curling up in my bungalow with a good book.

Well, that was my plan. I might be pacing the floor, counting my bank account and wondering how long I could take deciding on my next move. Even if I changed my mind about working for Carly, it was too late since she'd sold all her cattle and Baxter was in charge. Other options spun through my head, none of them ideal.

As if I'd opened a portal with my thoughts, my phone rang and Diane started speaking as soon as I said hello. "School's started obviously, so I don't need full time childcare. That means you'd have plenty of time to do interning here at the bank."

"How's the weather in Denver? It might be a wet Homecoming game."

Her heels clacked as she pounded on her way somewhere. "Okay, I get that the exciting world of finance doesn't thrill you. It should, by the way.

But it's a good place to start your career, get some money saved up, and then, if you still don't like it, you can find something else."

I wandered down Main Street, my cowboy boots hardly making a noise on the sidewalk. "In what universe do you see me enjoying living in a city?"

"The universe where you're making some bank and meeting interesting men." Voices greeted her. "I've got to go. I can set up the internship starting Monday. Let me know."

I'd barely hung up when Dad pulled his old Dodge into a parking spot in front of me. My heart jumped into my throat. Would he be happy to see me? Would he pretend not to know me? I gripped my phone as it vibrated.

Susan. She'd be all over me to move to Lincoln and go back to school. I didn't want that, so I punched her to voicemail. Staring at Dad, my heart hammered from my chest all the way through my stomach and weakened the backs of my knees. My phone vibrated before I got it into my pocket.

Dad's face was serious as he slid from his pickup and started toward me. At least he acknowledged he knew me.

I couldn't move as he got close enough to see the light on my screen. "Looks like Douglas is calling."

That broke my paralysis. "Oh." I lifted the phone and stabbed the key inviting Douglas to leave a message.

"Not going to answer it?"

I slid it into my back pocket. "I've had a raft of calls. They all have suggestions about what I should do next."

We stood awkwardly and he broke the silence. "The people who love you want to see you settled."

"Sid asked me to take over Frog Creek. It has some appeal."

He gave me an amused grunt. "Irritating Dahlia and Ted isn't good enough reason to take a job."

He was right, of course. "It keeps me in Grand County. Pays better than most jobs. I know the operation. And it would get the rest of them off my back."

He sucked his teeth. "They aren't used to worrying about you. It freaks them out. So, if you'll get your life sorted out, they can relax. And everything can go back to normal."

I looked away. "What's normal?"

"Good question." In a move totally not normal for him, he dropped an arm around my shoulder. "It's time we make a new normal, don't you think? I've been expecting your mother to show up. But I have to accept she's gone. And even if she appeared, I'm not sure I'd take her back." He shook his head. "I love her, Katie, but I need to find a new way to go on."

That was one ray of sunshine. "You're going to see Deenie again?"

As if on cue, a shout of hello came from around the corner at the Long Branch. Deenie waved with such enthusiasm I thought her arm might fly off. She yelled across the street, "Meet you inside. Bring Kate!"

"How about it, Katie?"

I waved back at Deenie. "Sure. You're buying, right, since I'm unemployed?"

He took his arm away and I missed it. "Happy to have you join us, but that's not what I was talking about. How about you finding a new normal? And you could start with forgiving Louise."

I bristled. "That's asking a lot.

We meandered across the street. "We've all lost a lot. Glenda, Marguerite. Jobs, marriages. Don't you think we ought to hold on to what's left? I want all my kids to get along. To be a family again."

I missed a step and the lump in my throat nearly choked me.

Dad didn't look at me. "I'm sorry I took off like that the other night. It was never about you. It doesn't matter whose little guy swam upstream to spawn. You're my Katie. And I hate to tell you I'm like the rest of the danged Foxes. I rely on you to keep us all going."

I didn't know what to do with that. Keeping the Foxes going. What did that mean? No one ever asked if I wanted that responsibility. Maybe he meant that to comfort me, but it landed heavy in my gut and rolled around.

I trudged after Dad, who'd seemed to gain a new spring to his step, probably excited to see Deenie.

My phone vibrated again and this time, Sarah's bird finger was enough to make me take it. I flicked my hand at Dad. "I'll be right in." Then I greeted Sarah. "Are you on your way home?"

"Robert's bringing the pickup around now. I should have been home yesterday after they finished the infusion. But they wouldn't release me."

I stood close to the side of the tack shop as a shield from the wind.

"Because you talked them into releasing you after Olivia was born and you nearly killed yourself."

She harrumphed. "That wasn't my fault. I suppose it's okay because they're releasing Dad now, too, so we can take him home."

I didn't think Alden would be strong enough, yet. "Is anyone there to help him?"

She sighed. "Sheila and Tony are going to stick around for a while until Dad gets on his feet. I think I'd rather die than listen to that bimbo prattle on night and day."

I laughed. "That's not nice."

"Listen, nice isn't my priority. But I'm grateful I don't have to worry about him. The lawyer told Dad that Mom's developed pneumonia. She won't get out of bed to rehab her hip and Dad thinks she's willing herself to die. I don't think she's got enough awareness to will anything. It's weird how out of it she is. It happened so quickly."

"They'll keep her there until her trial. Maybe she'll get more lucid."

Sarah sounded matter-or-fact about all of this. "I doubt it. According to Dad, she'd been slipping for a while and it was escalating. If I'd known how bad it was, I never would have let her around the kids. I'd have made Dad take her someplace."

Knowing Sarah, she'd filed her brother's murder, her mother's psychotic break, and her father being her father, in a recess in her mind. Right now, she had a newborn, a toddler, and a ranch to deal with.

Robert and I wouldn't let Sarah shove this all away for too long. But for right now, I didn't push back.

I heard a smile in her voice. "Get this. Robert, your brother who said Tony was a delinquent who couldn't be around his daughters, told Tony he can spend summers at our place. And here's the strange part, Tony hugged him and said he can't wait until next year."

A woman's voice shouted my name and Aria bounced out of Dutch's Grocery on her way across the street to me.

Sarah heard it, too. "Is that Aria? I really like that woman. Tell her hi." Sarah hung up.

Aria wore a form-fitting pair of jeans and a short leather jacket that looked softer than satin, along with her happy smile that invited me to mirror it. "I'm glad I ran into you."

Jealousy couldn't help but pool inside, but that didn't keep me from responding to her warmth. Like Sarah, I liked this woman. "I thought you and Baxter left a couple of days ago."

She had a cagey look on her face. "We did. But I had some business in Denver and, as it turns out, more business here."

I took in her glow. "Troy Stryker sold you the land?"

She giggled and made a little hop. "I told you he couldn't say no to me."

"Congratulations." Some people had a golden touch. Grandma Ardith said they pooped rainbows.

She took hold of my wrist. "Now I have one more piece to put in place."

A wave of excitement hit me when I realized what she wanted, and I couldn't help my grin.

She saw it and squeezed my hand. "I need a manager, and the land abuts yours so it's perfect. Please say you'll do it. Please."

"Of course." There was no hesitation.

Maybe this kept Baxter in my life, where I would see him from time to time and he'd continue to feed my soul and rip it apart at the same time. But it also meant working with Aria.

More than that, it sounded wonderful to raise cattle who wouldn't judge me, push me one way and pull me another, demand I do or be, or perform to their will.

And even better, I'd get to spend my days being outside on the land that I loved.

TAKING STOCK
Kate Fox #10

At the foot of the Rockies, Kate Fox and a billionaire lock horns.

During her visit to the bustling National Western Stock Show in Denver, Kate Fox's business partner, Aria Fontaine, expresses a grave concern. She is worried about her cousin, Jefferson Hansford, an enigmatic billionaire, who recently went through a tumultuous divorce. When Kate finds that Jefferson has been drugged and is in the hospital, Aria's worst fears are confirmed.

Pushed by her sense of duty and friendship, Kate reluctantly steps into the role of investigator, going undercover at a high-profile fundraising gala as Jefferson's "fiancée" to draw out his assailant. But when tensions between Kate and Aria's husband-to-be, Glenn Baxter, run high, she is forced to leave the fundraiser with more questions than answers.

In a dark turn of events, Kate's prime suspect is found murdered the following day, sending her scrambling to make sense of the details of Jefferson's complicated past. Kate's investigation propels her through a complex maze of dark family legacies, a hidden connection to the stock show, and trails of dirty money. Caught in a whirlwind of duty, forbidden love, and danger, Kate's resolve is tested as she confronts the chilling realization that the attacker will likely strike again—unless she can stop them first.

Get your copy today at
severnriverbooks.com

ACKNOWLEDGMENTS

I owe my biggest thanks to all the readers who have been with Kate along her journey. Because you've been faithful, I've been allowed to keep writing her adventures and it's the most fun I've ever had (in public). For those of you frustrated Kate hasn't found her happily ever after, stick with us. I promise you won't be disappointed.

As always, thank you to my amazing publisher, Severn River Publishing, and especially Amber Hudock, Mo Metlen, Julia Hastings, Cate Streissguth, Megan Copenhaver, Keris Sirek, and the visionary, Andrew Watts. I suspect there are others at work behind the scenes I haven't met yet, so a big thank you to everyone at SRP. You keep this boat afloat and let the rest of us play around in our made-up worlds.

I am edited by the best minds in the business. Thank you to my developmental editor for almost every book that carries my name, Jessica Morrell. I believe those books should list her as a collaborator. And Kate Shomaker, who knows Kate's stories better than I do. You've saved me from so many embarrassing mistakes.

A huge shout-out to Megan Tusing, audiobook narrator extraordinaire. You guys, if you haven't listened to the Kate books, or any of Megan's large repertoire, you're missing out. I'm not lying when I say she's exceptional.

Thank you for the technical expertise of Shawn Hebbert, from the Keith County Sheriff's office. If I've taken liberties with the procedure, it's not on him. He knows his stuff. And to Doug Dyer, who had to reach way back in time to remember how center pivots work. (I may have moved a few things around there, too, so don't blame him.)

I know for certain I wouldn't make it through the vagaries of the writing and publishing process without my posse. Thank you to Erica Ruth Neubauer, Lori Rader Day, Susie Calkins, and especially Jess Lourey, whose cries of "Sprint!" have spurred me to write so many days when I'd rather do anything else. These writers—with so much talent it's intimidating—are ready to saddle up anytime the call comes, and I'm more than grateful.

Thank you to Wendy Barnhart for so many things, from the tears and support, to the advice, and nudging. You're a brat and I love you.

Always and forever a thank you to my two phenomenal daughters, Erin and Joslyn. Children have a way of lifting you up and keeping you in check like no one else. I am so proud and honored to be your friend as well as your genetic donor.

And to Dave. There isn't a moment that goes by that I'm not grateful for you in my life. (Well, there was that *one* moment, but it was short.) You inspire every book and make me laugh every single day.

ABOUT THE AUTHOR

Shannon Baker is the award-winning author of *The Desert Behind Me* and the Kate Fox series, along with the Nora Abbott mysteries and the Michaela Sanchez Southwest Crime Thrillers. She is the proud recipient of the Rocky Mountain Fiction Writers 2014 and 2017-18 Writer of the Year Award.

Baker spent 20 years in the Nebraska Sandhills, where cattle outnumber people by more than 50:1. She now lives on the edge of the desert in Tucson with her crazy Weimaraner and her favorite human. A lover of the great outdoors, she can be found backpacking, traipsing to the bottom of the Grand Canyon, skiing mountains and plains, kayaking lakes, river running, hiking, cycling, and scuba diving whenever she gets a chance. Arizona sunsets notwithstanding, Baker is, and always will be a Nebraska Husker. Go Big Red.

Sign up for Shannon Baker's reader list at
severnriverbooks.com